FOR ALL OF US

A NOVEL

by Jillian Rose

NEW YORK
Stony Iron Publishing
2024

Printed in the United States of America

First Printing, 2024

ISBN 978-0-9998847-1-3

Stony Iron Publishing
Brooklyn, NY 11201

And I can't help
but to wonder,

how many times
have I loved
you this way?

1

FEBRUARY 1902

I had never seen a grey sky like this one.

I had seen grey skies that hung like a blanket, smooth and heavy and formed from misty air. I had seen crisp grey skies that spoke of the promise of first snow, the clouds telling stories of shifting seasons. I had seen electric grey skies, sparking and tinted with deep blue, the tiny hairs on your arms upright and swaying to its rhythm.

And then, there is this grey.

It doesn't hang in the air, and it doesn't deliver electric promise. It just moves around me, ominous and inexhaustible, permeating air and breath and bone. Inching inward until my heart squeezes. Until my lungs are threatened.

It's a grey that has been stretched thin with time, but somehow, still embodies the same density it did on that day.

I had never seen a grey sky like this one. But now, it never leaves.

The time is half past four. The in-between. A day nearly gone by, but not quite. An evening peering from beyond the horizon. The only color outside of the monotone is the starchy movement of my midnight blue petticoat, brushing the cobblestone. The only sound the heels of my boots with their clank, clank.

Clank, clank.

I've lived in this town for most of my life. An eighth-mile stretch of road contains every storefront on Main Street, and I know every fissure in every exterior wall, every octave of bell that rings over every threshold, every smile from every store clerk and what each one holds. Because a smile is always much more than a smile.

Mr. Hutchinson's is the smile I am on my way to see, but how I wish he wouldn't offer it up. It is filled with far too many of the things we don't say, try to smother behind curved lip. The General Store had been propped up on a small hill at the end of the road since as far back as I can remember. Mr. Hutchinson has always been there. Didn't miss a day for the birth of his daughter. Or his son. Has not missed a day during these dark times, and we all wonder if his superior work ethic somehow keeps him safe. Resilient. But I think it is something more than that, somehow.

Mr. Hutchinson had always been kind to us. The ring of the bell over his door has always been the most pleasing, with a hum to it that is nostalgic. When it rings this time, he looks up. Smiles.

"Ms. Juliette. What a pleasant surprise."

He places his wrinkled palms flat down on the aged wood countertop and holds them there.

"Good to see you, Mr. Hutchinson." I nod my head and once inside, pull the hood of my petticoat down.

"It has been a while," he says, making his way around the counter, taking one of my hands between both of his. "Will it be the usual?"

It stings when he says it and we just let it hang there. *Will it be the usual?* He's said that same thing, maybe hundreds of times. Every time. But this time, nothing is usual, and we both know it.

Mostly, we'd just come to look. Find joy in the small shop, the kind man behind the counter whom we called a friend, the eccentric little treasures that would make their way on trade from small villages much further away than we'd ever travel. This was the usual. It was usual for *us*.

Now, there is no us. There is only me.

I take my hand back and return the kindness with a small smile of my own. My face feels rusty, however, and I immediately regret it. I walk to the counter. There is a rectangular alcove covered by glass that lines its center, and inside, I see it—holding the light just right.

I move my finger slowly over the glass. "I'd like to purchase this."

Mr. Hutchinson's skin bunches up and brings his eyebrows to the center of his forehead. "Purchase it, Ms. Juliette?"

"Yes, please." I step back, giving him room to unlock the glass enclosure. I dip my hand into my pocket and the coins make a jangling sound as I gather them. "I have enough," I say, opening my palm and offering them up.

He cups his hands as I drop them in and stands there for moments, unsure of how to proceed. I nod, shaking him from his trance, and he moves to retrieve it, just as he did the last time.

He lifts it gingerly, because anyone could see how tender the moment is for me. He drapes it over my outstretched fingers, and for a moment, it dangles there, suspended in its in-between—what once was and what would be.

Mr. Hutchinson is gazing silently as I gather the necklace in my palm in a heap of delicate metal, touch it with the tip of my index finger and watch the hair-thin golden threads move around each other.

"Mr. Hutchinson?" I look up, eyes hollow, but still, reflecting more life than they have in some time. "I wonder if you might be able to help me with something else."

He nods. "What can I do for you?"

I dip my hand into my pocket again. Hold it there.

"I'd like to add a gemstone to this necklace. I know you have an expert hand."

He bites the inside of his mouth. "I have not worked with such delicate gold in some time. Have you considered journeying into the city center? The jewelers are most trustworthy. I have met them all myself."

I walk closer to him, my voice a whisper. "Trust is what I am looking for, most of all. And that is why I've come to you." I pull my hand from my pocket, grasp a small black pouch. I place the necklace down on the counter so that I can open the pouch's drawstring, and carefully extract the treasure. I hold it at first between two fingers, and then let it rest on my outstretched palm.

Mr. Hutchinson's eyes widen, and then turn into small slits, inspecting the iridescent item that rests there.

"It can't be," he says. "How?"

"I found it. I know it's hard to believe, but I found it, down by the creek."

"Do you have any idea?" he asks me. "Any idea how rare this is? And not just in these parts."

I move my palm slowly from side to side, watching the colors swirl in its marbleized off-white sheen. "I have some idea."

"They are mighty rare, Ms. Juliette. Hardly any to be found to begin with. And then they were hunted to smithereens. Why, that's fit for a queen, I tell you. I bet it's worth more than this whole town and the two towns over. All the homes and shops and streets and gems combined."

My eyes mist over, my throat clenches. "It's worth more than all of it, to me."

Mr. Hutchinson quiets, softens, his eyes knowing. He shakes his head slowly, from side to side, and exhales in his gentle way. "It's a miracle. That's what it is."

"She wouldn't have it any other way," I whisper.

He gestures me forward, stretches out his own hand. "May I?"

I nod, placing my whole Universe there on his palm.

"Trust me, Ms. Juliette. Your secret is safe with me." I hand him the pouch, and he places the pearl carefully inside. "I will give this all the soul I have," he promises, and I know that he will.

2

Present Day

The sky is velvet, a kind of impossibly deep blackness that isn't contrasted by the stars. Instead, the dichotomy comes from artificial light, the city stretching across the gaping horizon—acting as if it holds a candle to such vastness. Its confidence is applaudable, however. Its presence is undeniably mesmerizing, especially from this vantage point.

I teach on the rooftop on warm summer nights. We are twenty-seven stories up and the warmth is like a blanket, massaging our muscles to move with more grace. The lights don't go down for Savasana in the way they would in the studio, but they don't have to. The mood of the class is set from the start and weaves its way all the way through. It is quiet up here. And tonight, so still. An oasis of stillness plucked and nestled far enough above the rest that one can almost forget the kinetic energy that is buzzing below in every direction.

Savasana is the pose I am most fond of. A favorite pose can tell a lot about a person, and when I say that my favorite pose is one of rest, it feels like an admittance. But it's not that I'm apathetic. It's just that I find the most in stillness. When I can forget where my breath ends, and the air begins. When I am silent, it is like that with everything—all one moving thing.

I weave around the mats, stepping lightly between heads and torsos and toes, all limp and sprawled and breathing in scattered rhythm. So much quiet, it is almost overwhelming. So much connection. So little distraction. I take a deep breath and hold it just long enough to feel that subtle burn around the edges of my lungs. A pleasurable feeling with a trace of discomfort. The kind that reminds you that you are alive.

"Inhale," I say, my voice soft and melodic, meeting the moment where it is so that we can all move slowly out of it. "And exhale. Start to move your fingers, your toes…" The students roll over to their sides, and at their own pace, move up to sitting. I make my way back to the front of the mats.

"Namaste," I say. "Namaste," they reply, legs crossed and eyes closed, heads bowed and hands to their chests, pointing toward that dark night sky. And like being lifted from a trance, they are up and moving again, albeit at a slower pace than they had started. I rise to hold space for the class as they gather their things and make their way to the door, and then turn to gather my own.

I can hear her soft footsteps approaching amidst the quiet. "Cora," says Natasha, as I turn toward her. "Thank you for a beautiful class. I really needed it."

Natasha is made of stark contrasts and piercing stares. Her striking beauty is undeniable, with her dark hair, severe eyes, and shining skin. But it's her dichotomies that make her most attractive—her peaceful, whimsical power.

She embodies a fearlessness that I can't relate to, especially these last couple of years. Things seem easier for her. Maybe they aren't, but they seem that way.

"Natasha," I say warmly. "Isn't it wonderful up here? I'm glad we have the whole summer ahead of us."

"Wonderful," she agrees, looking out toward the skyline and inhaling deeply through her nose. "It's my favorite night of the week."

She turns back toward me. "I don't understand why Emerson doesn't join us. He probably needs it more than I do. And that's saying something."

She reminds me that even the most peacefully powerful still need to bring themselves back to center.

Natasha and my husband, Emerson, are partners at Noho Design Group, the architectural firm they founded together over five years ago, named aptly for its location north of Houston Street in Lower Manhattan. They worked together out of graduate school, followed the same trajectory and complimented each other's skillsets, and it became apparent that their next step would be to find a way to work for themselves rather than for someone else. And at thirty-four years old, they are already inspiring success stories, both self-made and impeccably talented.

"Have you spoken to Emerson this afternoon?" she asks.

"Not since this morning." I bend to grasp the end of my mat and roll it into itself. "He said he'd be back-to-back in meetings all day. Is everything ok?"

"Oh yes," she says, waving her hand in the air. "Everything is fine. I just wasn't sure if he mentioned it yet." She tilts her head to the side, lifts her chin. "May I make a proposition?"

"By all means," I say, stashing the mat under my arm.

"The Catskills Retreat Center," she says, and from the way the muscles in her face soften, it seems the thought of it alone brings her peace. "Have you heard of it?"

"I have," I nod brightly. "I've heard it's extraordinary." A coworker had attended a hatha training at the center last winter, and came back not only with reports of wonderment, but with an obvious glow. "Are you planning a trip?"

"We are sending one of the teams at the firm on a three-day *bonding experience.*" She shakes her black hair out of its ponytail and lets it drape over her shoulders. "Half of them work remotely, half of them work from the office half of the time, and it's all well and good, but there is something missing, from this team specifically. They aren't clicking. Creativity is lacking. We have a big job coming up and we need them at their sharpest. And we have all this travel and conference budget we haven't used up."

"A beautiful idea," I say, swinging my bag over my shoulder. "Emerson's on board? I'm surprised he hasn't mentioned it."

"I only just got his blessing today," she says. "He's rather open to the whole thing—agreed it'll be good for the team. But we need to move quickly." She exhales, tucks her hair behind her ear. "They are nearly booked for the season. The only availability they have is less than two weeks out, right after the Fourth of July."

My eyes widen slightly. "So soon. You think that will impact attendance?"

"I don't think so. Most of the team has already committed. The problem," she shrugs, "is more of a staffing issue. Their yoga instructor is going to be in Bali."

The roof has emptied, and we are the only two left in the open air. Natasha gestures toward the door leading back into the building, and I follow.

"There is other programming. We can go ahead anyway." We walk into the dingy light of the top-floor hallway. "But how can they attend a retreat center for three days without the full yogic experience? If only there was an enlightened instructor who could show them the path toward wholeness…"

I laugh and shake my head. "Enlightened is really pushing it."

She turns to me, smiles slightly. "I hate to ask for a favor."

"This is nothing like a favor." We step into the elevator, provide it with our second-floor destination. "It's an amazing opportunity." I place my hand on my chest. "I'd be grateful for it."

"You think you can take a few days off with such short notice?" she asks. "We are looking at Wednesday to Friday, after the holiday."

I nod as the elevator doors open, the air changing with it, smelling of patchouli and lavender. "My schedule is light that week. It shouldn't be a problem."

"Oh Cora, this is perfect." She places her hand on my shoulder, in a more affectionate way than we are accustomed to. It makes me glad that she does. My relationship with Natasha revolves around our mutual connection that is Emerson. Though I have known Natasha for long enough to technically consider her a friend, we have only ever scratched the surface. It's never been natural for us to connect in a deeper way. Though I think that connecting this way is normally something that either comes naturally or not at all, our disconnect may be partly my own doing. I spend a lot of time in my own head, with anxieties that are easier to keep buried.

"You'll be paid handsomely, of course," she continues. "I'll email you later tonight with the details." She removes her hand from my shoulder but holds my gaze. "This means a lot. Thank you."

"Thank *you*," I say. "Truly. I'm looking forward to the change of scenery." I bite at my bottom lip. "I need it."

We are quiet for moments, remembering. I don't plan on saying anything more about it, but whenever I allow it to surface, my breath is taken, and though unusual for her in this particular circumstance, Natasha fills the silence.

"You know," she says, gently clearing her throat. "If you ever want to talk… About anything…"

Tears mist the corners of my eyes. I look down, give myself a moment to settle. "Thank you," I say, as evenly as I can, offering a faint smile.

And then I am quiet, because right now, I don't want to talk about it. About the loss, two years ago, almost to this day, which changed my life irrevocably. About the pain, which has been threaded through my days ever since, that I am finally learning to live alongside. But I am grateful for the offer.

It has been some time since I have spoken of it, even with Emerson. About my womb preparing for new life and then suddenly, only empty space. It has become something he skirts around. I think he believes the reminder will break me all over again. What he doesn't realize is that in order to be reminded, I would first need to forget.

"I think," she says, cautiously but with just enough brightness to shift the weighted energy that is hanging over our shoulders. "That this can be a nice change of pace. New York City is the most magical place on earth and all," she shrugs exaggeratedly. "But…"

I think about the lights and the shows and the fancy dinners and the beautiful things that I have been lucky to experience. I think about all the nights I've spent with Emerson and Natasha after they leave the office, my stilettos matching their corporate attire, our clanking drinks blended with expensive spirits, laughing away my anxieties in the dark. And then I think about the soul of myself. I think about what it means to heal.

Distraction is enticing, but only for so long. Yoga is my meditation, a release that is healing, but sometimes it feels like a small bandage working to cover a gaping wound. Sometimes it just doesn't feel like enough.

"We all need a deep breath," she continues. "We all need it, from time to time."

I nod my head in agreement, my features soft with gratitude.

"Will you be joining the retreat?" I ask.

She huffs out the air in her lungs and shakes her head. "I wish I could," she says. "Timing isn't ideal. A big client is flying in from LA."

"A shame," I sigh.

"Don't feel sorry for me," she beams as we enter the studio. "I'll be in Bermuda next month. All alone for a week. My tan will be unmatched."

I smile and switch on the low lights.

"So," Natasha says. "Who gets to tell Emerson?"

I rummage through my bag until I find my phone, and hand it to her. "You go ahead."

She smiles again, grasps the phone and Facetimes Emerson as I place my mat and blocks in a cubby. Everyone else has gone for the night, and I love the quiet of it. Sometimes, I stay a while after the studio has closed. Meditate. Write. Dance like no one is watching, because they aren't.

Natasha is walking toward me with her arm stretched in front of her, and the phone grasped in her hand. "Good news," she says. "We have good news." She positions her arm so that we are both in view. The lighting is so dim, it's hard to make us out. Emerson, on the other hand, is doused in the fluorescence of overhead bulbs. But he is smiling that incredible smile and warming me up, along with everything around him.

"Still at the office?" I frown. "It's so late."

"You're one to talk," he says, his eyes narrowing in their light-hearted way. "You're almost done for the night?"

"I'm done, I'm done." I lean my head toward Natasha. "We were just chatting."

"You should have been here, Emerson," says Natasha. "The fresh air. The stars. The peacefulness. The poses." She holds the phone with one hand and accentuates her words with the other. "I'm telling you. Your wife is a dream."

I sigh appreciatively.

"Still trying to close the deal?" he asks Natasha with a sly smile.

"Oh, she's already on board," she says, flicking her hand in the air. "And it's going to be marvelous." She turns toward me, raises her eyebrows.

"It will," I nod, and then add with a smile for Natasha's sake, "it will be marvelous."

"Good," says Emerson. "Excellent work, Natasha." He moves his hand in a small salute. "You can sign off for the night."

"As if I needed your permission," she says, handing me the phone, touching each cheek to mine.

"You are going to be so perfect for this," she whispers as she turns to leave, sweeping her hair to one side, dangling her black leather tote on the other. "See you on Monday, Emerson," she yells as she walks toward the door, hand up in a wave he cannot see.

Emerson's smirk is sideways, and a bit of stubble has come in across his cheeks. Three years of marriage and five years of relationship later, and I still find him just as alluring as the night we met. For some of the obvious reasons—his chiseled jaw, his commanding shoulders, his deep blue eyes. But mostly for the important reasons—his gentle masculinity, his quick wit, his sharp mind, and his incredible kindness.

The night we met, we locked eyes across a crowded bar. He was four years older and he joked that I was four years wiser, and it all felt so fresh and exciting. We drank a bit too much and walked along the river, laughing until three in the morning. And we've hardly left each other's sides since.

He leans back in his seat, but my view stays stationary through the phone screen. I can see more of him now, watch the way he holds his hands behind his head, admire the broad set of his shoulders shifting with them.

"I'll pick up dinner," I say.

He shakes his head. "No. I'll pick up dinner." His eyes narrow. "You get in the shower."

I blush in a familiar way, a rush of heat not from embarrassment but from anticipation, and I'm sure he knows it, even if the dim lights won't allow him to see it.

"You'll meet me there?" I ask.

"I'll meet you there," he says.

* * *

The elevator doors open to our eleventh-floor apartment. I never thought I'd live in an apartment on the eleventh floor of a building in Manhattan, especially one overlooking Central Park, and I am awed by the reality of it every time I arrive home. I am a lot of things. I am made up of countless energies that are constantly vying for attention. But one thing I am grateful for is my ability to be grateful. It's something that doesn't waver.

I drop my keys by the door and remove my shoes, walking barefoot across our pristine wood floors. The light from tonight's half-moon is streaming through the floor-to-ceiling windows into the living room. The blue hue softens everything, draping over the space rather than lying in angles on top of it. I take it in with a deep breath, and then move to the kitchen. There are three bottles of wine lying in the rack, and I open an earthy Cabernet, giving it time to breathe.

I move to the bathroom and remove my clothing, a simple tank top and my favorite black yoga pants, which hug my small curves just right. I have yet to turn on a light but bring to life a few candles, instead. I don't like harshness: in lighting, in character, in life. I avoid it where I can. Once the ambiance is pleasing, and my skin is bare, I turn to look at myself. My reflection in the mirror is different in candlelight. It's more muted, but somehow, tells a deeper story. When the details fall away, I feel forced to look within. Tonight, I think I am seeing a bit too much. I wince and look away.

I turn on the shower, and water streams from two showerheads, meeting in the middle in a graceful clash of steam. I step inside and let the water cascade over me, drenching my long brown waves until they are stretched down the length of my back. When I was a child, my father would become angered by a lot of things, one being my lengthy showers. "Money doesn't grow on trees," he would bark, as he wrote out a check for the water bill. So, I shortened my showers by half at the least, and every moment was so precious it would slip by too quickly. The entire experience felt as if it was tarnished, ruined because all I could think about was how soon it would end.

I've learned a lot since then. I've learned to be grateful for moments. But the fear of endings will always be hard.

Either way, I allow myself the indulgence of an amply extended shower more often now. Especially when Emerson is on his way home.

I don't hear the elevator doors through the rush of water and shampoo, so his presence before me is a surprise. At first startling, and then every other wonderful thing. He steps forward, naked and perfect, and wraps his arms around my torso. I press my head into the curve below his neck, and we rise and fall together.

"I've missed you," he breathes. He lifts my chin and kisses me softly, our lips silken from the steam. "Too much working, too little playing."

"Let's make up for it," I say, my hands moving down his lower back.

He turns me around, rinsing the last remnants of suds from my hair. He runs his fingers over my scalp, massaging first the top of my head, and moving toward my temples, the sides of my neck, the backs of my shoulders. His fingers move slowly, intentionally, brushing my skin and then pushing into my muscles; moving out whatever my body was holding and replacing it with pieces of him.

He shifts my hair to the side, letting it drape over my chest, and kisses the back of my neck. "How was your day?" he whispers. The water and his lips and the heat tickle at my skin.

"It was ok," I say, leaning back and pressing myself into him, feeling as much of him as I can. My head is against his cheek, eyes closed and wanting.

"Not here," he breathes into my ear. "You'll need a proper congratulatory fuck after dinner." He turns me around and kisses my forehead forcefully, and then reaches over me for the soap.

I exhale audibly. "There is nothing proper about you. And what are you congratulating me for?"

His eyes widen and his lips pinch upward on the right side. "For being my newest employee, of course. Not many people get this opportunity," he says, as he rubs a bar of soap over his chest. "Once in a lifetime."

"It's funny," I reply, working conditioner into my hair. "I was thinking you should be the one we are congratulating. You just hired the best employee you will ever have."

He rinses the soap from his chest, letting it slip off his skin and circle down into the drain. "Maybe it's not such a big deal, after all," he shrugs. "You are only a temp."

I rinse the conditioner away, laughing with my eyes. I grab my towel from the hook and step out of the shower. A minute or two later, he turns off the water, and follows me.

He rustles his short dark hair under the towel and shows a side of himself others don't see. Slightly disheveled, eyes playful. Bare and nonchalant. Emerson is commanding in most areas of his life, but in an uncommonly balanced way. He's an amiable alpha. He finds strength in his magnanimity. He's striking, really. I see him this way, and each time, I am captivated. Because he is so beautiful. Because I get to embrace these sides of him.

Most sides of him. We both have walls. And we are working to break them. At least I know I am. I think I am more aware of these walls than Emerson is. Or maybe he is just better at seeing beyond them.

He hangs his towel on the rack and opens the bathroom door, a trail of steam exiting with him, glistening footprints appearing and then vanishing behind his bare, polished form. He walks toward our bedroom, and I follow.

I watch him slip on his grey sweatpants, the elastic lying low across his sculpted waist.

"I'm proud of you," he says. He moves from playful to sincere so eloquently, and sometimes they blend together, become one beautiful thing. "For all of it."

I lean my head to the side, smile earnestly, knowing how much is behind his words. Knowing how he means them. Knowing that past experiences paint the future and come alive in the present in interesting ways, and in this moment, our experiences are coming alive this way. With tenderness. With awareness.

And though we haven't been expressive about our shared pain in an outward way for some time, it is in these ways that we honor it, and each other.

"I'm proud of you, too," I say.

He winks at me, runs a comb through his wet hair. "And maybe I shouldn't tell you this." He places the comb on the smooth wood of the nightstand, walks toward me. "But I only hired you because you're hot."

"I can't blame you," I say, pulling a silk tank top over my head. "But one wrong move, and I'm going to HR."

He comes in close and pulls the tank top back over my head in the other direction, letting it fall in a small heap on the floor.

"I don't make wrong moves, Cora."

3

Present Day

Emerson is out of bed at five-thirty most mornings, and after hearing his alarm, I normally drift back for at least another hour or two, depending on my class schedule. He moves around the apartment silently, the only disruption a kiss on my cheek before he leaves. But today, I wake with him. It is a three-hour drive to the retreat center, maybe longer depending on traffic out of the city.

Whenever I do rise before the sun does, I vow to do it more often. Life becomes so routine. Not simply because of work schedules and mealtimes and moon cycles. But because of something much less tangible. The energy at this time of day feels like it exists outside of my usual life. Like I get a small peek into another realm of existence.

It's not for this same enigmatic reason that Emerson embraces early mornings, but because he is good at treating his body as the machine that he considers it to be. He eats well. He lifts weights. He runs through Central Park at least three times a week. And it shows. I'm good to my body, too. Just not in the same ways he is. I nurture other aspects of myself alongside my physical vessel, feeding my soul in a way that is foreign to him. It's the biggest difference in the way we see the world: the systematic versus the soul of things.

It's a difference that hasn't been a significant problem in a traditional or tangible sense, but it's a missing piece that I grieve sometimes. I wish, maybe just once, he'd come to one of my classes. Sit in meditation with me. Peer at the moon and think of something beyond the science of the phases.

Of course, I also understand the converse impact of our differences. That we each bring something to our union that we wouldn't have individually. That through our differences, we find a unique balance, fitting together in our own imperfect way. He is beautiful to me. He is the person I fell in love with, exactly as he is—and who I've decided to continue to grow with every day.

"Plan on moving in?" he asks, motioning to the stack of bags near the entrance. "Looks like you packed for a six-month expedition."

"Oh, shush. I need things for class," I shrug.

"You are going to be teaching at one of the most sought-after, not to mention expensive, retreat centers in the world, Cora. I'm pretty sure they will have everything you need."

"I need *my* things. I feel better when I'm prepared. Class is more impactful when I'm prepared." I zip my cell phone into the front pocket of my backpack. "I really want this to go well."

I don't teach yoga because I've transcended all earthy anxieties. I teach because I have plenty of experience with them. Aside from the monotonous tension that normally sits in my chest and digs at my shoulder blades, the thought of being away from home, away from Emerson for the first time *since*, and leading classes for some of his best employees, has been unnerving.

I feel inexplicably drawn to this experience, however. It feels important, by the way my heart swells with a warm and mysterious intuition. I believe the most beautiful parts of our journey can be paved by this type of trust—in this tingling excitement that feels truer than the fear. And though it is something I haven't felt in a long time, or simply haven't been able to notice, this time, it is determined to make itself known.

"You'll be great," says Emerson. "I'm sure of it. Everyone is going to love you."

"They don't need to love me," I say, moving on my toes toward the bathroom to retrieve the toothbrush that I forgot to pack, and returning to finish my thought. "They just need to allow me to provide the space for them—to receive whatever it is that they *do* need."

Emerson has his back to me, filling a bottle with cold water from the filtered dispenser in the door of the refrigerator. "Still," he says, walking back toward me as I slip into my sandals. "They are going to love you." He wraps his arms around me and rests his chin on the top of my head. "Just not as much as I do."

I tilt my face up to his, lean against his cheek. "Are you sure you can't come, even for a day? It might be good to bond with the team. See them in a different light."

"They'd see me in a different light, too, and I'm not sure if it would be a beneficial one. I'd be too out of place. Besides, I have more work to do this week than I have time for."

"I'll miss you." He releases me and kisses the top of my head. "I'll have the shower running when you get home on Friday."

"A good compromise, at least," I say, pressing the elevator button. "You'll help me get these things to the car?"

"Can you please just let Viktor drive you?" he asks, swinging one of my bags over his shoulder. He turns squarely toward me, makes sure I am looking into his eyes. "I would feel much better if Viktor was driving."

I'm still getting used to the idea of having a driver. Though I do enjoy Viktor's company, I often choose independent transportation. I'm just grateful that Emerson has a comfortable ride to the office in the morning.

The elevator doors open and we both walk inside, bags over our arms.

"I want to drive. I never get to drive. Besides, I want to have my car there. I'll have more freedom that way."

"We have different definitions of freedom," he shrugs.

"Freedom lives on a sliding scale," I smile. "It's not the same thing to everyone." He exits the elevator into the vast marble lobby, and I follow.

"Maybe I have gotten my ideas of freedom a little twisted up lately," he says. "There are a few changes I'd like to make."

"Yeah? Like what?"

We make our way to the front doors and the muted air falls over me. It is warm, and quiet, and I can see the first hints of color fading upward in the sky. There is a delicate melancholy that rests in the early summer sky, the warmth dancing with the promise of change on its lips. If only we could all dance toward life with such poetic grace.

"Like having more time," he says. "For other things. For us."

I take his free hand, squeeze gently. He wraps his fingers around mine.

"We have been working a lot," I say, though aside from this three-day engagement, I have not been working all that much. Not even full-time hours most weeks, unless I'm teaching a workshop. His schedule, however, has been incessant. I understand why, and I'm proud of him for it. Once-in-a-lifetime opportunities supposedly only come around once in a lifetime. But what other once-in-a-lifetime things are we foregoing because of them?

I hand the valet my keys and we wait.

"When you get back, we'll have the whole weekend to ourselves," he says. "I won't open my computer. I'll turn off my phone. We'll go to La Sirène on Saturday night. We'll lay in bed until noon on Sunday. And then we'll take a walk down by the waterfront and eat ice cream."

Even in the muted air, I can see the light in his eyes.

"Burnt honey ice cream and enough sunshine to make our cheeks rosy?"

"Oh, you bet," he promises, as my car pulls into the vestibule. "Now please, be careful, ok? You'll call me when you get there?"

"I'll call you when I get there," I nod, anxiety tingling at my throat.

The SUV pulls up in front of us, and Emerson leans against the back door. "Natasha sent you the full brief, yes?"

I nod again, mouth slightly dry.

"Remember to ask for Kai," he says. "He owns the place. He's been Natasha's main contact."

"Thanks, Em. I'll be ok." I take a deep breath and we stack my bags into the trunk. Emerson opens the front door for me, drapes his arm over it, waits for me to come in close.

"See you," I say, leaning my head to the side.

"See you," he smiles, pushing his soft lips against mine, smelling of pine and sunrise.

4

JULY 1893

It was always about him. Sometimes, it seems to me that all of life before him was navigated by an undeniable magnetism, leading me down paths toward our synchronistic merging. If I veered off, I felt it— the tug, the friction, the swimming upstream—nudging me back toward what some may call my fate but of which I believe is only half the story. Though I don't disregard fate's hand, a stronger force directs us through this life, through lives before and after and in between. Love is stronger. Love is the strongest force of all. Because without love, there is no inertia. It is the foundation of all kinetic energy. Of all forward movement.

Asher's hand grasps around mine so tightly it is as if together they are one thing. He is breathing with me, shouldering the pain, holding as much of it as he can. His eyes are focused, adoring, deep and endless seas. I focus on them, on the truth in them, on the life in them, and I am strong. And I push. I push until it seems I may burst at the seams, until I see it in his eyes and I hear her cry and I know that she is here. And it feels as if the entire Universe just passed through me. Just showed me what it means to be eternal.

I look down at her, and I know now that love has no shores. It is endless and deep and cascading. Because now, the love I have with Asher that seemed to reach the very edges explodes around us until we are sure that edges don't exist and it goes on and on forever like the shimmering night sky. All wonder and awe and deep presence come from the same place. Is all built from the same core. Without love, there is no inertia. With it, the world spins around us.

I look down at her, and I know we are at an arrival point. A pinnacle moment amongst so many. And I wonder if perhaps life is like a staircase of such moments, and each time we arrive we rest there a while, only to rise again. Again, and again.

Even in the deepest embracing of youth, in these first breaths of life, her eyes tell stories. They are the color of blue crystal, of vast iridescent seas. Wisdom must be something we are born with. Something we grow into as we age, but in youth, something not to be disregarded. It is where it is most pure.

I am moved from my trance as the midwife bids us farewell, having scrubbed her arms and the floors and packed her things, rolling them neatly into her satchel and tying it off with thin rope. And then it is just the three of us, me laying damp with sweat and tears against my bedding, arms cradling new life, Asher leaning over us, breathing through his reverence and moving his thumb back and forth against my shoulder.

"What should we call her?" I whisper, knowing Asher is privy to something I am not and having known it all along. And now it is time to ask, and I am buzzing with it. Knowing her name exists already and soon I will too be speaking it with my lips.

"Did you know?" he asks me, so quiet and sure, "that pearls are the only gemstone to come from a living creature?" He moves his thumb now to her face, gliding it so softly across her cheek it must have felt like a warm breeze.

"I did not," I say, looking up from her captivating eyes and into his that are in fact grown into.

"They are extremely rare," he follows. "Their existence the true workings of a miracle. They hold the wisdom of the earth and the purity of the heavens."

I smile, the type of tired contented smile that is laced with a peace we may only know in moments, but which carries with us thereafter.

"It's beautiful," I whisper. "It's perfect."

He moves to kiss her forehead and then my own. We are one moving piece now. Three parts of the same heart.

"Our little Pearl," I say.

"Our little Pearl," he says.

The glimmering core of our existence.

5

PRESENT DAY

Three and a half hours later, I find myself weaving through a dense canopy of lush forest on a road just wide enough for my SUV, but not quite wide enough to separate me from the branches scratching up against my windows. How quickly the bustling city transforms into wilderness in New York. If you stop paying attention for even a few minutes, you cross the threshold without seeing where one thing ended and the other began.

I pass a small convenience store, propped quietly on a hill against a majestic deep-blue mountain backdrop. I see a young woman exit, hugging a to-go cup, even in the summertime warming her hands against the crisp morning air. There is a small child with her, a teddy bear under her arm, a pair of pink rain boots on her feet even though it's not raining. I feel the pang. The hurt of the surfacing reality. It's an orbicular thing, one that comes at me from all directions.

Emerson and I hadn't planned on any of it. So, I don't know why it had to go this way. In this unnecessarily convoluted and painful direction. But life can be dreadful and complicated. Sometimes, it's really that simple.

I shake my head, hoping to scatter the thoughts like dust. Like a dog disseminating the wetness from her coat. And I keep driving, but not for long, because five minutes later, I'm turning onto an even smaller dirt road onto the grounds of my destination.

The land is stunning, even at first glance. I pull in to see a large structure, grandiose, while still buoyant and airy, comprised of large glass windows, two stories framed by tall columns, and pristine white walls. It is surrounded by a circular clearing, probably 25 feet in each direction, with a large pond to the East. The clearing ends at the tree line, an enchanted scattering of pines and maples and white birch that seem to stretch on forever. There are narrow paths chiseled into the lush periphery, with no telling as to where they lead.

To the left of the dirt road is a modest parking lot. I can hear the gravel moving beneath my tires, the leaves whirling around me, the birds singing their songs under the morning sun. I take a deep inhale when I open my door and realize how tense my muscles have been. They can't help but to retreat in the mountain air, moving down from near my ears and settling into their proper space at the base of my neck.

I gather my bags from the trunk, all but one I cannot manage, and make my way to the entrance. It is quite a distance from the parking lot, separating the mundane from its enchantment. The front door is wide open, letting the crisp outside air in, and me along with it. The interior is just as grand as the rest of it, with two-story high ceilings in what they call *The Citrine Welcome and Living Center*, judging from the sign above the front desk. The floors are crafted with light wood, the kind with extra grain. The walls are crisp white, the beams along the ceiling rustic and aged. There is life everywhere. Plants and trees and flowers and moss softening the empty space.

There is incense burning, subtle and sweet, and I wonder how something that scorched and smoky could smell so fresh. It is a scent I have never smelled before, and I would have to remember to ask about it. There are wall hangings, a tapestry of Lord Ganesha, paintings of the beach and of the woods and of dancing flames and lovers and seven glowing chakras. And there are candles, lit even in the sunlight. Dancing with it.

A woman sits behind the counter, smiling softly. "Welcome to the Catskills Retreat Center," she nods. She exudes peacefulness in an all-encompassing way, but with an edge to it, accented by a spirited buoyancy. I wonder if this is her natural state, or if she must work at it, but it is surely intoxicating.

The anxiety I felt this morning is lifting. I notice the difference in the weight of it. The energy here feels pure, and kind, and I want to make more space for it.

"My name is Maralyn. How can I help you today?" It seems more a song than a sentence when she says it, and I can't help but to respond with more brightness myself.

"It is so lovely to meet you, Maralyn," I nod. "I'm here with the NoHo Design Group."

"Wonderful," she smiles. "We are so glad you are here. The rest of the group isn't expected until later this afternoon, but you are welcome to settle in and explore the grounds until then. Can I have your name, dear?"

"Oh, yes," I say, cheeks blushing awkwardly. "My name is Cora. I'm here as a temporary yoga instructor for the group. I believe Kai was expecting me?"

I feel a buzzing warmth in her presence; or perhaps it is the space itself that hands me over to this lovely sensation. Either way, I'm not used to it, and the vibration leaves me slightly winded. It's a breathy excitement that feels like a lustrous rush of adrenaline.

"Oh, Cora," she smiles warmly. "Cora, of course. I should have known. Yes, yes. Kai is expecting you." She reaches over the desk and takes my hands. She squeezes my fingers, holds there for a moment, as if she is searching me. It is so gentle that I am lulled by it—by her presence, by the coolness of her hands. And then she releases me and continues in her warm way.

"Let's get you settled, first and foremost," she says brightly. "Please, put your bags down. Soloman will take them to your room."

She nods to her left as a startlingly large man appears in the doorway near reception. He is large in the tall and muscular sense, with broad shoulders bursting from his t-shirt, no hair on his head, and a stance that seems to mean business, but before any first judgments are solidified, he speaks and wipes all my preconceptions clean.

"Cora," he says, in a friendly and exuberant voice. "You are absolutely wonderful." He turns to Maralyn. "Didn't you have a feeling she would be this absolutely wonderful?"

"I did have a feeling," she says, as whimsically as ever, and I am finding such joy in imagining their daily interactions.

"Welcome to the team." He joins me in front of the desk and extends his hand. "I'm Soloman. I'm a bit of a jack-of-all-trades here. I teach baking classes. I lead sound baths. I carry bags. Right now, you may notice I am wearing my bag-carrying hat. It's not very stylish. But it does the job."

"It suits you," I smile. "Thank you both for the warm welcome. I was nervous on the drive up. I wasn't sure what to expect. But I have a feeling I'm really going to like it here."

"How quickly the unknown can become, well..." Maralyn moves her hand in an arc in front of her. "The present moment."

"Almost like magic," I smile again.

"Well, come on then," says Soloman, as he picks up one bag and then another. I don't mention the bag I'd left behind in my trunk. I'd rather not put him out.

"I'll tell Kai you're here, Cora," says Maralyn. "I'm sure he'll want to give you the tour." She leans her head to the side and smiles. "He loves giving the tour. Just get settled in and come down whenever you're ready."

"Thank you, Maralyn," I say, as she settles back into her space behind the computer screen. Soloman leads me to the left toward a sweeping staircase that wraps upward toward a lofted second floor. It is vast at the top of the stairs, with a view of the grounds from the two-story windows. There are plush couches with billowing pillows on each side, and two small wooden tables. I imagine sitting here at sunset with a cup of chamomile tea and pouring words onto paper. I am comforted by the quiet. By the sound of my own breathing. I'm sure the space will be bustling when everyone else arrives. But for now, it is blanketed by silence.

"The bedrooms are down this way." He ushers me down a long, wide hallway. The lighting is dimmer. Softer. "There is another hallway on the other side. They wrap around the exterior of the building and meet around the back. This way, each room gets plenty of natural light. But over here," he says, motioning to a space to our right, centered down the length of the space, "is what we call the Eye. A *calm center*, if you will."

The Eye, as Soloman called it, is an oasis. A spiritual haven. I can feel it as soon as we enter. It is dim and very, very quiet. The only light comes from a large salt lamp on the back wall. As my eyes adjust, I can make out more of the details. There are candles placed around the periphery, and a fireplace in the center, none of which are lit. There are plush meditation mats on the floor, 25 or so, but the room is so large that they don't crowd it. It is carpeted. Soft. Comprised of the deep colors of the earth. And again, I smell the incense, dancing around my awareness, gracefully bringing my senses to life.

"There's a lot more to see, but there is plenty of time for that." He speaks more quietly in here. It seems he has no choice, as the energy creates an instant reverence. I can feel it moving in me. Energy finding spaces where it can become tangible.

Soloman moves his head to the side, urging me to follow, and directs me through an arched entrance away from the Eye and to the Northwest corner of the square hallway configuration. "A corner room. For our new teammate."

"Oh, thank you," I say, and then add, "temporary teammate, at least," in case he doesn't know my place here, for only a few short days.

"A teammate is a teammate, Cora. And that's what you are today."

"That's what I am today," I mirror. And I feel welcomed in a way that makes me believe that I belong here, in that warm and intuitive space in my chest.

As if, in this moment, I am where I am meant to be.

Soloman opens the door, and I can see why the corner room is sought after. The windows wrap around the far edges as if the sunshine is holding the room gingerly in the palm of its hand. The bedroom and living area take up the same grand space, with wood floors and fluffy white carpets. There is a nook near a large chair with a yoga mat stretched out on the ground. Above, shelving, with, as Emerson had imagined, everything I might need.

Soloman places my bags down atop a chest at the foot of the bed. "Bed, here," he points. "Sitting area, there. Washroom..." he says, as he directs me there, "here." The soaking tub, the cement floors that extend from the shower and outward in a way that creates one wide open space—it is all so awe-inspiring, and incredibly well-designed. This delicious mix of mid-century modern simplicity, antique grandeur and luxury, and something so natural and connected and kind. "There is a sauna room down the hall, also. An infrared and a steam room. You are not only free to use the space and the amenities at any time, but we beg you to enjoy them. We don't look at our work here as work. We are all here to heal, and to grow, and to meet our souls. Our practice is an extension of our passions, and we are meant to embrace the space as much as the guests who grace us with their presence. Yes?"

"Yes," I say, and that is all that I say, because roused emotions are threatening to crack my voice. I don't know exactly what it is that inspires this, but it has something to do with how naturally he seems to move through the world, and how it reminds me that it is ok to be myself. I am touched by how genuine he is. And it makes me more aware of the ways I am not.

I am also awed by this way of embracing work as an extension of self—not as an arduous thing, but as a healing thing. To see the human first, and the employee second. To remember that humanity is at the core of this work. Or any work that someone is passionate about, for that matter.

"Yes," he repeats with kindness, as if he knows even from my short response, that there is a lot that I am holding.

"Whelp, I'll leave you to it. Here is your key." He passes me a wooden card with *Catskills Retreat Center* and *Room 11* etched into it. "Just scan it at your door. Whenever you feel settled, come back down to reception, and Kai will show you around the grounds and get you acclimated. The group won't be here until later this afternoon, and there is plenty of time."

"Thank you so much, Soloman. I appreciate your help."

"Of course, of course." He bows before me in an exaggerated way, and then closes the door behind him.

Alone now in this delightful room, I take a very deep breath, and move toward the windows. The grounds seem to stretch on forever, lush with early summer sun. I open one of the windows, and the thin white curtains move with their breeze. I stand there for minutes, staring out at the trees, a waking meditation—roused only when I realize I haven't yet called Emerson.

I reach for my phone and find that it is not in my pocket. I must have left it in the car, and I know I should go down and retrieve it before I do anything else, as he may be starting to feel concerned.

I quickly tidy my hair and leave my room, fighting the desire to walk through The Eye and sprawl out on one of its cushions, head down the hallway, down the stairwell, and back toward reception. No one is at the desk, and I slip outside and toward my car. The phone is sitting in the front console, the GPS screen still lit up. I hop into the front seat and see that Emerson has called twice already.

"Cora," he exhales, moments after I dial. "I was getting worried."

"I'm sorry, my love. I only arrived a little while ago. I got up to my room and realized I left my phone behind."

"As long as you're in one piece, I'm happy," he says, and I can envision his sideways smile, one I have seen a thousand times but that never loses its charge. "How are the looks of it?"

"Oh God, Em, it's gorgeous." I take a deep breath, let myself fall into the smooth contours of my seat. "And I haven't even seen the half of it yet. The main building is terrifically soothing. Majestic, really. The aesthetic is beautiful. A unique design style. Modern and luxurious, but also spiritual, connected, so close to the earth."

"I had a feeling you'd love it. Kai supposedly designed the whole place himself. Natasha told you he worked as an architect in Manhattan?"

"Really? No, she hadn't mentioned it. That's how they were connected?"

"A few of our colleagues worked with him in the past. I never met him personally. Supposedly he was a wizard. Super talented. Not sure why he abandoned it all and went to hide out in the woods," he says quizzically. "But, to each their own."

I look over my shoulder at the structure behind me, and I am sure this is nothing like abandoning anything. "I can't speak for someone I haven't met. But looks to me like he's fulfilling his dreams."

"Well, good for him," Emerson says, rather enthusiastically. "And speaking of dreams, we have plenty to fulfill when you get back. So best hurry it up."

I shake my head but smile anyway. His charm tends to buffer what may come across as condescension, but of which I know is more innocent than that. "I'll be back before you know it," I say.

"Try to find some time to enjoy yourself, ok?"

"I will," I nod, peering out into the lush woods. "It doesn't seem it'll be very hard to do here."

"I love you, C," he says, deeply and absolutely, sincerity always waiting there on the tip of his tongue.

"Love you," I say, hanging up the phone and leaning my head back on my seat.

I exhale. The closed windows exaggerate the heat of the early sun, and it lulls me, holding me there in its embrace. I am cradled by the air around me, and very suddenly, with the heat and the quiet, I feel tremendously peaceful. My limbs are heavy, but in a luscious way. In a way that I have not felt in some time. The mountain air must be making its way into my cells.

And I think that hiding out in the woods might not be such a bad thing, after all.

I peer out my windshield, squinting my eyes and using my palm to shield them from the light streaming down. I want to take in as many details as possible of the naturalness around me, the sweet open air softening my sharp edges. Much of the forest beyond the tree line appears untouched and raw, and it reminds me that perfection doesn't come from flawlessness but from life itself. Each leaf and flower and passing cloud exactly where it is supposed to be. The leaves are swaying in the soft breeze, their melody one that must inspire all other songs. I sit with their sweet sounds for some time, until I notice a unique movement amongst the trees. It is one that appears just as natural but shows itself in a different way—as a connected piece, from the same soil, but standing out with an energy all its own.

I tilt my head to the side, watching, and then, I am sure of it—the movement I see in the woods in front of me is of a man weaving through the trees, stepping through high grass while, somehow, not disturbing it. I get out of the car, shut the door, give the man a small wave. He is closer now, and I can see that his chest is bare. His shirt is draped over his shoulder, with an ax leaning atop it. He must be the groundskeeper, and I think that every person that works here must be more stunningly beautiful than the next. He is slim in stature but strong. His skin is sun-kissed and glistening. His long hair is pulled back and secured breezily at the top of his head. He raises his hand, waving back without motion, holding there in a sort of kind and reverent welcome.

I find myself staring in a way that may be inappropriate, but I have never seen anything quite like it. Like this entire picturesque frame. The woods in the background. The sun's rays scattering down through their canopies. This gorgeous, half-naked man moving from light to shadow and back again with such grace it makes my chest swell.

My breath was caught up in it, and I find it again as I turn away. I wish I could have captured the essence of it and bottled it up. It's something I'd like to see again, and not just in my memory.

I go to the trunk of the car and retrieve my final bag. It's heavier than the others, and I swing it around to rest on my hip. I turn to walk toward the building, and he calls to me. From the softness of his voice, I discern that he is now only feet away.

"Hello," he says. "Can I help you with that?"

His tanned skin is shining in the morning sun, sculpted muscles expanding and contracting in a way that I can't help but to admire, once and then again. He moves the ax from his shoulder and lets it hang from his right hand, and then rests it on the ground. He swings his t-shirt off his shoulder and pulls it back over his head, a loose-fitting grey-blue cotton V-neck that looks like it's been worn hundreds of times and made better for it.

"Oh, thank you. I'm all right." The world suddenly seems to hold a slight sheen. My words are spoken but they sound far away. My heart is beating rhythmically in my throat. "That lovely man, Soloman, helped me with the rest. I had just left this one behind."

"Please," he says, extending his arm. "It would mean a lot to me."

I smile slightly, wary of the blush that is appearing on my cheeks, and pass him the bag. He takes the strap from a place where my hand is not. I notice that I notice it.

"I appreciate it, thank you." I close the trunk and we walk, the only sound our feet and the gravel.

"You must be Cora."

He doesn't pose it as a question but as a statement.

"Yes, I just arrived a short while ago."

"Welcome." He smiles warmly but his eyes are intense, somehow creating profundity from the mundane. And then he stops walking, and just looks at me that way—with the gentle smile, the bag over his shoulder, the ax hanging to the side of his calf, his deep brown eyes penetrating in a way I am unable to avoid. It's a strange gesture, to stop this way, but his pure presence is comforting. It's perhaps only strange because it's not strange. Because it seems so natural for him—a trend that I am quickly noticing here, at this place, and that I hope I can embrace just the same.

And then he walks again.

"The center is remarkable," I say, filling the silence and somewhat disappointed in myself for it.

"In this moment, there isn't anywhere else in the world I'd rather be," he says.

"I can understand why. I've only just arrived, but the energy here—I can tell it's unique."

My arms are crossed over my chest, though the morning chill is no longer in the air. There is just a lot swirling within me, energy that was once stagnant moving under my skin in a new way, and I think I am trying to keep myself contained.

"It is very special to me. This land holds countless stories." He stops again. "Do you see those flowers over there?"

He points to a cluster of pale pink blossoms scattered across a small open meadow, stretched out to the left of us, right beyond the tree line.

"Peonies," he says. "They are my favorite. As delicate as tissue paper. They only bloom for a short time each year. Maybe 7-10 days, at most. They came to life just this morning."

"Beautiful," I say, stretching my neck, eager to get closer. "How sad that they are only here for such a short time."

"Yes, it is sad," he says, his face soft and thoughtful, "though I think that's part of what makes them so beautiful. They hold the whole Universe in their petals, and then, with just as much grace, they are content to fall back to the earth."

I look at him with a soft smile.

"There are messages everywhere," he says, his gaze still falling across those elegant pink petals, and then turning toward me.

"If we only remember to look for them," I say.

His eyes seem to deepen, like they are endless. He lets them fall shut, for longer than is expected, and when they open, appear black from their depth. The way the infinite sky does, scattered with stars.

"Do you remember?" he asks me.

His words are delicate but there is no lightness there. My breath catches, lost somewhere in their gravity. I look away and back again. "Not often enough," I whisper.

He is terrifically silent, almost tragically so. A prickling heat materializes in my chest. It feels like sadness but with more nuance; a beautiful type of sadness that comes over me like a warm ocean wave. I don't understand why it comes, but it only lasts a moment. A remnant of something I must have forgotten. Something showing itself with this enigmatic reminder and working itself through. Things tend to live in our cells. Get processed when we least expect it.

"Do you care for the grounds here?" I ask, unable to bear it and again breaking our quiet.

He takes a slow breath, walks forward again. "I can't resist getting out in the early morning when the sun is just starting to warm things up. We were running low on firewood. It often gets cool at night, even at the peak of summer. I'll have to go retrieve it later, but I've prepared a large bundle. Ronan will help me when he arrives."

"Ronan?"

"Our full-time groundskeeper."

"And your name?" I ask, unsure why I'd waited.

His features are intense in this striking early light, obvious in their perfect symmetry, delicate and angled and exceptionally graceful, as if they were painted in depiction of the perfect form. His head leans slightly to the side, the sun creating a glowing frame around him, dancing in his wisping hair.

"I'm Kai," he says.

6

PRESENT DAY

Once we know who someone is, it's hard to remember who we thought they were before. The mind replaces what it no longer needs—the imagined details with what's real. It doesn't feel that way this time, however. It seems to me my imagination is dancing with the tangible details to create a new reality altogether, as if my preconceived notions haven't gone away. They've just been augmented. They've changed form.

This doesn't make sense to me in a logical way. It just seems my soul is at work, recognizing another soul in a way I am unable to comprehend. Even though I don't remember how I'd pictured him before, for some reason, it still feels like I pictured him exactly this way.

"Oh, you've met," sings Madalyn. "That's good." Kai and I walk through the entrance to the Welcome Center together, my bag over his arm. Maralyn leans her head to the side and seems to study him for moments before continuing.

"I was just emailing you the schedule, Cora," she smiles gently. "The group will be arriving around two o'clock."

"Plenty of time," says Kai. "I'm going to show Cora around, and then we can ready for our visitors." He turns to me. "Does that sound all right, Cora? I know it's been a long morning, so if you'd prefer to rest, please—I can introduce you to a few of our quiet spaces and you can recharge."

"I'd love to take a walk, if you don't mind." I'm not feeling tired, and I'm surprised for it. "I'm looking forward to seeing the grounds."

"Beautiful," he says, and then turning to Maralyn, "Thank you for your thoughtful work, as always." He puts his hands to his heart and bows his head. She mirrors him, and I am sure this is not the first of such exchanges.

"Cora. Do follow me." He places my bag at the side of the desk, and then motions for me to join him, and we head left from the entrance toward the pond. It is sprinkled with lily pads and framed by tall reeds and the water is still and clear and glistening with sun.

"We are on 47 acres, though much of the retreat center is framed within a 10-acre radius. The rest is hiking trails and some lush forest in which we've scattered nooks built for quiet contemplation. They aren't on the map. I think it's fun to stumble across them. Meditation benches. A labyrinth walk. Those kinds of things. We won't hike out that far today. I'll just show you some of the structures."

We turn onto a narrow trail at the north end of the pond.

"The buildings where we lead most of our sessions are built along a connected path, similar to the interior of the main building, which we call Citrine for short. All connected, all woven around a cohesive core. Did Soloman show you the Eye?"

"He did. What a beautiful space. I am looking forward to spending more time there."

"It is one of my favorite spaces on the property. I spend time in mediation there in the evening. Late at night, when most others are asleep."

"The quiet sounds intoxicating," I say.

"It is. Even when there are many people here, it's still quiet. You can't force that kind of thing, but you can beget a space that allows it. And it's something that I am grateful for. That the space itself has created this. That we're here as a part of it."

I do feel as if I am a part of it. As if the woods have welcomed me with a warm embrace. We can't see anything but forest now, stretching in every direction at the edges of the trail. The air is fresh and pure. I inhale deeply and let it tickle at my throat and the edges of my lungs, making its way through my dusty capillaries. "That the space itself has created this—what a beautiful, though modest thing to say. I'm told you've designed everything."

"I have put so much of my heart into it, but I can't take all the credit. It guided me, once I let it." He pauses, looks out into the forest. "And the whole team took part. They've been here since the beginning." His words are gentle and alive. "We started small. A tent and small groups that visited on the weekends. And the more soul we poured into it, the more it grew."

He smiles, a peacefulness falling over the angles of his face.

"I can imagine that's the reason the energy here is so unique. The soul that was poured into everything."

Kai tilts his head to the side, sinks his hands into his pockets.

"May I ask how it feels for you? First impressions can be quite illuminating."

It's a good question he asks, and I'm not sure how to answer it. Because the land is already doing something to me that I can't quite explain. There are aspects of these sensations that are familiar, as I've felt the unique impact that energy work can have on the body and the mind in my yoga and meditation practices. But this is new to me in its intensity. I am not afraid, because there is something pure and calming in its power. There is a deep presence in the swirling movement.

"It's peaceful," I say, all too succinctly, leaving out the rest. I had learned at a young age that expressing my vulnerabilities led to feelings of loneliness or frustration, because I so often felt misunderstood. "I've come from the city just this morning, so you can imagine the dichotomy."

He nods his head, and looks up at the sky, seeming to search for something. There is only a vast and stretching blue that can be seen, but I am sure, infinite answers to be found there. He looks back at me.

"I can imagine the dichotomy. But I wonder—and please, tell me if I am being too bold or intrusive—but I wonder, how does it make you *feel*?"

I can tell that small talk means nothing to this man, because there are more important things to be discussed. The truth of it is that there are always more important things to be discussed. It is something I must be reminded of, but of which seems to come naturally to him.

"I don't find that intrusive. People don't usually seem to care about the vulnerable bits. The things underneath. Or maybe I'm just too afraid to share them."

"You don't need to be afraid here," he says. And I believe him.

I exhale. "I'm grateful, first of all—that you are asking me a real question, and that it is ok for me to answer it." A stray leaf wanders down from a tree, makes its way gracefully to the ground below, settles there. "I am sure that things are different here. Lighter and weightier at the same time. And it's ok to be myself, and both of those things at once."

A strand of hair has loosened from its band, and I tuck it behind my ear. I feel flushed. The energy continues to move under my skin, but the pressure is demanding now. Like it wants to burst through my chest. He waits for me to continue.

"I feel this stirring, one that runs deeper than I am accustomed to. Perhaps I could call it inspiration. But that's not it... Not quite." I pause, searching. "It feels like it's sparking on my fingertips. It feels as if I am somehow more myself in this moment than I have been in a long time."

He doesn't smile now. He looks down at his feet, and then at me, and stops walking again. I am already accustomed to his starting and stopping, and I appreciate that he is holding space for my sharing in such a profound way.

"Who are you, when you aren't yourself?" he asks.

I am quiet. I am fumbling for an answer, but my mind seems as if it is suddenly wiped clean, and I can't find the truth of it.

"I don't know," I say.

He is breathing evenly, and not just looking at me, but into me. It takes my breath, and we just hold there. It is comforting now that my mind has cleared. It doesn't feel numbing, but more like a meditation. Like I am more than just my mind, and my body. Like I am remembering other parts of myself.

"Your soul always knows the truth, Cora. It's the rest of our selves that must keep practicing. Keep learning." He nods. "Your soul is wise. It is strong and soft, and exceptionally compassionate."

My eyes are misting over, and I slowly shake my head. "I don't know," I say again.

"I do," he says. He is gazing at me with a penetrating stare. One of recognition. For maybe the first time in my life, I feel *seen*—in a way that isn't about the words we spoke or the way he looks into me. In the same way that I am feeling this deep presence, in the same way that this energy moves under my skin, it is an abstract but powerful knowing. It bubbles in my chest, and I clear my throat, wary that I am losing myself in it.

"But how could you know that?" I ask, breathy and searching. "We've only just met."

We are still standing in place, facing each other. He brushes his sandal against the powdery trail beneath us. "You can tell what my soul is like, can't you?"

I think about things like wisdom and benevolence and tenderness and benign power, and I cannot disagree with him. I nod and keep the rest to myself. He is still looking at me, and I am awed by his ability to be so present. I am overwhelmed by his gaze but I refuse to let my anxieties pull me away, and I force myself to stay locked there for as long as he does. I teach the importance of presence in my classes every day, but my own practice wavers. I am human after all, but so is he. He just seems to vibrate differently than me. Different than most.

"These deeply stirring states are a beautiful gift," he says. "Some of my most soul-provoking states—they arrived without known premise. A wildness that couldn't be named or contained and of which I held only an awareness of its presence. I've learned to trust the stirrings, and not demand answers before they arrive. Those can be discovered in time. We must embrace the journey itself. Accept wherever it is that it may lead us."

He swallows hard and rubs at the back of his neck. It is the first time I notice hints of anxiety in his eyes, and I wonder what moves in him. I want to ask him, but it seems these are answers I'm not meant to have. I need to remind myself again that we have only just met, because it does not feel that way at all.

I believe there are some people in this world we can know for a lifetime, and never really know. But there are also those whom we can see deeply at first glance. The latter is incredibly rare, and something I have yet to experience to this magnitude.

"Come," he says.

We continue on in silence, and I allow my space to settle, recalibrating around the energy and awareness of the last few minutes until we come upon the next structure, a pristine wooden a-frame propped up on a small hill. The front façade is comprised of only glass, segmented by perpendicular beams, and painted the most luscious and surprising shade of deep blue-violet. The roof matches in color and leans from its pinnacle down toward the grassy grounds below.

"Lapis Lazuli," he says. "Our creativity center. Each structure is named after a naturally occurring and supportive substance, making the structure itself not only a natural extension of the earth, but a space that creates the energy to elicit and harness these powerful forces within us." He ushers me forward toward its entrance.

Being well-versed in supportive gemstones, I know that Lapis is said to help one tap into their creativity and support inner peace, spiritual awareness, and collaboration. "I am awed by how deeply considered these spaces are," I say, and that is all I say, as I am truly enveloped in awe, and most of my energy is focused on taking in my surroundings.

Inside, there is a large rectangular table at the back end, surrounded by stools and covered in splashes of paint. To the right, patterned floor cushions are arranged around a circular carpet. To the left, a scattering of floor easels, pottery wheels, and shelving with fine art supplies and craft items, brushes, paints and pencils, fabrics and yarn and thousands of colored beads. The small but airy structure is alive with color, the blue-violet highlighting lighting fixtures and ceiling beams, complimenting the subtlety of the rest of the interior structure, built of light wood and glazed cement floors. The glass façade opens to a view of the forest, bringing the outside in and saturating the space with light.

We walk next to the dining hall, about 50 yards to the right. Appropriately named Raw Green Opal, the dining hall serves nourishing plant-based meals, meant to support gentle detoxification and vitality. True to its name, it is built of moss and overflowing with life. Near the counter, there are fresh herbs, growing straight from the soil, and a robust garden unfolding from the back porch that can be seen from the window. Kai grabs two bananas from the counter and hands me one. "We'll get you a proper meal before we head back."

Tucked a little further up into the woods is Tiger's Eye, a physical fitness center. This space is more clinical when compared to the others, housing exercise equipment, treadmills, stationary bikes, and weight machines. It is softened by dark wood and ivy and deep orange granite.

"We promote outdoor physical activity as much as possible, but we feel this is a beneficial addition," says Kai. "We don't want to keep people from their workout routines if they find them beneficial, and we find this space to be great for energy release after some of our more intense meditative sessions. The lighting changes depending on the weather and time of day or night. Ambiance can be so important for reaching a flow state, in physical activity or otherwise."

"Dependent on the weather?"

"Imagine a cool, rainy evening, navy-purple-hued low lights, the sounds of melodic thunder through the speakers. It helps with flow."

He moves to a touchscreen on the wall and the room falls into a quiet space of deep purple hue, rumbling thunder sounds complimented by a melodic flute echoing through the space. "A contrast to today's sunshine, but you get the idea."

"I'm overwhelmed, Kai. By how wonderful this all is." I close my eyes for a moment, listen to the sounds of the rain. "I'm so grateful for the opportunity to teach here this week."

"I am glad and humbled to hear that," he says, putting his hands to his heart. "I had a strong feeling about this arrangement being..." He pauses, holds my gaze again for a fleeting moment, but then looks away. "…being one that unfolds with the utmost grace."

I think about the intuitive pull I felt toward this experience. I wonder if Kai is leaving something out, not because of the words he chooses but in the way he says them—as they seem truthful but carefully chosen, eloquently avoiding the rest.

"So did I," I say, and then add, much less eloquently, "Natasha had the most wonderful things to say about the center. And Emerson had high praise for your work."

"They are too kind." He picks up a pair of loose free weights and places them to rest on their rack. "They obviously shared high praise about you and your work, as well."

"Emerson mentioned knowing you through mutual connections in the design space?"

"Yes, we hadn't crossed paths back then, but we know a lot of the same people. It's not a very big world, once you're in it."

"How long have you been removed from that world—of the traditional architectural firm?"

"Has been, oh…" He pauses, bringing two fingers to his chin. "Has to be almost 5 years now." He leans his head toward the doorway. "Walk and talk? The yoga studio will be our last stop."

I nod, and he continues. "I had to make a change. The pull was so strong. The messages so insistent." He gingerly moves a branch to the side and ducks beneath it as we walk down the narrow path toward the studio.

"Did you like what you were doing?" I ask him.

"I loved it," he says. "It was less about where I was, however, and more about where I needed to go."

"Did you envision that this was where you were headed?"

"Not in the details," he says. "Only in the way it felt." He takes a deep inhale, followed by an exhale, long and silent. "It was a leap without being able to see the ground beneath me."

There is a rocky patch of earth before us, and we balance across the undulating terrain. His gracefulness is so extraordinary that I find it hard to comprehend. It seems his soul is doing the walking, and his body is just following its lead.

"I was following the path one enlightening moment at a time," he says. "I still am. It didn't make sense to anyone but me."

"It makes a lot of sense to me," I say, understanding this soulful resolve, inspired by it, wishing I had more of it.

"Have you experienced something similar?" he asks.

"I've only been teaching for a short time. Less than two years. My story is nowhere near as glamorous," I sigh, "but I do understand the demanding nature of necessary change. In my own ways."

"In what ways are those?"

We continue to walk without urgency, gliding along the now smooth trail to the rhythm of the bird song.

"I didn't listen in the way that you did. It seems that the choice was made for me, rather than by me."

"By who?" he asks.

I shrug. "The Universe? Karma? The manipulative reality of pure happenstance?"

He mirrors my shrug, but whereas mine was questioning, his is somehow wisdom.

"What started as subtle nudges," I continue, "they became something else entirely."

"They got too loud?" he asks, looking toward me as the earth stands firm beneath our moving feet.

I am quiet for a moment, allowing the all-too-familiar surge of pain to pass through me. I've learned to stop fighting. I've learned to just let it burn. "They got too loud," I confirm, in an ironic whisper.

I am looking down as he puts his hand on my shoulder. The purity he emits removes feelings of inappropriateness—his presence and how he delivers it is absolutely a kindness, and it is not for that reason that I feel the rush of heat on my skin, centering around his touch and reverberating outward. My vibration feels too small for his presence; my body not accustomed to his unique frequency. He only rests there for a moment, but even after he removes his hand, the shockwaves continue to echo.

It seems we are both catching our breath, relaxing our heartbeats, recalibrating around an unspoken reality. We continue walking, the sun decorating our faces with patterns seeping through the trees.

"I worked in mutual funds. I fell into it. My father set me up with an internship while I was in college. The hours were absurd. I was sleeping only a few hours a night near the end. There wasn't a time when I wasn't experiencing high levels of stress and anxiety. I resigned when I had no other option, so I don't consider it a courageous leap," I shrug sadly. "But I suppose it was a leap nonetheless."

"These things follow their own timelines. We both experienced that same pivotal shift in different ways. You had no choice for your reasons, I had no choice for mine." He doesn't ask me about my reasons. I appreciate that he waits for me to offer them up. His patience and presence make me feel safe. "If not courageous, what was it?"

A beetle lands on his forearm, and he watches, still and gentle, until it flies off.

"Honestly?" I ask.

He tilts his head to the side, lets it rest gently in the air. "What other way is there?"

I can't possibly disagree, and I wonder how he can speak these resounding truths with such tenderness and simplicity. Any knee-jerk reaction or habitual defensiveness doesn't seem to exist in response to him. There are only kind offerings of broadening perspectives and reminders of my humanness—of what it means to be truly present and authentic.

"Desperation," I say, responding with my own simple truth.

"Is navigating through desperation not courageous?"

He asks in such a sure way that I find tears threatening at the corners of my eyes. I can see the truth of it, but it doesn't fit in the spaces between my cells. They are too filled up with other things that are much heavier, and the only ones that I know how to feel.

He waits, giving me the space to decide if I will continue. And though I never continue, though this is where my silence usually falls, where I choose new words that are far too light and in total contrast to the choked-up feeling in my throat, this time, I do. I want to.

"We never meant to get pregnant," I say, my head down, hearing only my voice and the swaying trees and our feet against the gravel. "We didn't think we wanted children. But it happened, and that quickly changed."

A bluebird flies across our path, lands on a nearby tree branch. For moments, we watch. And then, with as much grace as when it had arrived, it departs, singing its sweet song.

"I didn't slow down. We lost her at seventeen weeks."

When I say it, every cell in my body is grasping at something that is slipping away. I have nightmares where I am running and running but don't get anywhere. Everything is sinking. Everything is out of reach. The guilt is too great. I avoid it because the panic is normally too thick to wade through. But in this moment, I am still breathing. And it surprises me. So, for this reason, I say the words I know every intricacy of, but which have never actually crossed my lips.

"I blame myself for that," I whisper.

We continue our slow pace, the yoga studio in view, fifty or so feet further up the dirt path. We are fully in shade now, the foliage so thick that the sun's rays can't make their way through, and it smells a bit like rain and feels like the damp softness of a cloud resting on my skin.

"I am so sorry, Cora," he says with deep compassion. And then, he is exceptionally quiet, turning toward me and looking into my eyes in a way that is pure presence, and then somehow, looking even deeper still. It seems his gaze is penetrating me, burning through layers of skin until they can find the truth of things.

"This has been tragically painful for you," he whispers, gripping his chest in a way that seems to demonstrate not just empathy, but pain, and when he speaks this truth, a single tear that had been threatening falls down my cheek. I can feel the heat of grief in my chest, but it mingles with relief. Because the pain feels less there, in his empathetic hold. Like I have someone not just to speak it to or hand it over to, but to share it with. His presence feels like something ethereal. Like my body is transparent, and in seeing my pain through my skin, he can mirror it.

"I am awed by the way you experience this hurt," he continues. "The light you have. The way you move with such grace..." He moves his hand away from his chest, and lets it hang by his side, and I can imagine how comforting it would be, to hold it.

"There is..." he starts, trailing off. He holds his shoulder, squeezes there, his muscles shifting under his grasp.

"What?" I ask, wiping the dampness from my face. "It's ok. Whatever it is, you can say it."

He shakes his head in such a small way it is almost imperceptible. "There is so much I'd like to say to you," he whispers, and then finds his voice again. "I know that this is not my place, but I wish I could tell you." He looks up toward the sky, searching, straightening, accessing something, his shoulders rolling down and his heart pulling him forward. "I wish I could tell you this is not your fault. That there are so many powerful truths that make up your story, and I am sure this particular shame is not one of them."

He takes a deep breath and comes back to the ground, grips at the muscles of his shoulder again, and I feel a shiver run down my spine. His words come to me like riddles meant to be unraveled, mysteries that are too enigmatic for this language. They have a weight to them, holding us to the earth in a new way. I am lightheaded. The energy is roaring, screaming out under my skin and spinning around us. There is a part of me, a spirit-led part, that craves agreement. But I very quickly quiet that part of myself, sure I am not deserving of even one moment of its kind respite from the guilt I am meant to feel.

It seems the only response that I can access is one that is orbiting our periphery. With so much moving inside of me, I'm surprised I can find my voice at all.

"Thank you," I choke, "for your presence."

"Thank you," he says, "for yours."

He releases his hold on his shoulder, lets his muscles settle back into place. I take a deep breath and try to let myself settle back into place, too. It's useless to attempt to fully come back to center in this moment, and I don't have to. I allow myself to stay in this heightened space of consciousness, let the pain simmer under my skin, and continue to walk forward anyway.

When we come upon the final structure, whatever forcefield has been created around us begins to crumble. There is more room to breathe, bits of light falling over our faces again in lacey patterns. I am reminding myself to focus on the way my feet feel upon the ground, and to take sufficient air into my lungs.

The building is architecturally profound, comprised of dark wood and surprising angles, high ceilings and open air, built into a nook surrounded so closely by forest that the tree branches brush against its thatched roof. There is a large outdoor space with wood-planked floors, open walls, and a bamboo overhang.

"There are two spaces dedicated for yoga classes—out here on the veranda, or in the studio inside. The interior is split into two sides—a contemplation room, and a yoga studio. The contemplation room is used for meditation. It is a silent space. The walls are soundproof. And this," he says, opening the door to the yoga studio, "is your office." It is, not surprisingly, sensational. Minimal and soothing, gentle and alive. There are candles and salt lamps not yet lit, an altar at the front, shelving with blankets and blocks and mats, and large windows that look out toward the forest. The atmosphere is similar to the Eye—quiet, penetrating, inspiring, and deeply comforting.

"Does it have a name?" I ask, my voice a revering whisper.

He walks toward the window and places both his hands on the thin sill, his back to me. He stands that way for moments, looking out toward the forest, reminding me that silence does not need to be uncomfortable. And when he turns around, there is a glimmer in his eye, though one I have trouble pinning down. There are tears that have made their way through, but I don't know what they represent—his reaction to deep presence, or emotion on either end of a wide spectrum, from deep pain to an astounding appreciation of beauty.

"Not yet," he says. And that's all he says. So I don't say anything more.

7

APRIL 1899

I walk down toward the creek without haste. There is no need to rush, and the sweet afternoon sun is meant to be felt in an unabridged way. The first breath of the spring season is not just an air, but a mood that permeates every cell. Sparking, enlivening, lightening, dancing on inhale. Primrose and their sweetness. Fresh laundry swaying in the swirling breeze. Still-crisp air melting around cascading rays of an awakened sun.

The creek, until that time of year trickling down from the far reaches of the mountains, is now more like a small but rushing river, a haven for the ice-cold water born from winter snow caps. The sound is my favorite part. Each stone turned and smoothed under the babbling movement. The jutting rock that stretches over the water looks even more majestic in the springtime, solid and dignified, a source of grounding amongst the rush of new life.

I dip the bucket and feel invigorated by the quick numbing of my fingers. I dip another, and let the water splash over my wrists, kissing the edges of my sleeves and dispersing through their lace. With the weight of the buckets balancing me on each side, I walk the 150 feet between the creek and the empty house, my neck warmed by the sun and exertion, but the rest of me cooled by the dampness that hangs gently.

The back porch is littered with wisps of pollen. It swirls around my boots and makes footprints upon the wooden planks. *She would love this*, I think.

I place the buckets down and move to the side of the house to retrieve the laundry from the line. And then, I am done, and everything suddenly seems too quiet. But it won't be, for too much longer. And there will be halibut and grits and stories to tell. So, I find a seat on the front porch, watching the sun slowly make its way across and down until my eyes get heavy.

"Mama!" I hear and awake with a jolt. She is running, her curly blonde hair seeming to catch the sunset before it has even shown itself. She has that way about her. A life beyond the rest. A depth and lightness that lives in one place at the same time and it is perfectly natural and easy. For most of us it is not natural, but something we are always wishing for.

"Mama, look!" She dives onto the porch before I have a chance to make my way down, her hand clutched around something I cannot see. Her eyes are wide and alive and blue like crystal—so filled with light and so pure that you can see right to the bottom. She opens her hand and sitting there on her palm is a small silvery-grey and shining stone.

"Sphalerite," she says, slowly and carefully, turning her head toward the path. "Right, Papa? Did I say it right?"

"You said it just right," he says, his smile crooked and gentle as he walks, easy and sure, with his very slight limp and his exceptional grace. "Just right," he repeats, rustling her hair as he joins us. And my heart exhales, because I can't breathe right until he is here with me. There is never enough air without the both of them near.

"It's a true treasure," she says. "A real and true treasure. I didn't find it, really. Papa found it. But I led us there to the creek, so maybe a little bit of me found it, too."

"She's got it all turned around, Mama," says Asher. "If anything, I was just there to retrieve it. Her treasure-hunting senses, they never fail. She can sniff out a gem from miles out, I'm sure of it."

My face starts to hurt from all the smiling. My favorite kind of hurt.

"I am so proud of you, my little one," I say, lifting her up and spinning her around. "Treasures for my treasure."

"Do you know what they say about Saph...about Sphalerite, Mama?" She is in my arms, speaking close to my face in a whisper.

"I do not but I sure wish you would tell me."

She turns to Asher. "Should I tell her, or should you?"

"Oh, you should most definitely tell her," he nods.

"Right, I'll tell you," she says, turning back around. "Well, this here gem will keep us safe. All you have to do is believe it's so."

"Well, I just have one question then," I say. "Do you believe it's so?"

"Mama," she giggles. "I don't even have to try."

I tickle her under the arms to extend the mesmerizing sound of her laughter.

"So, my dear girl, what do you think?" asks Asher. "Should we stash it away for now?"

"For now," Pearl nods. "But only for now. Because when we go out adventuring tomorrow, I'm bringing it with."

Asher nods in agreement. "A very good plan."

The two of them scurry inside to place the gemstone in Pearl's steel capsule, where all her most precious treasures are held. There is a piece of dark-colored labradorite, two calcite crystals, the glistening half of an oyster shell, a handful of speckled and sparking stones that caught her eye in the same way that they catch the light.

The steel container was a gift from Asher on Pearl's sixth birthday. A place to keep safe the things that keep her safe.

I sit watching the sky turn a deep orange, listening to their reverent whispers.

8

PRESENT DAY

After stopping for a quick but delicious lunch of kale and farro patties drizzled with tahini sauce and iced lemongrass-hibiscus tea, I part with Kai by reception and go to my room for a shower. The light is streaming in through the windows in its full afternoon splendor, and although the bathroom is in shade, I leave the lights off to embrace the naturalness of it all.

It is so quiet. So peaceful. The only sound the splashing of water, moving across my skin, falling in wet clusters to the smooth concrete below. I think back on my morning, the beautiful respite from my usual routines, surroundings, and experiences. And I have many reactions that have been vying for space.

I was calmed by images of the forest, the stunning structures, the purifying aromas. There is a lightness, one that leaves me feeling electric—with a tingling under my skin, and a tickling at my throat. It feels like inspiration, possibility, an excitement without preconception of what it is that I am excited about. There is heaviness, too. It is made up of fear and longing, mingling with an all-too-familiar grief. There is the memory of the sharp pain and how it was buffered. The truths that I try to avoid and the way I spoke them.

Most noticeable is this burning sensation in my chest. This is separate from the rest, neither heavy nor light, or maybe it is both of these at the same time. It is hard for me to tell, because it is an abstract thing. It is soul-inspired and alive, sad and kind, and I don't know how to make sense of it.

When I had my miscarriage, I did not shed a tear for two weeks. For fourteen days, I moved about the world in a numb stupor. I quit my job and sat in front of the television, looking but never watching. I ate but I didn't taste my food. Slept but did not rest. And then, on the fifteenth day, a package arrived at my door—a sweet pair of croqueted booties I had forgotten I'd ordered—and something in me broke. I convulsed under its weight.

Emerson held me through it. He became my foundation when I was totally undone.

He never seemed to come undone, however. I think he found solace in my need for him. I think he was afraid of me when I was the emotional walking dead. He never spoke about his own pain. He used mine as an excuse not to.

While in the trenches of this trauma, Emerson's support was self-less and generous and kind. I was never alone in it, and it is something I will be forever grateful for. There was just something about sharing this pain with Kai that felt undeniably and strikingly unique—not necessarily in what was spoken, but in the way that it *felt*. Like his presence traversed the endlessly cascading layers of my experience that lurked well below the surface, and in being acknowledged, they were finally able to exhale.

I bring my focus back to the moment, to the water, to my breath. I think of Emerson. I wish he could see the grounds, the architecture, the way the breeze moves through the trees here. I know he would not appreciate these experiences, or be impacted by them, in the same way that I am. That they would mean something different to him. And that's ok. But this longing feels more poignant now—the wish that he would care to see the world through a different, more connected, more spiritual lens. That we could share in this depth and passion together.

It is not this longing that creates that burning under my ribs, however. I take a deep inhale and a long exhale, and I am reminded that with every cleansing breath comes the excavation of some of the stagnant dust that is always waiting in the wings. My interactions with Kai were of pure presence. I have never experienced presence in that way, and I understand that such a profound energetic experience could have lingering effects. I do feel guilt around the intensity of my experience, wondering if Emerson would see my interaction with Kai as inappropriate. He has never presented himself as a jealous person, though I don't know if he would quite understand the purity with which the interaction was expressed. Without understanding that, my time with Kai may have appeared to be far too intimate.

But was it far too intimate? I can try to deny that I was drawn to him, but it is futile to lie to myself. What I can truthfully embrace is the fact that I was not drawn to him in any kind of usual way, and that the allure is likely intensified by the unique nature of our interaction, and my need for this soul-inspired kind of connection. It feels frivolous to allow myself to look at it in any other way. I was seen and opened by the true presence of another being, one who is further along on their awakening journey than I am. I'm sure he would impart the same presence and wisdom to anyone else who was in my place. It was special, and important, to me—but only because it was unique for me. I have a feeling that this kind of interaction is anything but unique here. That it is woven into its tapestry.

My heart was opened in moments, and there was relief there. An exhale. There has been so much constriction. So much pretending. And, amidst my admittedly beautiful life, so much pain. It's not that I can't talk to Emerson about these truths and pains. He is supportive in all the ways he knows how. But that doesn't mean it is in all the ways I need.

Not only did the interaction with Kai rouse something within me and create movement amidst my dusty wounds, but it also allowed for an uncomfortable clarity. I cannot escape the knowing that today represented something that I have been missing in a profound way. The fact alone that it was such a unique presence in my life feels suddenly tragic. I see it now, so clearly. I long for connection in the deepest and most holistic way, and I have been existing predominantly on the surface of things.

I don't blame anyone but myself. I've accepted these dynamics in my life without doing anything to change them. But, in my own defense, I couldn't truly know what it was that I was missing without knowing what it felt like.

I turn off the water and wring out my hair. Suddenly aware that I may be running behind schedule, I shake myself from my revelry, give myself a brisk towel dry, and tie my hair on the top of my head. I look toward the clock on the wall, the kind that looks like it would make a monotonous tick-tock but of which is kind enough to not impart such torture, and see that we are meant to greet our guests in around 15 minutes, give or take. They will be traveling together by bus, the high-end kind with televisions and bathrooms and gourmet snacks. Gourmet or not, it sounds rather uncomfortable to me. I'd so much rather have my own space.

I dress myself in a pair of form-fitting grey athletic pants and a matching short tank, with a loose-fitting, button-down draped over, meant as a coverall until it is time to teach. I pour a glass of water from the filtered tap by the window and find my phone.

Will be busy for a while, I text Emerson. *Will call later. Love you.*

I love you too, he responds moments later, and I place my phone on the charger by my bed, check myself in the mirror and head downstairs.

Kai, Maralyn, and Soloman are in the lobby, standing around the front desk and laughing about something I am not privy to. There are also three others I have yet to meet—an older woman with a flowing skirt and waving silver hair, a young man with strong arms and bronze skin, and a middle-aged gentleman with kind eyes and a white apron.

"Cora," Maralyn smiles. "I hope you are feeling refreshed. Come, meet the family."

She introduces me to Avery, the Creative Arts Therapist who smells of Patchouli, Ronan, the full-time groundskeeper, and Alexander, the kind-eyed vegan chef.

"Such a pleasure to meet you all," I say, and when they bow, similarly to Kai and Maralyn earlier, I follow suit.

"Transport is running a little late," Maralyn says, "but our guests should be arriving soon. In the meantime, let's go over the agenda for the next few days."

Maralyn proceeds to read through the schedule, ensuring everyone is comfortable with the week's structure. I am to lead four yoga classes over the next three days. I am told I have full creative control, but I am also reminded that with this team comes full support—and if I need direction or have any questions, to never hesitate to ask.

"Remember that the overarching goal of these three days is to impart creative inspiration and team building," says Maralyn. "But it goes without saying that from these overarching goals, we always aim to go above and beyond for our guests, meet them where they are at, provide safe spaces, and impart whatever it is they desire for the next stages of their growth."

And then, to my surprise, the team chants in perfect unison, "Presence, patience, intuition," followed by a venerable bow of their heads.

When their eyes rise again, Kai's find mine as if they have something to say. But before I can read their messages, they have turned away.

9

PRESENT DAY

The guests are ushered inside with warm welcomes, coconut and mango-infused water, plush slippers for their feet, and name tags to hang around their necks. The team works together with graceful precision, seemingly hyper-aware of every space and utterance and empty water glass that needs attention, but without any indication that they are exerting energy in their consideration. I assist where I can, following their lead, almost envious that I am not as at home here as they are, craving their naturalness and experience.

It is an eleven-person team, and the whole group has joined, which to me seems quite a show of dedication, considering the distance and short notice. A few of the guests are familiar, as I sometimes visit Emerson in the office, and I'm sure I've seen them before. It is common for Emerson and me to speak about the intricacies of our days over a slow dinner, and I've heard plenty about his teams and their strengths and struggles—at least from a professional standpoint. He rarely gets personal, and it is ironic to me that I am given the chance to know everyone in a deeper and more personal way these next few days, when he has been working with many of them for years.

I say *hello* to everyone, receive *hellos* and kind nods in return. Muhammad, the only of the group whom I have spoken with in the past, extends his hand. If Emerson was ever to get personal, his relationship with Muhammad would be the closest thing. He is his most trusted employee.

"How wonderful, that you are here with us," he says. "Natasha seems thrilled about it. She referred to you as 'marvelous' more than once in our team brief."

I laugh, grateful for the welcoming words. There is a part of me that feels like an outsider, but I hope this will dissipate as the days progress. It could be a strange dynamic, being here as both the yoga instructor and the wife of the CEO, but it doesn't have to be. We are all here with a purpose.

"I'm glad to have the opportunity to be here with you all," I say. "Hopefully we can all take from it what we need."

He scans the vast and light-filled room and then smiles broadly. "I, for one, am feeling better already."

The team is cued up to lead guests to their rooms, and I'm glad I've found a way to help. We usher them upstairs, hand them key cards to their single rooms while they marvel at their temporary dwellings, and soon there is no one left in the lobby but who started there before the group's arrival. Aside from Kai, who is preparing for the first session.

Soloman tells me that this upcoming session is a sort of icebreaker activity—a way to welcome guests and get them comfortable in their new environment, where they will be living amongst their colleagues in a whole new way. "Kai normally leads this group, though the rest of us join as active participants. You are welcome to do the same."

"I'm a bit nervous," I admit.

"You are amongst friends," he says.

"And eleven of my husband's star employees." I bite the inside of my mouth.

"I bet they'll be friends soon, too," he shrugs, and then he smiles, and so do I.

Twenty minutes later, the guests start to filter back into the lobby, and once everyone has returned, they are guided to a door to the right of the front desk, where Soloman had first appeared when I met him. I had no idea it would open to such a vast space, but behind the wall of the reception desk there is an arch-shaped room that is grand in both size and magnificence. The wall that separates us from the lobby is comprised of floor-to-ceiling bookshelves, the arch-shaped wall at the other side made predominantly of glass. The space is large enough to account for the Eye and individual dwellings upstairs, as the far wall doesn't denote the edge of the structure, but it opens to an outdoor space with an overhang and seating area, and then out further to a lush patio garden.

There are floor cushions set up in a circular shape in the center of the room. Kai takes the seat at the far center, and everyone follows his lead, choosing a cushion and settling in. Once everyone is seated, silence and stillness fall over the space. Kai takes three deep inhales, followed by three slow exhales, and then removes his phone from his pocket. After moving through a few quick steps on the screen, shades descend covering every large window, low lights are switched on above us, and a gentle chant plays over the speakers. The space transforms in moments and I am comforted by its grace. The others look around in awe, not yet privy to the level of pristine magic they are in for, and already taken by it.

Kai directs us to breathe as he does, holding deep inhales, releasing slowly, and we are soon breathing to a singular rhythm, with each other, with the melodic sounds that fill the room. His energy is striking in its quiet and compassionate command. He is undeniably beautiful as he sits there, directing the energy of the space with closed eyes and an obviously open heart. He asks the rest of us to close our eyes too, and I do so reluctantly, so mesmerized by this space that has been created that I don't want to stop looking at it. But once my eyes are closed, it becomes even more powerful, and I feel safe there.

"It may seem you are all here for a specific reason," he says. "What might that reason be?"

Silence follows.

"You are safe to respond with whatever your truth is. In this space, there is no judgment. No expectations. There needn't be any pressure to do things in a certain way. There is no right, and there is no wrong. There is only now, as we are."

Silence again follows, and he directs everyone to open their eyes.

"Why are you here?" he asks again.

A middle-aged woman with auburn hair and thick-framed glasses, hazel eyes and a matching scarf, raises her hand. Kai smiles with kindness, squints at her name tag. "Jennifer. Why are you here?"

"Our boss made us come?" she smirks.

The group laughs quietly, some looking down, some raising eyebrows.

"Ah ha," he exclaims. "Precisely. Your boss requested it, and here you are. Is that the common thread for all of you?"

The group shakes their heads in agreement, seemingly growing in comfort concerning this honest response.

"Now, the same question, again, but slightly different. Jennifer, why are *you* here?"

She is quiet for moments, fiddling with her fingers, and then looking up at Kai. "Well, because I'm supposed to be," she says. "I want to do the right thing."

His eyes are locked on hers, soft but penetrating, a gaze that I have already learned from him. They change color to a deeper brown, the reflections in them swirling slightly like a kaleidoscope.

"Why are you *here?*" he asks this time.

Her eyes mist over, and it is not surprising. It makes sense to me, in this moment, not knowing what is going on under her skin and in her heart but feeling that something has been penetrated. Because this is how I felt earlier. This is what a moment feels like when your emotions haven't been let out in so long, and someone hands you a compassionate invitation.

She takes the tip of her scarf and dabs at the corner of her eye. "Because I am lonely," she whispers. "Because I am hoping these days will bring me something to hold onto."

Kai takes another very deep breath, his eyes still locked on Jennifer, her eyes still locked on him, and he brings his hands again to his heart. He looks around the room then, and nods his head, prompting the others to follow his lead. We all oblige, giving Jennifer our presence. Our understanding. Our support. Whatever it is we each have to give.

"Beautiful, Jennifer. Beautiful. Thank you for your courage." She smiles, and I wonder if she feels a bit less lonely already.

"Now, we will go around the room, and each of you will be invited to share your response. Why are you *here*? Because I am…"

He adjusts his position on the cushion, settling in deeper.

"You are never required to do or say anything during your stay here. If at any time you have something to express, you can do so safely. If at any time, you don't wish to speak, then you may remain silent. But I do ask you one thing. Please do aim to be aware of your motivations. If you don't want to respond to this question, why don't you want to respond? Maybe the answer lies there. *Because I am …embarrassed? Because I am …unsure? Because I am …afraid?*"

He closes his eyes again. He is quiet, and we wait. When he opens them, he looks to Maralyn. "Would you speak next?"

"Of course," she says. Kai nods.

"Maralyn, why are you here?"

"Because I am a widower. And you all are my family."

My breath is taken by her honesty, and then brought back once my hands are to my heart. So much of a story can be told in so few words, and I have love for this woman I have only just met.

Kai doesn't respond in words, so neither do we. The group does their best to practice presence in the way he does. In the way he is.

"Bradley, why are you here?"

Bradley takes an exaggerated breath, rubs at the stubble on his chin. "Because I'm angry as hell," he says.

Our hands are to our hearts again, and in following Kai's lead, we are silent for longer than I had expected. The longer we are silent, the deeper we sink into it—as if true presence can't be avoided if we just give it the room to be itself.

Kai raises his eyes slowly and speaks again. "Jacob, why are you here?"

Jacob seems prepared, the momentum of the moment creating a rhythm.

"Because I'm losing grip on who I am."

And we are silent for just as long but it doesn't seem that way, once we are truly in the moment.

"Makenzie, why are you here?"

"Because I am always afraid."

"Jade, why are you here?'

"Because I have breast cancer."

Hands to heart, hands to heart, but the energy is so big inside me and around me that I think it may burst through my seams. Tears are prickling at the corners of my eyes, and it is something I am not alone in.

"Greg, why are you here?"

"Because I drink too much."

"Gabby, where are you here?"

"Because I've lost touch with the soul of things."

"Dustin, why are you here?"

"Because I am a shit father."

"Muhammad, why are you here?"

"Because I struggle with depression but I hide it well."

"Aniyah, why are you here?"

"Because my husband had an affair."

"Emily, why are you here?"

"Because I have an anxiety disorder."

The room is bubbling with emotion now, as there is something about this outpouring that is so novel, so raw, so true. An experience, for most of us, I'm sure, that is like no other. The chant-like music still hums over the speakers, but it is far away—giving us a rhythm to hold to but not leading us. Kai turns then to the rest of the team, and I see that it is a practiced dance. Practiced and pure, the way a dance should be.

"Soloman, why are you here?"

"Because my family doesn't accept me for my sexuality."

"Avery, why are you here?"

"Because I tried to commit suicide when I was younger."

"Alexander, why are you here?"

"Because I gambled everything away."

"Ronan, why are you here?"

"Because I was homeless for over a year."

And then his eyes move to me, and I feel heat rising under my skin, like I am being roasted from the inside out. He gazes at me, just as he has gazed at everyone else, but for some reason, it feels different, again laced with words that are unspoken and of which I can't hear beyond the clattering in my chest.

"Cora," he says. "Why are you here?"

And as though in a trance, every possible *because* that I had listed in my mind—*because I carry so much pain, because I don't know who I am anymore*, even the most difficult admission, *because I lost my little girl and blame myself*, all crumble and get lost in a puff of smoke. And instead, I speak from somewhere else. Somewhere from which my mind is not involved, my heart taken by surprise, my body totally unaware. Even my voice sounds different, deeper, vibrating against my rib cage. The room starts to spin, but nothing is moving. It is just inside my head that the energy is twisting around so quickly that I must grip the sides of my cushion with both hands and utter it with eyes open wide.

"Because I have never felt seen. Until you saw me."

10

PRESENT DAY

The group responds wordlessly, just as they did for every other admission, just as they held presence for everyone else's truths. Eyes first to me, and then down toward the ground, and then closed with reverence, just as every other time. Hands are to hearts which beat against them. But this time, mine pounds hard inside of me, gathering up the blood from my veins and draining my cheeks.

Kai, however, does not look down. His eyes do not close. He does not look away. I am the one who breaks the gaze. I am the one who rips myself from the seemingly impenetrable energy that tries to hold me there, gripping the edges of my seat and accumulating in sweat against my neck, my chest, the curves of my legs. The silence now feels deafening, so prolonged, so obvious, so weighted. I try to control the curves of my face. Try to appear as unphased as I can, while feeling guilty for this deception after such a brave outpouring by a group that I am meant to be supporting.

After what seems like an eternity but is likely less than half of a single minute, Kai speaks.

"I am awed by you. Awed by all of you, your courage, your graceful honesty. You are here for these reasons, and so many others. Let us grow together, heal together, awaken to our potential together as we navigate these few days of true presence with care and reverence."

He proceeds to lead everyone in a chant, while we hold hands around our circle, but the final minutes of the session blur together, and I only follow the motions, my thoughts ricocheting out in every direction.

"Namaste," he says.

"Namaste," most of us follow, while others are still learning a new language.

"In your room, you should have found a schedule detailing the rest of your time here. Maralyn will stay back to answer any questions you may have. I will return shortly to lead you on a tour of the grounds. Feel free to use this time in whatever way feels comfortable for you. There is seating outside if you'd like to rest in the sun, and there are small bites in the lobby if you are hungry."

And with that, Kai rises, and the rest of us follow.

"Thank you," he says to the group. "Thank you for being here."

The team turns to make their way back to the lobby, and I follow. The rest of the guests scatter, some stay back in small groups, some head for the garden seating outside. Sweat accumulates on the back of my neck as I watch them break off into their clusters, whispering under the late afternoon light. What have I done? I'm afraid of what the intensity of my words meant to them, fearful of how much they cared to notice. I don't know how I let those words slip, but it didn't feel conscious. Conscious or not, did they find my admittance as bizarre as it felt to me? Was the energy in the room intense enough to allow for this strange admittance without explanation? Or did it sound as wildly inappropriate as I believe and fear?

"I appreciate you all," Kai says to the team. They nod, and then they are on their way, seemingly aware of their next steps and where they need to be. I turn to walk back to my room, internally admonishing myself and desperate for a quiet breath, but as I do, Kai speaks in my direction.

"Would you have a moment to talk?"

I have trouble swallowing around the lump that has built in my throat, and I only nod, my fumbling fingers revealing my anxiety.

"This way," he says, leading me toward the stairway, and up.

I nod again. I am quiet as we walk, but only on the outside. On the inside, there is so much noise. Too much movement. I wonder if he can see this in me. He is walking at my side, facing straight ahead, breathing slowly, but I can't help but to think I also see more.

We find the entrance of the Eye, and he makes room for me to enter first. Once inside its dimly lit haven, we find a seat on two of the far cushions, the salt lamp nearby exuding a pleasant glow. Kai pushes some loose strands of hair behind his ear, softens his shoulders, lets his head fall slightly to the side.

"I don't know why I said that," I utter, too abruptly for the softness of the space. "I'm sorry," I say, much more gently.

"Why are you sorry?"

I am sorry for many reasons, but I can't seem to pluck one out.

"Cora," he says, my name on his lips creating such a rush of heat through my body that I am mortified by how much my senses are betraying me. "You have absolutely nothing to apologize for." His voice is deeper, more defined, less enigmatic. It is sure and passionate and raw. And it only makes things spin faster.

"You are so connected," he says. "Do you know this about yourself?"

I shake my head in sad disagreement. "I only wish that I was. I am feeling confused. And I am obviously erratic."

"Cora," he says again, his eyes somehow finding an even deeper space to inhabit. His face now, however, looks pained. Looks as if it is holding onto something for dear life. I know it because I can feel it. I don't know why, but I can feel it. I can feel the pain of it.

For minutes, we are both utterly silent. The only movements are in the rise and fall of our chests. Our eyes are locked and our hands are at our sides, resisting a sort of magnetic pull toward the center of things. The top of my head is tingling, burning as if it can't house something. My chest is bubbling over, my throat taut and dry. My eyes are blurring, the soles of my feet aching, the hair on my forearms moving as if electrocuted.

Whereas earlier, these physical manifestations of my energy were fascinating and mostly pleasing, now, I am afraid. The intensity is too overwhelming, and it is hard to comprehend its sudden and uncontrollable force. And it is not just the physical sensations that I am afraid of. It is how my heart feels when I am close to him. It is that I want to be closer.

"What is happening?" I ask, replacing our protracted silence with a whisper so soft I can hardly hear myself.

Whatever is working through the muscles of his face now seems to transform to something else, forcing his eyes to shut and his features to contract, pursing his lips, stilling his breath. When he opens his eyes again, he tries to speak to me, but there are no sounds. It's like I can hear him, but I can't make it out. Like the language is slightly outside of my frequency.

"Please," I say, suddenly desperate for answers as my body seems to want to crumble from the outside in. "What is happening?"

"Exactly what is meant to happen," he whispers. "Just as it always is."

"This feels nothing like always." I put my hand across my chest, trying to contain myself. "I can hardly breathe. I feel too big for my body."

"That's because you are. You are so vast."

"I am nothing," I say.

"You are everything," he says.

I sway, unable to hold myself still. The energy pushes against my insides, trying to find more air.

He takes a very slow breath. Rests his palms atop his legs. Closes his eyes again. When he opens them once more, they look pained, but soft. I wish mine could look so wise. Could look so patient.

"I know how overwhelming this feels," he says. "I know."

"How what feels?" I swallow hard, my tongue moving against a dry throat.

"This," he says, and I wonder how one word could be so absolute and simultaneously enigmatic.

"You have felt it?"

He nods slowly. Closes his hand into a loose fist and then opens it again.

"There is so much," I choke.

"So much of what?"

My hands are shaking. I place them under the weight of my legs but they do not still.

"So much movement. The energy inside of me has become tangible. I feel it all over. Everywhere, all at once."

He nods again, brings his hands together in his lap. "Take a deep breath with me?" He leads the way with an inhale, and I follow, once and again, the air vibrating as it enters and retreats.

"There is…" he says. He stops. It does not seem usual for him, to hold back this way. I am sure it is not usual for him. "There is upheaval when…" He trails off again. Sighs. Shakes his head.

"When what?"

He squeezes his hands together. "When there are things begging to be seen," he says, as if he is exhaling an admittance.

I squint my eyes, looking at his blurred edges, knowing these moments usually allow me to see deeper. But I am clouded, my body too overwhelmed for clear seeing, and I find no answers there.

"What is that you see?" I ask him, not even sure what it is I am asking.

"I want to ask the same question of you," he says, but he does not ask it. Instead, for the first time, he turns away, looking not into my eyes but beyond them. "It will be ok," he says. And I'm not sure if he is talking to me or to himself.

I sit, transfixed, disoriented, simultaneously soothed and afraid. We sit for minutes this way, wordlessly and searching. I am studying the curves of his face, wondering where it is that his soul resides. If it drapes itself over his skin, too big for his body, glowing around him in every direction. I wonder too, where mine can be found. If it hides somewhere in the dark. I wonder why I have not looked for it.

I am silent because I don't know what to say, too unstable and muddled to make sense of things. I believe that he is silent not because he can't find the words, but because he doesn't want to say the wrong ones. As if there are words that could make this delicate air evaporate around us and leave us gaping.

"We should go back," he finally says, with gentleness but far too suddenly. And I am grateful for it. Not because I don't shatter around it—this time together needing to end—but because I do.

I want to stay here. I want to stay here, with him. And this is not something I should want.

I nod my head, trying to get my bearings, rising to a stand. I am so lightheaded. I can't tell where my feet end, and the ground begins. I don't tell him this. Instead, I try to find my balancing point, gripping myself there so that I don't stumble.

I look up to him, eyes wide. His dark features are becoming one with the soft glow, blending into each other.

He nods once more.

"It will be ok," he says.

He says it like a promise that he doesn't want to break.

11

JULY 1901

It's hard to choose a favorite part of the day because each one has its hold on me. When the sun first shows itself over the evergreens, waking them both with a slow yawn, and I am reminded yet again of the heart-burning type of love that may have seemed like a dream overnight but is real and lit up by early sun. Her little fingers at midday, covered in butter and ripping apart crusty bread. The sun moving back down against the gentle row of birch, a blanket big enough for three, and telling stories with wide eyes. The way he moves toward me when the house is silent and dark, his eyes matching—slow and deliberate until he is in front of me and his arms are tight around my shoulders and I feel the familiar fire in my belly that never wanes.

It's hard to choose a favorite part of the day, but today, as I am hanging our laundry on the line, the breeze blowing through the fabrics, moving them in waves, I am sure I don't have to choose. Because I'm noticing, right now, that each beautiful moment is all there is. And if I can't bottle them up, then I might as well appreciate each one as the best one that will ever again exist. And as I look out into the field where Pearl and Asher play, I know it's my favorite. It's my very favorite, over and again.

It's the height of summer. Pearl's eighth birthday. The sun is high in the sky, the sunflowers following its lead, moving up through the air and opening. The warmth is delicious, and the golden light meets their skin in a way I've never seen light behave. Pearl is laughing, a wide-mouthed joyful kind of laugh. Asher has his arms out wide, spinning through the air. The butterflies dance around them, trusting they are in the presence of benevolent forces. And it seems they are one—Pearl, Asher, and the butterflies, dancing in the golden warmth of the afternoon.

I don't want to disturb this moment. I only want to watch it from where I stand. Let my senses soak in every detail, and hope that I remember for all of eternity.

It would be tragic for these memories to disappear. I think that's the thing I am most afraid of. That when I die, this all becomes dust. And once they are memories, inside of me is the only place they can stay alive. When I am gone, where do they go?

That night, when Pearl is the type of tired that you only feel after a day in the sun, and sleeping soundly earlier than she usually might, I sit outside with Asher on the porch and watch the watercolor sunset being painted beyond the tree line—another favorite moment, the air still warm, the lightening bugs waking from their slumber. Asher has this way about him, so otherworldly you'd think he's lived in a thousand other places. Atop a thousand other stars. But my eyes would tell me he's only ever been right here, that his wisdom comes from someplace else.

Pearl gets it from him. She is special, like he is.

"I've been thinking about memories," I say.

"Memories?" he asks, turning his gaze from the setting sun to me. "We have made many good ones." His smile is so kind. So contented. It never seems to leave his face.

The thought of these memories makes me feel warm all over, our love story an always growing, always shining thing. And then the fear tickles at my throat. "Many good ones. And that's why I've been thinking about them." I brush the day's dust off my lap, take a quick breath. "Where do our memories go when we die, Asher?"

His face softens, his head falling slightly to the side in the way that he does it. "I can't be sure. But I can tell you how I see it."

I nod my head, asking him to go on. How he sees it is all I need.

"I believe the memories become a part of us. They get etched into our cells. Kind of like we're branded by them. And when we leave, they come with us. When we become a part of the great beyond, so do they."

"How?" I lean in closer, ensuring I don't miss a thing. "How do they come with us?"

"As a part of the soul of us, Juliette. In the part of us that never dies."

I think for a moment. Another. Asher can see the concern on my face. "What's the matter?" he asks.

"I've been thinking about death. How I've been afraid of it for that reason." I feel the crinkling of fear in my throat. "I've been afraid of it because I'm so happy, Asher. Because I don't want any of these memories to disappear."

"My love." He moves closer to me, kisses me softly on the cheek. "They can't disappear. They are an act of miraculous creation." He puts his hand to the side of my face, holds me there and whispers. "They are made from the soul of things. And the soul of things never dies."

I place my hand over his, feel the soul of him.

"That's how you see it?" I ask him.

He nods. So I'm sure of it. That these memories will always be ours. And I'm not so afraid anymore.

12

PRESENT DAY

The sun is still lingering hot in the sky at this time of year, and I welcome it on my cheeks. My backpack hangs on my shoulders, my mat rolled under my arm. I am still unsteady, still blurred, but as I walk the ten-minute hike to the studio, the physical intensity slowly recedes, leaving behind simmering nerve endings like burning embers in its wake. The surge in my mind and in my heart, however, roars as strongly as ever, and I'm not sure how I will teach through it.

Kai and the team will conclude their tour at the studio, where I will greet them. I'm to lead a single session today, two tomorrow, and one more in closing on Friday morning. I decide to lead this session indoors. The aim of this first class is to create a welcoming container, and as stunning as the outdoor space is, the sun still hangs heavy, and I want to avoid the possible distractions that come with the glare and the sweat and the uneven distribution of heat. The studio is so lovely at this time of day, glowing with the edges of the afternoon, and I first take to placing eleven mats across the floor in an alternating pattern. I unfurl my mat at the front near the altar, perpendicular to the others. And then, realizing the team may be joining as well, I add another six mats at the back.

I wonder if Kai will claim one of those spaces. I wonder if my body will be able to move the way it must, if my words and thoughts will be here with the group or forced to wander somewhere else if his gaze lays across me. I fear what it is I am wondering. I fear what it is I am trying to understand. I fear how quickly my existence seems to have transformed into something foreign, with languages I don't comprehend, sensations that I have no control over, and this pull—a longing so deep there is no word or descriptor, but a longing for exactly what, I am not sure. It seems to be coming from every direction. My soul is screaming out for him, my body wants to be close to him, my heart is recalibrating around his particular rhythm.

I open my backpack and retrieve two sticks of incense and my favorite knitted blanket. I gather armfuls of rolled blankets from the shelves and distribute them. I light the candles surrounding the altar, others perched on their tiny little platforms lining the walls. The incense starts to fill the room with its earthy essence, and soothing sounds are spilling from the overhead speakers.

The group arrives as one moving mass, floating slowly down the path toward the studio. They are exuding new calm, and a unique wonder that I too experienced a short time ago. I am privileged to hold this space for them in these moments, while they are experiencing this sense of connectedness. I want to provide them what these moments deserve, and that determination helps me to ready through the tumult.

When I see him, he is misted with the heat of the early evening, a bandana wrapped around his forehead, his eyes again on me. The room jerks forward and back again, my visual perception warping in a way I'd only felt if I'd drank too much wine or jumped out of bed too quickly, and even then, not like this. Not this way.

I take a very deep breath, and then another, steadying myself, focusing myself. I am not looking at him, but I know he watches me. His gaze is penetrating, made of heat, of fire, of the particles of the earth's core.

"Welcome, everyone," I say, standing in the doorway at the side of the room. "How was your tour?"

"I've never seen anything like it," says Dustin, a 50-something man with black and grey hair and a smart jawline. Dustin doesn't look at all like a shit father. But that doesn't mean he's not.

"Me either," says Gabby, a young woman with waving blonde hair that has expanded in the day's heat. "It's wonderful."

Maralyn is with them, as well, but the rest of the team is not. I do not know if she and Kai will stay. I do not ask.

"Please," I say, my voice gentle but shaking beneath the weight. I don't think they will notice, though I am exerting strength to keep it even. "Choose a space for yourselves." I extend my arm, urging them ahead. "I've provided you with a mat and a blanket, but if you feel you may need blocks, or decide you need them at any time during the class, you can find them at the back of the room."

"What are the blocks for?" asks Greg, a young man with broad shoulders and a reddened complexion. "I've never done this before."

I explain the purpose of the props, demonstrate their use, and ease worries for beginners as the group finds their places. Kai sits cross-legged on a mat at the back, quiet, solemn, sacred. His eyes are closed, his palms facing upward in his lap, but his jawline gives something away.

Once everyone is settled in, quiet falls over the group, and the energy shifts. I take part in creating it—the container, the peacefulness, the allowance, the presence. But it is Kai who seems to hold it for us. Like he has the whole Universe lit up there in front of his closed eyes. Like he paints it all with a light that streams from his fingertip, creating us, letting us unfold around him. His energy reverberates through the room and I am sure I am the only one who holds this awareness. Everyone else, they look too nonchalant. Too curious. Too ready to move and stretch and forget that they are light beings painted by the most beautiful, perfect hand.

I close my eyes for a moment and metaphorically shake myself out of this overwhelming state, one so gorgeous and connected and powerful that it is difficult to leave. When I open my eyes again, I see that he too has opened his, and I am released.

We start the class with a deep breathing technique, in for four seconds, hold for four seconds, out for four seconds, repeat. We move through a very slow vinyasa. I demonstrate each pose at the front of the studio, holding each for an extended time, allowing the beginners to take the time they need to settle into these new ways of moving their bodies. I circle the room, walking through the alleyways created by the mat formations, my bare feet silently gliding heel to toe against the light wooden floors, crouching down to gently adjust arms and legs and pressing down into muscles where they need it most.

The poses get deeper as the class progresses, muscles more confident, massaged, warmed. The sounds over the speakers are soothing, moving us to a slow rhythm, helping us to breathe consciously in and out as our bodies open.

"You have all heard of the mind-body connection," I say, striving for a peaceful but sure voice that is aligned with the moment, bringing myself back into my body in any way I know how. "Yoga puts this into practice. It gives us the power to connect these parts of ourselves more deeply. It allows us to choose the direction in which our energy flows." I shift into Warrior Two. "It allows us, perhaps most importantly, to open our minds by simply moving our bodies, holding ourselves in ways we didn't think we could, nurturing ourselves through the burn, learning about ourselves through things like balance, poise, and strength. And of course, growing through the discomfort, when we shake and stumble."

I move into downward-facing dog and continue. "But mind and body, they are only two aspects of our selves. There are whole dimensions to be found in each of us. Entire Universes housed in our skin. We can connect to ourselves more deeply here. We can access the places our souls reside."

We move then into a restorative version of pigeon pose, one that I like to land in after an introspective moment. From a seated position, we bend our right knee in front of us, stretch our left leg behind, drape our torso over our right shin. The container that it creates, the heat of the stretch, the darkness of eyes to the ground, elicits a beautiful depth and opportunity for awareness. "These next couple of days, we will explore this connection to self. Let's allow ourselves a few moments now, to meet ourselves right where we are."

I allow myself to settle into this space, muscles taut, eyes closed, darkness swirling around me. And in my quiet, something opens. The tears fall and I don't stop them. I hide them behind the pose, I let them bubble over. They just want to keep flowing, like they had been damned up for years and can finally surge toward open air. They fall for the pain of the last couple of years, for any pain I have felt before and kept locked up. They also fall for things that aren't painful, but raw and wild—like what is happening to my soul while it resides in this place, amongst this land. Amongst his presence.

I lead the group to move to the same pose on the other side, mirrored and legs switching places, and when I do, I see that Kai is not to the ground like the rest of them. He is sitting up straight, looking at me. Staring with an impenetrable gaze, watching my tears fall. And though he sees me catch his stare, he does not falter. He only holds his ground more intensely. More passionately. With an all-encompassing grip. And while the rest of the group has their eyes to their mats, I sit there with him, unabashed tears rolling down my cheeks. Only sit there and stare across the room, like we are the only two beings in existence. My heart is pounding, thudding hard against my chest. There is a fire under my skin, running up the lengths of my arms, my belly, and between my thighs.

"Everyone rise slowly," I say, wiping at my cheeks and ripping myself away from him with everything I have in order to continue, to remember that there are people here who need me to proceed. We stretch the limbs on each side of our bodies, and then I direct the group to Savasana, ten minutes before I am meant to, move to turn down the sounds from the speakers and dim the lights to hide my face. Kai moves to Savasana too, closes his eyes and gives me room to breathe, and though I know I need it, I don't want it. I retrieve lavender essential oils, I circle the room, use my thumb to apply oil to foreheads, bless each member of the group as I move through.

Except for him. Because I am afraid that if I touch his skin, I'll burn us both up.

And then, the class is over and everyone rises and they appear peaceful but animated with gratitude, as made evident from their graciousness as they exit the room. Maralyn shows them the rest of the meditation space, and then directs them toward the dining hall for dinner. Kai is seated on his mat again, just as he was at the start, legs crossed, eyes closed, appearing peacefully confident aside from the tight set of his jaw. I move about the studio with supreme slowness, tidying the way the blankets are folded, nudging mats back into their places, blowing out candles, one by one, and shaking, all over.

I am arranging my belongings near the altar when I feel him. He does not touch me, but he is right behind me, breathing soundlessly, and I feel him. I straighten, but I do not turn. I look toward a statue of Goodness Parvati glimmering before me in her antique gold against the setting sun.

We stay that way for minutes. We don't move. I hardly blink. I am so still that the thudding of my heart sounds like a cacophony; the blood moving through my veins an anxiety-producing invasion of the moment. As time passes, I am sure he will not shift until I do. I am sure that he leaves this choice to me.

I don't turn around. I speak in a whisper.

"I'm married."

"I know."

"And still," I exhale through shaking lips, "somehow, that feels like such a frivolous thing for me to say."

"I know," he repeats.

"I don't know what is happening to me," I say.

Silence.

"But you do?" I ask.

He is quiet. He does not respond. Again, minutes go by. Two, maybe three. And I finally turn, slowly so as not to disturb the air; afraid if I move too fast, I will send myself reeling. Crumble into a trillion little particles. He is so beautiful, standing there in his sadness. I don't know the story of his pain, but I see it on his face, and he is so beautiful. His arms hang to his sides, his chin slightly raised, his eyes telling countless stories, holding more wisdom than I knew could exist in one shining place.

"But you do," I say.

He nods.

"It happened so fast," he says. "Just like I knew it would. But I am weak, because I stand here with you. Because there is a war raging inside of me. An atom bomb in my heart, threatening to blow everything up with one wrong move. But that's not who I want to be, Cora. It's not who I am."

"Then who are you?"

"I'm a man with an eternal question of which I have two answers to, and of which I cannot remedy the paradox."

"If you can't give me answers, then please," I say, holding my hand tight to my chest, "at least tell me your questions."

He is thoughtful for moments. Then, he moves to the raised altar and sits down. I find a seat next to him, grateful for the foundation to steady me.

"The rules of the physical world and the pull of the soul can be at odds." He moves his hands over his thighs, and I can imagine the friction he creates. Like the warm rush I still feel moving under my skin. "When they are, which do we follow?"

I do not respond. I wait for him to continue.

"The soul can hold wisdom beyond what our minds can comprehend. But we have chosen to be here, in these bodies, as a part of this physical world. In making that choice, there are certain things that are meant to be respected. Answering the soul's call may not always be wise or noble. Sometimes, as far as the physical world goes, these soulful acts can be selfish, indulgent, reckless."

I swallow hard around the lump in my throat, not confident I understand what it is he is referring to with these paradoxical theories, but simultaneously feeling the weight of the truth, on both sides.

"Resisting. Navigating extraordinary pain. This is sometimes what we must bear. This is where our conscious growth sometimes lies." He turns to me. "What do you think about this, Cora?"

I feel a rush in my chest. Another opening. I may have thought

I had opened as far as I could, but there are always new layers. Always deeper ones. And it seems I am only just scratching the surface.

"I think," I say, voice shaking, looking up toward the ceiling, and then back down again. "I think that whenever I have followed my soul's call, I have not been led astray. Though, too often, it is a call that I have ignored. I believe there are different types of discomfort, and that if we are aligned, the pain we feel is one of growth—the way a seed must be ripped open in order to reach toward the sun. If we are not in alignment with our soul's call, we experience a different type of pain—the type that means we are swimming upstream, living a story that is not our own."

I shake my head, slowly back and forth. "I don't know. Maybe it is naïve to think this way. Or maybe it is selfish, after all. I can tell you what I believe, but when it comes down to living it, I can't seem to get it right."

I exhale a shaky breath and look down at my feet upon the wooden floor. I wonder what it would be like to reach for the sun.

Kai turns toward me, twisting his body so that his heart faces me and I do the same. We are close, probably too close, because I can feel his heat and his knee is pressed up against mine. It burns there, where they meet. Like that very spot is the center of everything. The other things, the rest of us, just spin around it, not realizing what it all comes down to.

"You are beautiful, Cora." His head hangs to the side and rests there a moment. "You are so beautiful."

His words pour over me like hot honey. An explosion of emotions is stuck under the sticky confines, and I am terrified of what will happen when there is nothing to hold them back. How much passion I will find there. And how much bone-shattering guilt. The desire is undeniable. It is an uncontrolled flame, scorching every inch of my insides.

"I'm so sorry." He says this so passionately, I can feel the emotion of it radiating from his skin. "I just want to protect you," he whispers, and then exhales.

"If you want answers," he continues, straightening, "I shouldn't be the one to give them to you."

I swallow hard. It seems an imperative to know what is moving through his mind, what experiences he hasn't shared, what wisdom he has that I crave to discover.

"I can't. Not like this." He moves his thumb across the bend of my leg, the same one that is already burning against his, and I shiver, my entire body seeming to recalibrate around the heat of it. He leans in, speaking closer to me, smelling like dusk and oak.

"But if the time comes that you feel ready, sure it is these answers that you seek, come to me. I may not be able to give you the answers. But I will lead you there." And then he whispers, "I will show you."

He takes his hand away and I am hollowed. And I want to tell him that I am ready. That I am sure.

But nothing comes.

"Only then," he says. He closes his eyes, breathes deeply.

And I sit there in my silence.

13

PRESENT DAY

We both rise wordlessly and walk out toward the now subsiding day, sunset skies swirling around the tops of trees like an oil painting.

"Are you hungry?" he asks. It feels too common a question after these feelings of being doused in something otherworldly. And I think that it must be purposeful. I think that he must be giving us room to be human.

I shake my head. My body tells me that I need sustenance, but my anxiety tells me that I do not, and this time, I know which truth wins out.

"Will you bring something back with you, at least?"

"Yes, ok," I stutter, and we continue toward Raw Green Opal, silently, one thousand thoughts undulating in waving patterns through my mind. The whole of the group is seated, enjoying mealtime together down the length of a long communal table along spliced and glossed wooden benches. Maralyn looks up toward us and nods, and I wonder what she has seen, what she has noticed, what she knows. It seems that she and Kai are quite close. I am also unsure how obvious these interactions have been to the outside eye, and who in this group might go back to Emerson with their observations, even if innocently. I think about my confession in this morning's group. The thought of someone sharing the words I spoke makes my stomach turn.

"Come," he says.

I must look like I've seen a ghost. I'm sure my face is as pale as it feels.

He directs me to a lovely spread, and when I don't move toward the empty stack of plates, he grasps one for me. "Do you like mushrooms?"

I nod, and he places two small portobellos stuffed with quinoa and spinach on my plate.

"Mashed garlic cauliflower. And eggplant with Calabrian chili. Ok?"

I smile gratefully, feeling soothed by his nurturing kindness. "Thank you. Yes."

"Hey, Alexander," he says over the room's chatter. "Mind covering this up so that Cora can take it to go?"

"By all means," Alexander replies, tipping his hat and smiling a broad smile. He adds a white cardboard cover that fits perfectly over the plate, and hands it to me. "Bon appetite."

"Thank you," I smile weakly, grasping the plate underneath so that it doesn't teeter.

"Will we see you at the social circle tonight?" he asks. "We're going to project a movie and make herbal tea concoctions. Rowdy bunch, we are."

I find a small laugh and surprise myself. "That sounds lovely, yes. I will be there. I'm just going to go rest a while."

Kai nods, and so do I, and I turn to walk out of the dining hall and back toward my room. Each step that takes me further away, I feel it—the pull, the tide, the tugging weight of the distance.

Once at the door, I turn and see Kai has not moved. I see the rigid angles of his jawline, the stories in his eyes. And then, I walk.

The evening is still and quiet. The sun has now dipped below the tree line, and the sky looks like beach glass—a muted grey-blue held against the horizon. There is so much moving inside of me that I feel numb. I embrace the blanketed color of the sky and become it. I don't let myself look at the rest of it. Become undone.

The lobby in Citrine is empty, as there aren't any more guests expected. I'm glad there is no one to make small talk with, as I only want to go back to my room and be alone for a while. I don't have the space for conversation. For anything else.

I open the door to my room with the wooden key fob and place my dinner into the mini fridge. I open the rest of the curtains and watch the sky turn to a deep purple. I fall onto my back on the billowing bed, and lay there, arms outstretched. And then I roll over to grab my phone from the bedside table.

I have two missed calls from Emerson. He must be out of the office by now and going home to an empty apartment. I am wary of returning his call. I don't know how to speak to him right now. I've never not known how to speak to him. Whatever it is that happened today, I am sure of one thing—I can no longer deny the inappropriate nature of my actions.

The phone rings again in my hand. I take a deep breath before answering. The kind that hurts the edges of your lungs.

"My girl," he says, sweet and sure. "Finally. I've missed you."

"Emerson," I exhale. I say it as a reminder. As a relief that is also stabbing. "What a day it's been."

"Tell me all about it," he says. He is bright and airy, and it feels foreign.

I know there is no way I could tell him all about it. Even if this experience with Kai did not exist, it would be difficult to articulate the impact this place is having on my soul. I feel guilty for so much omission, but in this moment, I don't know any other way.

"I don't even know where to begin," I say, attempting to sound as light as he does, but the weight of it all pulls my words down an octave.

"Well, how was your first class? Did it go well?"

"It did. It went well. They are a lovely group. I'm already quite sure that you are lucky to have them."

"I think so too. I'm glad they are having a new experience. A break from the intensity of these past few months."

"I don't know about a *break*," I say. "Maybe just a different kind of intense."

"The intensity of spa life?" he laughs. "Exhausting."

It is the kind of joke that I don't want to hear from him right now, and I am afraid to confront it. Afraid, for the first time, that even the smallest crack in our structure can lead to complete and utter destruction. I respond with a small laugh. It makes my chest hurt.

"I miss you, C. Any way you can come home a little sooner? Weather will be great on Friday. We can start the weekend early. I'll take the day off."

"I need to lead a session on Friday morning," I say, "and there's a bunch of assimilation and closing practices later in the day, before the group leaves. I shouldn't miss those. But I'll be home by evening."

"Patience is a virtue," he sighs.

"You're not usually the patient type," I reply, more playfully. Accessing a side of myself that usually comes so easy with Emerson that I can find it even amidst the clutter.

"Waiting is such a waste of time. I know what I want. And do you know what that is, Cora?"

"You'll have to tell me," I say, fumbling with a loose string that hangs from the thread of my shirt.

"You," he says, in a way that is seductive in its unembellished ease. "Right here. On the kitchen counter."

My cheeks flush, my body practiced in these responses. It's a flush that is expected, even valued. A passionate response to the promise of my husband's skin against mine. To his words, these private and intimate words that are spoken only for me. But with them, a sweat breaks out along the nape of my neck. A new piece of my response that does not belong.

"Tell me you'll be all mine, all weekend," he says, his voice deep and stirring. "Tell me I can do whatever I want to you."

I close my eyes, hold my lips together, the shame more obvious in the darkness behind my closed lids.

"I'll be all yours," I whisper. I repeat it again, with more strength this time, because I am making sure it is true.

I am making it true.

"I'll be all yours."

We hang up the phone, and the emotions that I have kept locked in my organs, in the spaces between my breath, in every capillary that navigates the length of me, are starting to make their way up to the surface.

Guilt has such a weight to it. It feels like it's suction cupped to my insides.

How could I let myself get so carried away today? I can't even blame this on time, wearing at my resiliency. There was no build, only crescendo. It seems my entire life has transformed in the span of a single day. Something new has infiltrated the carefully crafted picture of my existence, one that has never been perfect but has always been beautiful—more beautiful, perhaps, in its imperfections, because there is pain, and it is real, and it is human.

But in that humanness, there is this one great flaw. And it is one that I am now seeing more clearly.

Where has my soul been?

There may have been times I thought it was leading the way. But most often, it has been silenced, forced to watch me make choices that might seem like they make sense but don't encompass that bit of ethereal magic—a walking down the true heart-centered path that my longing has always been built around. My purpose has floundered. I've grasped at change only when I was desperate. Not from a trusting space, but from a fearful one.

These thoughts enlighten a dreadful and panicked feeling that comes with the honest realization that my chosen path might not be my own. And the impossible position that would leave me in.

I take a deep breath. Another. And then another.

When it comes to Kai, the biggest problem, in this very moment, is not the draw I feel toward him. It is not the excruciating intensity of my experiences in his presence today. It is not the answers that I am both begging for and avoiding, the reasons behind all of this that feel so much deeper than any usual attraction. *Attraction* is not a word that describes this. This is something totally unique and foreign and its own. These monumental things are not the biggest problem, as hard as that is to fathom. The biggest problem is that what I want, more than anything, in this very moment, is to go to him. To fall into his arms, feel his heat against me, hear him whisper into my ear, allow myself to come undone around him. I've never wanted anything, *anything*, so deeply, with such all-encompassing abandon. I didn't even know I could want anything this deeply, in this whole way. Not just my body, not just my mind. But with the whole of my soul. Right down to my core. Into the depths of myself. Places I have never seen before. That I didn't know existed.

And now, the light shines on them for the first time, and they can't be unseen. They are alight. And I am left in darkness.

I roll over onto my side, pull my knees up to my chest and hug them tight. I consider leaving. To just pack my things and drive home tonight and put this all behind me. But I know it wouldn't be right to abandon my responsibilities. I have made a commitment, and for the sake of the team and the group, I must see it through. And what would I tell Emerson? I have met someone I am so inextricably and deeply connected to, that I can't bear to spend another day in his vicinity or else I'm sure I will destroy everything we have built together?

The predominant reason I can't leave, however, is much more glaring, and one that is difficult to admit, even to myself. The reason I can't leave is that I don't want to. More aptly, *I can't*. I truly cannot imagine walking away. This doesn't feel like an excuse for my desire. It feels like an actual imperative in a way I truly can't understand.

The sky is dark now. The blackness is blanketed over the trees, but the walking paths are illuminated by the soft light of lanterns, leading the way outward, or back to center. I push myself to rise, change my clothes, ready myself for the evening's program. I let my hair down, a deeper brown in this dim light, allowing it to cascade over my shoulders. I wear a long floral dress, my back bare, the flowing skirt hugging down around my waist.

I retrieve my meal from the refrigerator, planning to take a few cold bites. But it is so carefully prepared and considered, and deserves my consideration, too. So, I brush my teeth, gather my things, and bring it downstairs with me to warm.

The group has returned. I pass by Muhammad in the hallway with a nod and hello. Maralyn is back behind the desk, clicking behind her computer screen.

"Cora, you look absolutely lovely."

"Oh, thank you, Maralyn. You do, as well," I smile. "I needed a little time to recharge."

"Oh, yes. The first day can be…a lot."

I nod.

She directs me to the micro kitchen to the left, and once the plate is ready, I move toward the seating area in the lobby. I eat slowly while looking out on the grounds, though the sights in front of me only linger there, undefined, blurred in my whirling thoughts. I am wholly inside of myself— thinking about Emerson and my love and my guilt, about Kai and the intensity of being in his presence in this excruciatingly short period of time, about my soul and why I have not listened to its whispers. It is an overwhelming feeling, the friction of the ricocheting thoughts fogging my periphery.

When I finally turn around, I notice that the room has filled, guests congregating, ready for the evening's event. I shake myself out of my daze and rise, moving toward the kitchen to clean my plate.

"Would you happen to have a few moments to help me set up the room?" asks Maralyn. "Soloman got sidetracked helping a guest with something."

"Oh, absolutely," I say, grateful for the distraction.

We walk through the door to the arch-shaped room that already holds memories for me. "We'll need chairs instead of the meditation cushions," Maralyn says, gesturing toward the center of the room, "and we'll need to pull in a couple of tables. Alexander is bringing over the rest of the supplies for the tea ceremony now."

A projector is facing the windows, the shades pulled all the way down. There is a closet to the far right, and from it we haul chairs in stacks of three toward the center, placing them in a semi-circle around the screen. We place two long tables behind and cover them with silken Tibetan-inspired tablecloths. Alexander enters with a cart filled with deep-blue mugs and tin canisters holding a myriad of tea leaves, herbs, and flowers for tinctures.

"We'll get started in ten minutes or so?" Maralyn asks Alexander.

"Ok with me," he says, arranging the tins in a considered way, and then looking toward me. "A rainbow, from the earth. So beautiful to see it all laid out this way, don't you think?"

"Beautiful," I say. "Truly."

I am drawn to the colors and the aromas, but even more so to the attention to quiet, beautiful, often overlooked things. It is ironic that this focused attention has a way of expanding my perspective, reminding me of how much there is to be present for. In my whirling thoughts, I have been contracted. In the smoking friction of rumination, truth can't be found—at least not in the soul-infused way that I am craving. Though I admit my thoughts are still spinning, it is relieving to have some space for them to shake themselves out.

Maralyn turns and cocks her head to the side. She opens the door and walks out toward the garden, and I know she wants me to follow.

I am apprehensive. I know she has something to say.

The garden is wonderful at night, the way the lanterns create a tapestry of light and shadow amongst the foliage, the smell of lavender and moss wafting into the cooling, dark air. Maralyn takes a seat at a small, round metal table, and I have a seat across from her.

"How are you doing, Cora? How was today for you?"

Whereas a concise confirmation that *everything is fine,* or *all is well,* would most often suffice in response to questions such as these, Maralyn's questions are asked in a genuine and deeply present way. I am sure she is looking for a true expression of my current reality, if I choose to offer it up.

One can tell when they are being invited to pour their souls out in the details.

"You don't have to talk about it, if you don't want to," she says, her face soft and kind. "But I just want you to know that you can. Anything you might want to express, well, it's very safe with me."

I exhale in an exaggerated way. "How can you all possibly be this spectacular? So present and kind." I run my finger along the edge of the table, study its intricacies. "I have never experienced anything like it."

Maralyn smiles gently. "We can just be ourselves here. There isn't as much in the way. Do you know what I mean?"

"I know what you mean," I nod, biting at my bottom lip.

"I'm not trying to be nosey. Really, I'm not. I just know *life-altering experience* when I see it." She pauses, lowering her voice. "And I know it's hard to talk about what happens in here…with anyone…out there."

I fall back against the chair. "It seems as if it would be almost impossible."

Maralyn nods slowly, hands folded gracefully in her lap.

"I'm having trouble understanding what is happening," I say. "It feels like I've experienced years' worth of transitions within a single day." I shake my head, exasperated, and take to a whisper. "It has been no time at all, but everything feels different. I'm totally changed by something I can't understand."

"The soul doesn't care about the artificial timelines we create," she says. "Or think we need to stay within the confines of. The most powerful and pivotal things are *that* way, right away. They wouldn't be what they are if they weren't."

I nod, holding Maralyn's gaze, resonating through our enigmatic conversation. "I feel like I've lost control of myself." I look down into my lap. "I can't help but to think I must be a terrible person."

"Oh, but you can't be," she shrugs. "Because you aren't. It's really that simple. And don't ask me how I know that. I just know. Just like you know that I wouldn't lie to you."

She is speaking softly, but with that particular edge; that beautifully exuberant energy that is unique to her, and it makes me smile. "I know you wouldn't."

"Do you want to know how I met Kai?" Her question makes me understand that she has seen more than I'd hoped, but I feel comforted by it now. Grateful that I have someone to talk to.

I nod my head, leaning in.

She crosses her legs, rests her elbow on the table and leans her chin on her fist.

"Well, when Bryan died, I was utterly devastated. The grief was all-consuming and quite possibly life-ending, to be honest with you. We had only been married for a little over a year, we were madly in love, and we had our entire lives planned out and ahead of us." She pauses, her voice solemn but even, and infused with such a deep affection that it makes me think that her love and pain must be of equal depth. "It was a car accident— a horrific and sudden thing with no warning."

My body is weighted by my depth of compassion, my heart burning with its empathetic hold. "Oh, Maralyn. I'm so, so sorry." She places her hand over mine, gratefully, and continues.

"We had been planning to build a home in the woods, leave the city, be out in nature, get a dog or two or three. Just a week prior, Bryan had met with an architect to start laying out the plans. I was in Connecticut for the weekend for a friend's bridal shower, so I hadn't joined him, but he came back thrilled by our prospects. After Bryan passed, I had to reach out to said architect and cancel our agreement. As you can imagine, said architect was Kai and as you can also imagine, he was so incredibly kind and empathetic, that I became quickly dependent on his wisdom and presence."

She fixes her skirt, changes which leg is crossed over the other. "We were fast friends, really. Took to each other quickly. He was at that time just starting to dream up his plans for this place, and I needing somewhere, *anywhere*, to direct my soul, I wanted nothing more than to be a part of it. He tells me now that we saved each other, because without his drive to impart within me a sense of purpose, he may not have been as ambitious with his plans. Either way, here we are, all saving each other on a daily basis."

"Now, I tell you this for a few reasons," she says, lowering her head but keeping her eyes on me. "May I tell you what those reasons are?"

I nod, absorbed in her sharing and grateful to be privy to these parts of her story.

"First and foremost, if it's not too bold, I'd like to think we too can become fast friends. I wanted to share with you a little bit more about who I am and what brought me here, as friends do."

"As friends do," I repeat, the corners of my mouth rising graciously.

"But I also wanted to share because I too had my first experiences with Kai, and I know what an incredibly unique presence he is in the world. You see, I was in fact taken by him the moment I met him. Just being in his presence tends to change people's lives. He is a healer. And with that incredible healing power can come some turmoil."

I feel suddenly tense, wary of the warnings she may give me. Wary that from her perspective, what I am experiencing is not unique at all, and what I had considered from the start: that this would be anyone's reaction to his presence.

"It's not that," she says, leaning in, her air deliberate and sure. "I'm not saying what you think I am." She must have seen the way my eyes darkened. The way my shoulders moved. "What I am trying to tell you, it is quite the opposite."

I am frozen in place, hanging on her words.

"We are all taken by Kai, yes. He has a unique presence, of course. Even his baseline interactions are extraordinary. But there's his *always*, and then, there is *this*."

I am watching her now, her body language one with her words, like what she is telling me is an imperative.

"I have never seen him this way," she says. "This is new. And I have never seen a reaction like the one you are having. I'm a rather empathetic type, Cora. It's a blessing, and a curse. But this is something with unique magnitude, and I'd be remiss if I didn't discuss it with you."

She leans back in her chair, her head falling to the side. Her every move is graceful. Slow. As if the air is the same as water, but she has learned to breathe there.

"I saw it, the way the light changed this morning. It was like a rush of fresh air. And believe me, Cora. The energy here, it is always sensational. But what it is now, with you here with us, with him—it's different." She pauses for a moment, nods her head. "His eyes," she whispers. "They are alive. Alive in a way I have never seen them. And though I don't know what yours looked like before you arrived, today, I am sure they look the same as his."

I am simultaneously buzzing and exhausted. Inflamed and afraid. My heart opens and its warmth rushes through every passageway under my skin. I hate myself for it, but it is visceral, undeniable.

"And with you saying you're a terrible person? Well, that is the last way you should feel. You're just being swept up by miracles and trying to keep your feet on the ground. And that, my dear Cora, is a terribly difficult thing to do."

Tears are falling down my cheeks again, and it seems unfathomable to me how many times my body has begged for such emotional release today. I am utterly overwhelmed, and not sure where to place any of it, or what words to let fall.

"I don't know why this is happening," she continues. "I'm just telling you what I see." Her voice and the rest of her softens, and she says with utmost tenderness, "and letting you know I am here to support you."

"Oh, Maralyn," I cry, placing my face into my hands.

She comes around the table and rests on the arm of my chair, placing her arms around my shoulders. "I know. I know."

I lift my face and speak through the tears. "I don't know what any of this means. I can't understand why I am reacting this way. I can't even have a legitimate conversation about it without excruciating guilt. I'm married to a beautiful, kind, loving man, and I am being unfaithful even in this discussion. But this is not anything like a whimsical attraction with Kai. It's this ripping sensation—a fiery ache I feel whenever I move away from him, and a disintegration of self, the self I've become accustomed to, whenever I am in his presence."

She wipes a tear from my cheek, the way only a friend can.

"And here I am, being terribly selfish. You shared your deepest experiences with me, and I'm crying over nothing at all." I straighten up, my eyes still heavy. "I'm sorry, Maralyn." I place my hand on her shoulder, hold there for a moment. "I'm just very glad to have met you."

"That is the silliest thing I have ever heard," she says, rolling her eyes. "I'm the one who wanted to talk about this. You're just indulging me. You're a yoga instructor with quite a sense of humor." She winks, pinches my cheek. I smile, a confusing but fascinating mix of emotions painted across my face.

"You can't figure it out until it's figured out," she says. "It sounds too simple to be true, but those things are the most truthful of all."

"I'm not even sure what it is I am trying to figure out." My voice is small and disheartened.

"Or maybe you're afraid to look?"

I cast my eyes down. "I'm definitely afraid to look." I think about Kai's offer. His offer to show me, if I'm ever truly ready. I think about my avoidance. I think about the betrayal. I think about the desire.

Maralyn rises to a stand, finds her seat again. "I believe that we can't move toward the next stage of our consciousness until we are in agreement with our soul. Until every part of us says that we are ready. We can say we are, but it's not about what we say. It's about what's true."

I readjust myself in my chair. "What do you think happens if we aren't ready?"

"We'll get other opportunities. In other ways. That's how I look at it, at least. One door may close but there are infinite others. Though…"

She bites her lip, leans her head to the side.

"What?" I ask. She hesitates. "It's ok. Your thoughts are very important to me."

"I just wonder," she says. "I just wonder if there is a type of doorway that is, in fact, one of a kind. That is built by fate's hand. That is at the edge of an infinitely winding road, that we've navigated toward all our lives. One that it all comes down to."

I swallow hard, sweat prickling at the back of my neck. A fear takes hold, and I feel as if I am reaching, reaching, losing my grip. A portal has opened and it's getting smaller and further away. I sit here, feet adhered to the earth, watching it fade into the distance.

"I'm not saying that's the way," she says. "I just wonder."

I lean my chin into my hands.

"I wonder, too," I say. "And I wonder, if we find this fateful door but we don't walk through, what happens? Are we forced to backtrack on a solitary path, until we can find ourselves back where we started? Can we ever go back? And if we can't, what is the way forward? There's got to be another way. A crossroads. Another choice."

"Two roads diverged?"

"Maybe," I say. "Maybe."

We are silent, listening to the sounds of the forest. A song that is sung without wondering. Only wonder. Everything in its place.

I look up. The lights inside are dimmed. "Looks like they're ready to get started."

"Are you ready to go inside?" she asks me.

I nod my head, and she takes my hand. And just like that, I'm not alone.

14

PRESENT DAY

When we walk in, Kai is stationed near the projector, adjusting knobs until the screen comes into focus. He has changed his clothes, and wears a pair of loose-fitting pants, tied around the waist and hanging low, with a black V-neck t-shirt. His hair is down around his shoulders, and if I ever thought impossible, he is even more striking in the evening light.

I choose a seat on the opposite side of the room, leaving as much space between us as possible. It is no use trying to fight these surges of energy, the sloshing movement of it through my veins. But what I can do is act on these things as appropriately as I can, keeping distance while I try to decipher what comes next, and doing so one small step at a time.

I create a soothing tisane of chamomile, chrysanthemum, lavender, and valerian, hoping it helps to bring even a small amount of calm to my erratic nervous system. We are watching a documentary, following the stories of three young people's spiritual awakening journeys. I am sure it is spectacular, but I can't focus, and I may as well be staring at a blank screen. My brain can't process this much information so quickly. My heart can only hold so much. I am fogged, after this year that is a day, without sleep. I look forward to closing my eyes. Letting my subconscious take control of something the rest of me cannot possibly comprehend. Letting my soul speak in my dreams.

When I was younger, my father called me Dreamer. He didn't mean it as a compliment, which to this day makes me sadder for him than it does for myself. He is a dreadfully practical man, which may not necessarily be an awful thing on its own. It's just that his practicality is paired with bitterness, especially toward those who crave that spark that he spent a lifetime snuffing out.

What a sad thing, to grow up believing that dreaming is a weakness. Once I was old enough to know otherwise, I tried to reject those old and tired ideals. But we all know how it goes. That conditioning is not easy to break. And as much as I wanted to, as hard as I tried, there was always a voice inside me, berating me when I didn't believe I was being properly responsible, pragmatic, or reliable.

My father was proud of me when I worked at the firm, got engaged to a talented architect, and moved to a penthouse in Manhattan. He hasn't spoken to me at all about my work since I started doing something that I love, leading people through vinyasas and honoring my passions. And to be honest, that reality made me want to rebel against his ghastly conditioning more than ever.

The thing is, I didn't marry Emerson to make my father proud, or to fulfill some self-imposed life's mission. I didn't do it because I thought I *should*. I did it because I loved him. And I do love him. But the fear that I've held, nestled somewhere between those longings for a depth to our interactions that has not been present, is that maybe there are other types of love. And maybe, because of my apprehension toward embracing my visionary musings, I didn't give myself a chance to find out.

This conditioning and who I truly am at my core have always been at odds. But the dichotomy screams at me now. It's created enough pain to push me to uproot my life entirely, at least when it comes to my work, but it was far too late. And now, that spinning web of pain and loss that has built itself around me has become suffocating. Perhaps my whole life I have lived Kai's fear: that in following my soul's path, I was doing something wrong, selfish, irresponsible. That I would hurt people that way. Hurt myself. In truth, it has always been the opposite. The *correct* and *proper* life that I was living created a loss beyond imagination. It ended a sweet, innocent life before she even had the chance to live it.

The film ends, and my eyes are hanging heavy. The group is rising from their seats, placing their mugs into the provided trays for washing, stacking the chairs to be returned to their original place. Some are congregating to continue the evening's discussions. Others are winding down, heading back upstairs to their rooms. Kai's seat is empty.

Before I have a chance to wonder, or wait, I say goodnight to Maralyn, to Alexander, to anyone else who is in my vicinity, and retreat to the stairs. It is a climb that should not be burdensome, but my limbs are so tired, and I am craving the cradling of the comforter, the plush of the pillows, the relief of sleep, hours spent processing today's happenings somewhere beyond waking thought.

When I get to my hallway, I look down the corridor and toward the Eye. In that moment, I am sure where he has retreated to. That he is there waiting. That if I choose to turn in that direction, if I ask him to lead me, he will show me the way. I am sure that this enlightenment would create new ripples, these answers create new questions. And I am sure that everything, again, would change.

I steady myself, take a deep inhale, and turn toward my room. If the strength that it takes to move me beyond that entryway is any indicator of my resolve, this choice is anything but inconsequential. And even amidst all the deceitful choices I have made today that could rip my marriage apart, I feel bolstered by this resoluteness. Bolstered, and yearning.

Once inside, I flip on the lights, change into a pair of satin pajama pants and a loose-fitting cotton t-shirt, and pin up my hair. I turn the lights out again, close all the shades, and sink under the covers. I lay there on my back, staring up toward the ceiling in the pitch blackness, not seeing anything but empty space. The blackness is comforting, numbing the places where it burns, and where it burns is everywhere. Desire and guilt are a fiery pair.

And then, my phone rings, the artificial light infiltrating the room and making me want to squeeze my eyes shut. I reach over and feel around until it is in my grasp and answer moments before it's too late.

"Hey you," he says over Facetime. Emerson is leaning against the back of the couch, a glass of red in one hand, his other outstretched to hold the phone. "Are you leading a séance next?"

"I do look eerie, don't I?" I ask, my features contrasting against the harsh light. "I'm exhausted. Just laying in bed, staring at the ceiling."

"I wish you were here, in bed with me. I'd give you a massage, you know." He lifts his eyebrows. "And I'd crank up the air conditioner to 43 degrees just so that we could huddle under three blankets. After we finished our tacos, of course."

"There'd be tacos?" I ask.

"Of course," he says, eyes wide.

"That sounds so nice," I sigh. And it's true. It sounds comforting. And it reminds me that life before this chaos was not lifetimes ago, in the way that it feels.

"Was it really only this morning that I left our apartment?"

"You aren't used to waking up that early," he says. "Throws off the internal clock."

"Yeah," I sigh again, and then change the subject. "How was your day?"

"Just another day. But now it's much more obvious that you aren't here, being that there is only one wine glass, and your very cold feet aren't tucked under my legs."

"What a shame," I say. He has no idea what this conversation really means to me. How important these small details are when it comes to holding myself together.

"Is that it for tonight?" he asks. "All tucked in?"

"That's it for tonight," I say. "We were watching a film downstairs, and drinking tea, and the tiredness came over me, and here I am."

"Double shot of chamomile?"

"You know me too well."

"What's the deal for tomorrow?"

"I teach in the morning and in the evening. And I'll join a bunch of the sessions in between. Looking forward to Art Therapy. And the group meditation."

"Does everyone seem to be playing along all right?"

"They do," I say. "It's sensational, the effect this space can have on a person."

"I wasn't sure if a few would warm up to this stuff. Bradley, Dustin…a lot of different personalities."

"It really is fascinating, how they meet people here. Everyone finds their own comfort level. There isn't a right or wrong way to experience things."

"Well, I'm curious to hear how tomorrow goes. I look forward to the full report."

"What happens at the Catskills Retreat Center, stays at the Catskills Retreat Center," I say.

"Oh please. You wouldn't do that to me."

"I'll show you my confidentiality agreement."

"I should have hired someone with much less backbone."

I shrug. Emerson rolls his eyes. He takes a long sip of wine with his eyes to me. He knows how sexy he looks. He effortlessly exudes sensual masculinity.

"So how is everything else? How is Kai?"

"It's fine. He's good," A prickling heat materializes across my collarbone.

"Is he as good at this as he was in the real world?" he asks.

I am glad the darkness is cloaking my face, because I am quickly irritated by this question and I'm sure it's showing itself quite obviously, with far more prominence than would make sense to him.

"The real world?" I ask, keeping my voice as even as possible.

"I mean, come on," he says, shrugging his shoulders in an exaggerated way. "The guy was on top of the world. Imagine if he was still at it, and not wasting his time in some spiritual amusement park?" He laughs, but I don't find it funny.

My eyes narrow. "That's obnoxious," I say.

"What is?"

"Just because this isn't your world, doesn't mean it isn't real."

"Oh, come on, Cora. I'm kidding around. You know I'm kidding."

I exhale hard. I am aware I may need to swallow this or else risk falling into a discussion I am nowhere near ready to have.

"I know," I say, holding the tension closer to my chest. "I'm just really taken by this place. It feels like a missing piece for me. And I wish you could understand that."

"Understand what, exactly?"

He is mostly unprovoked. This conversation doesn't hold a charge for him, like it does for me.

"That there are things that I need to experience more deeply to feel fulfilled in my life," I say. "I wish we could experience them together, but if we can't, I'll at least need to be more diligent about embracing them myself."

"Are you forgetting that I am the reason you are there?" He places his wine glass down and leans forward. The slight frustration in his voice gives way to kindness. "I know how much you love these kinds of things, Cora. That's why I made it happen."

I am shaken by the fact that I have overlooked this gratitude. That, even in his lack of shared experience, he is supporting my passions in his own way. I'm disappointed in myself for letting my overwhelm get the best of me, and for taking it out on him.

But still, there is something in this that doesn't feel right. That puts it all in a neat little box and takes out fate's part in it. My part in it. But this is not what I want to say now. Not now.

"You're right, Emerson," I exhale, turning over onto my side and bringing my knees up to my side. "I'm sorry. I'm grateful for this experience, and for you. Truly, I am. It's just been a long day, and we don't normally sleep in separate beds."

"If you're saying what I think you're saying," he smiles broadly, playfully, "then, I miss you too, Cora. And I love you, very much."

I smile weakly. "I love you, too."

"You're exhausted. Try to get some rest, ok? Fresh new day tomorrow."

"Fresh new day," I repeat. "Goodnight, Em."

"Goodnight, C."

In minutes, I am asleep.

15

SEPTEMBER 1892

I'd always dreamed of a bigger life. Not a fancy one but a deeper one. A life with meaning.

The first time Asher and I make love, it is on the grass. The sun is setting and the air is soft and all the edges of my Universe fall away.

And I am sure that for the rest of my days, I will live only in our open space.

There is a certain type of disbelief that comes with the realization of a dream that comes true. I am not sure if this means I was not truly open to it before it arrived. If I imagined I could have this bigger life but didn't really believe in it. If my world was too small to hold the possibility of such grandeur. But in this moment, Asher is here with me, and my life is expanding. *He* is my world deepening, in every direction. He is my dream coming true. Together, we are a life with meaning.

And I pinch my skin, reminding myself that this is real. That he is real. That he is loving me the way he does.

He leans his head to the side, his flowing hair settling on his forehead, the color of the dipping sun gracing him in all the right places. He catches me reddening the pale skin of my forearm once more, closing my eyes to appreciate how tangible I am. I feel his hand cover mine, soften me.

I open my eyes, and he is right there.

"What's the matter?" he asks. He looks down at his leg, readjusts in on the grass. It had been badly injured months back, but it is healing.

"It doesn't hurt anymore," he says. "If that is what has you worried." He wraps himself around me, his eyes close and warm.

"I am always concerned about you, but it's not that." I graze my nose against his, feel the tickle across my skin. "I wanted to be sure," I say, reveling in the feel of him against me. "That this wasn't a dream."

He takes my hand away from my skin, holds it in his, brings it to his lips and kisses it softly.

"I do see you in my dreams every night," he says, his voice like sweet nectar, one with the wildflowers. "Sometimes it *is* hard to tell the difference."

I still for a moment, thinking it through.

"What if we are dreaming right now?" I ask him in a whisper, as I run my fingertips across his shoulder.

"Well, my dear Juliette. That is the beauty of it." He lays his head down in the grass, and I follow. "That it's hard to tell the difference."

He pinches my cheek. "For peace of mind," he says, smiling gently.

I smile, too, relishing in the gentle burn. The sunset sky that was so fiery becomes a deep purple. I lay my hand across my stomach, and I am not sure why, but it seems I am needed there. And he covers my hand with his. And I feel more love inside of me than I imagined a human heart could hold.

"Life is but a dream," he says.

16

PRESENT DAY

I dreamt many things last night, and I know they were important, but they slipped away when consciousness slipped back in. What I do remember is waking with a sweaty jolt after seeing the blurred face of a little girl. Perhaps one who never had a chance.

I am on my way to the studio, a cup of decaf chai with oat milk in hand, the sun having just risen over the tree line. It is a beautiful, clear morning, smelling sweet and new the way only an early summer morning can, and I decide to host today's session outdoors. I put down my drink and my bags on the veranda and go inside to collect the necessary items. I feel more buoyant this morning as I arrange the space, unroll the mats, stream music from the outdoor speakers. We will practice sun salutations. We will keep things light and airy. We will energize ourselves for the day ahead.

The group starts to trickle in, some arriving in small clusters, others individually. Maralyn is there, and so is the rest of the team. Everyone is there but Kai.

They choose their spaces and there is one empty mat in the back and I can feel his absence like a hole in my stomach, raw and demanding. And we turn our faces toward the sun.

When class is over, the group heads to breakfast, and I decide to join them, having yet to enjoy a communal meal. The energy is wonderful and there is laughter and a lot of light and I am reminded of the other sides of healing. The parts that feel like relief. Like exhales.

I sit near Maralyn and Ronin and eat a bowl of warm oatmeal sprinkled with cinnamon and a colorful assortment of fruit. My muscles have that pleasant way about them, tension released after morning movement. It helps me to stay present, though I'm sure Maralyn notices how many times I look over to Kai's empty seat.

After breakfast, we move to Avery's Creative Arts Therapy session in the Lapis Lazuli room. I have been looking forward to this session, and I feel excited to work with my hands in a way that I haven't in so long.

Avery's long gray hair is pulled up in a bun, her skirt long, colorful, and flowing. She introduces the session, explaining that it will be led in part as an open studio (where we have free use of the space and materials to create in the way that we need to) and in part as a directed experience (with Avery providing an inspired focus for us to create from.)

She presents us with a question: *if you were a tree, what would you look like?*

The group looks at her quizzically.

"What do you mean, what would we look like?" asks Emily.

"Try looking at it this way." She crunches her eyes together, preparing for the profound. "If you were a tree...what would you look like?"

I smile, because I like her style—she exudes ways of being that may seem contradictory but work flawlessly together. Softness and strength. Playfulness and profundity. A reminder that we don't have to choose to be one way in the world, or another. That we can embody all these things at once. That we can be whole in dichotomy.

I find myself in front of an easel. I have not used paint in far too long, and I allow myself to see what comes. I paint an oak tree, branches outstretched, reaching up toward the sun. The trunk stands on the grassy ground beneath, the sky blue and clear. The leaves are lush and vibrant, and there is a hollow knot in the center, where a white dove lives.

A half hour later, the group makes their finishing touches, and we are invited to bring our art over to what Avery calls the Sharing Circle.

We pin our creations to a board on the wall, and one at a time, we share our experience and what our work means for us.

Whereas this may have at first seemed a lighthearted experience, I am awed by the depth of sharing. Avery is incredible at holding space, opening each artist to the possibility of finding their own answers.

Mackenzie's tree is empty of leaves, branches silhouetted against a winter sky. "It's my anxiety," she says. "It's showing itself here, in the cold."

"Tell me about trees in the winter," Avery says.

"They lose their leaves."

"Are they waiting for something?"

"For Spring, I guess," Mackenzie shrugs.

"And what happens in the Spring?"

"New growth. New life."

"Does Spring always return?"

Mackenzie nods cautiously. "Yes."

"Do the trees trust that?"

"Well, yes. They don't question it."

"And what about potential?"

"What do you mean?"

She looks down at her drawing, bites the inside of her mouth.

"At what time would a tree hold the most potential?"

Mackenzie thinks about it.

"Um. I'd say, maybe winter. Because there is the most opportunity for growth. They are just slowing down to prepare for it."

"How does that feel to you?"

"That feels good," she smiles. "It feels good because I think, perhaps, it gives me a new perspective. I have a lot of potential right now. And Spring always returns."

Maralyn has drawn a sycamore with a missing branch, but with new growth in another direction. Jacob, a weeping willow that is too beautiful to be sad.

When I tell the group about my tree, I tell them that it is reaching up toward the sun. Because I need the light to bring me life. Because there is something about the sky that makes me feel that anything is possible. So, Avery asks me about the ground.

"I don't know about the ground," I say. "Oak trees are meant to be strong. Stable. But I didn't draw any roots."

"What inspires you about the sky?"

"It makes me think of infinity. Of the cosmos. Of magical, beautiful things."

I look down at the painting, notice the lightness of my painted sky, powder blue with specs of white shimmering across the horizon.

"And what about the ground?"

"Well, that makes me think of beautiful things too, but their reflections. It makes me think of depth, of quiet, of my physical self in the world."

"Where are your roots?"

"I don't know," I say. "I thought I should have strong roots, considering how tangible my life has always been. But lately, I am feeling untethered. I wonder how I can be close to the earth, while craving the sky this way."

It is undeniable. I am drawn to the sky like a plant leaning toward the sun. I am not sure how to embrace dichotomy in my life, in the way Avery seems to. Instead, I feel stretched. Pulled this way, and then that.

"Maybe, they aren't separate things," she says.

"Maybe they aren't separate things," I repeat. "Maybe…"

Avery nods, urging me to continue.

"Maybe reaching for infinity means reaching in both directions at once—forever expansive in both directions. Maybe the belief that we need to choose, well…maybe that's an illusion."

I am quiet, and she sits there with me. The silence is therapeutic. It allows me to integrate these ideas that still feel so new. I am learning that my foundation was not keeping me balanced. It was only keeping me in place. I don't yet know how to balance my earth and sky, but I am sure there must be a way.

"And what about the white bird?" she asks.

"A beautiful little white dove." I look up from my painting and at her and I whisper, "She lives here with me."

Avery smiles softly and we let the quiet hang there, and I can feel it drifting. Up toward the sky, down into the earth.

When the session is done, there is a refreshed cohesion evident within the group after learning about themselves and each other from new angles. It warms my heart as I rinse paint brushes, roll up my canvas paper and stash it in my backpack.

Maralyn touches my arm. "That session was really beautiful."

"It was," I agree. "I've never participated in an art therapy session before. I'd like for it not to be my last time."

"Oh, Avery is a dream. You can always talk to her about private sessions."

"I think I just might. It felt good to use my hands again." I look down and notice the speckles of paint on my palms, but I have no desire to wash them off.

"How are you feeling?" she asks, after we thank Avery and move toward the exit.

"Oh, I don't know," I sigh. "I'm confused, Maralyn. I really am. But I do feel a little bit lighter this morning."

"Yesterday must have come as such a shock. It will take time to work it all through."

"I think so," I say, as we walk down the trail back toward Citrine. "I wonder if I need to change the way I am looking at all of this. Stop striving so hard for answers, and instead, look for contentment in the experience itself. A rare experience that should be appreciated for what it is—one that I can grow from and move on."

"Is that what you want to do?" she asks, leaning her head to the side.

"No," I say, honestly. "I don't. Maybe I *want* to want that. But I can't force that kind of thing. I can't force myself to feel a certain way."

"An exercise in futility," she agrees.

I nod. "But I do have control over my actions."

"Most of the time," she shrugs.

"Most of the time," I say, focusing out beyond the trees.

"Have you thought about what it will be like when you go home?"

"Yes. And I don't know the answer to that." I take a deep breath and look up toward the powder blue sky, wishing I could be so clear. "I wonder if it'll be like a switch turned on and off. If I will quickly go back to the way things were. Or if I will be irrevocably changed."

"It's strange to think about you leaving. You are such a part of things now. And you'd love Jarrett, the yoga instructor who is usually here."

"He's been in Bali, right?"

"Yes, he's been dreaming about a trip for years. He sent us a postcard telling us he's never coming back. We all rolled our eyes. He can't keep himself away."

"Hopefully I get to meet him someday. I have a feeling I'm going to be a frequent flier at the Catskills Retreat Center. I'll need a membership card."

"VIP access. Accumulate points for attendance at Art Therapy sessions and get a free massage."

We laugh and it feels good, and then I clear my throat.

"Maralyn? Do you know if Kai is all right?"

"I haven't seen him since halfway through the movie last night. Haven't heard from him, either. I must be honest, it's very unlike him. He tends to not miss a single session, if he can help it."

"I hope he's all right," I say, biting at my lip.

"If I had to venture a guess," she says, as we move slowly along the path, "it would be that he's giving you some space."

"Maybe," I say, looking at my feet brushing against the earth.

Maralyn holds my shoulder, gives it a small and compassionate squeeze.

There isn't any programming planned for a few hours. Guests have been invited to explore the grounds, and with the sun warm and gentle, a slight breeze rustling the leaves and creating its organic sym-phony, there is no reason to be indoors. I tell Maralyn I'm going to do some exploring of my own. She walks back to Citrine, and I walk in the direction of the studio space and up a winding path with a gentle incline. The woods get denser as I walk, the birdsong louder, the dampness in the air even purer. I can hear the rumbling of a creek nearby and move off the path in its direction.

It is a robust creek, cascading down from somewhere at the top of the sloped land. I wonder if I am on a small hill, or at the bottom of an enormous mountain. I crave to know how it came to be, and where it is going. It might not change the way the water drapes over the land in this very spot, but it would help me to understand. It would change the way I see it.

I walk along the creek, the movement of the water over the stones as soothing to my ears as it is to my eyes. I see a small bridge in the dis-tance, which leaves a lot of breathing room over the water, and I wonder how plentiful this creek becomes in the Spring. If it spills over into spaces that are now dry and waiting.

Though the water is shallow enough to cross at nearly any point, likely only ankle deep at most and scattered with plenty of stones to be used for leverage, I walk toward the bridge anyway, wanting to see its construction, feel the sensation of walking from one side to the other. It is a tidy wooden bridge, sturdy and simple. I run my hand along the rail and notice small carvings there. It is hard to make some of them out, but they seem to tell a story. There are objects; a humble home, a necklace, a river. There are people, carved without detail but with life to them, all the same.

I wonder if many hands have added to the art on this bridge, or if one person alone sat here, carving, day after day. I wonder about Kai. I wonder how much heart he has poured over this bridge. If he built it by hand, sweating in the early sun, creating something that may not have been a necessity in the moment, but which he knew would be, someday, when the water rises.

I hear the clanking of my feet over the wood. The hollowness is pleasing. On the other side, the foliage is different, with more color, and more lushness. There is a jutting rock that floats above the moving water. I step to the edge of it, and though the physics may seem intimidating, I have no fear of falling in. It is solid and durable, but it makes me feel light as I balance on its edge, floating high above the rest but grounded, one with earth and sky, in the way I want to be.

At the foot of the rock, sits an intricately carved altar—a wooden statue of the goddess Aphrodite atop an ornate platform. I kneel before it with my knees to the earth, drawn to its art and benign power. I move my gaze along her sculpted peaks and valleys. I reach my hand out to feel her smooth protective glaze delicate against my fingertips, but when I do, it is like she is electrically charged and sparking against my skin. I am startled by a sudden shift in my vision, a swimming sensation in my head, a buzzing in my crown and a rush of warmth in my heart space.

I take my hand back, and still for a moment, leaning my palms against the earth before rising to a stand. *Woah*, I exhale audibly, speaking to the forest.

The energy on the outskirts of the land feels even more intense, and I must remind myself that I am safe, that there is truly nothing to fear. My soul is reaching for such connectedness, and it seems wasteful to experience these enchanted states with anxiety, rather than appreciate the rare touch of their ethereal embraces. Kai has inspired these states in me, but so has the land, and it makes me think that he and the forest are one thing. Connected as one breathing, beating entity. And in that way, I can feel him here.

After a few slow breaths, I move further into the woods. I continue onward on the path and go off trail again once the creek is out of sight. My shoes are not appropriate for this piece of land, which is rockier and more overgrown, but I take it slow, aware of the unevenness of my heightened state and holding on to tree trunks for balance. I see a robin and revel in its song. Two butterflies, fluttering in playful circles around each other through the air. I feel so at home here. The city feels like a world away. Maybe that's why my thoughts seem so loud. I am accustomed to them being drowned out.

I move back to the trail, wary I will lose my way. I am appreciative of the calming effects of the forest because it is helping to keep me grounded amidst the intensity of the energy. Emotions and thoughts are cycling through my consciousness in a fast and erratic way, each one seemingly attached to exponential others. I feel deep gratitude in recognition of the unique depth of my experience, no matter how uncomfortable. It feels like growth, and something my soul has been begging for, though it is hard to tell which direction I am growing in, and where I am meant to go.

In this moment, I also feel a vast sadness. Sometimes sadness can be a beautiful thing. On the spectrum of emotions, it is not always one that holds a negative connotation, especially when it is paired with things like longing and nostalgia. And I do feel nostalgia, as if my soul is aware of something that I am not. It is a type of sadness that moves through me like the mist at dusk after a rainy summer day, navy blue and slow.

I turn at a bend in the path and come upon a vast field. It is covered in wildflowers, the delicate whisps swaying in the breeze. I inhale deeply the scents that are dangling in the air. It is so lovely, the sun now high above me, coating everything in its gold, and countless other colors glistening within it. In this moment, at just the right one, I am grateful to come across this wide-open space, because I feel unwell—the type that comes on suddenly as a sloshing in the head, something heavy in the gut, legs that beg for a rest. I take a seat on the small stone bench at the edge of the field, looking out upon its splendor, perhaps in my new favorite place on the grounds. And I admit to myself how much I miss him.

I wish I was thinking about Emerson, and I am not. I miss a man I hardly know, have met only yesterday, have not seen for only one morning. It frightens me, how much I long to see him again. Truly, how even just seeing him would fill me. Just being close enough to lay my eyes across him. Just a moment to prove the existence of him, that his heart beats, that he is whole and human and alive. I long for him in every way someone can long for someone, and then in other ways that I didn't know existed.

It is my soul that is screaming out for him, I am sure of it. That, in and of itself, is a magnificent thing, and maybe that is enough. Recognizing the call. Nodding toward my soul, and letting her know I see her, feel her, honor her. A truth that I can hold and that connects me to the ethereal—to a thing that I have always yearned for, in a way I didn't expect it to arrive. This is a gift that can aid in my healing and growth. And maybe, even enhance my relationship with Emerson. Because, at its core, such purity of experience can create a deeply inspired tapestry in this life, touching everything that matters. I don't need to be near Kai, in the physical sense, to embrace this awareness and the expansive impact it can have on my life.

I will brace myself to go home tomorrow night and put this in the past. But not all of it. I will stash the longing away. And I will embrace the growth. I will give it all the veneration it deserves and transform around it. I will love from my own truth in a wholistic way. In a way that I never have before.

I remember a quote from a favorite poet, Rumi, written hundreds of years ago and of which I have read probably a hundred times and never truly comprehended, at least in this way. That's what makes true bits of wisdom so innately wise—we resonate with them differently depending upon our depth of consciousness. I swing my backpack over to the front of my body, and lean it on my lap, zipping open a front compartment and pulling out a notebook and pen. I write down the words, rip out the page carefully along its edge, and fold it neatly into my pocket.

Feeling better now, I rise. I walk for fifteen minutes, away from the field, back along the trails, over the bridge, and past the creek. I am buoyed by the relief that has come with even just the beginnings of processing these emotions, and the reminder that sits folded on my hip, giving me permission to trust myself and this process. Taking action, or even the promise of it, can be a suitable salve—a kind of panacea for the discomfort that comes from so much clouded uncertainty.

17

PRESENT DAY

When I get back to the lobby, I don't need to ask Maralyn. She answers me, anyway.

"I haven't seen him," she whispers. "And Soloman told me that he'll be leading this afternoon's meditation. Which is Kai's usual group, and his favorite session, at that."

"Are you worried?" I ask, worry painted across my own face.

"Kai is extraordinarily aware, and always considered. Whatever it is he is experiencing, I'm sure it's what he needs in the moment. And that he's ok."

I shake my head, turn to go, and then stop.

"Maralyn?"

She lifts her eyes toward me.

"Does Kai stay in one of the surrounding guest rooms, as well?" I realize in that moment that I have no idea where he goes when he is alone. It's such a strange thing, to know so little about a person's day-to-day details, but everything about their soul. Maybe I shouldn't have asked, but it will help me to know if he is still very close by. I think it might help me to know.

"Sometimes," she says. "He likes to stay in a room on occasion, when we have guests. But he lives on the property. He has a home up in the northeast corner. He built it himself. Completely on his own. It's really something."

"I'm sure it's incredible," I say.

"This is his home," she smiles. "For the rest of us, it's a home away from home."

"Where do you live?"

"Oh, not far from here. A thirty-minute drive east on the highway. Most of us stay in the guest rooms when we have programming across multiple days. We don't have to, but we like to."

"I think that is wonderful," I say.

I turn to go but return one last time.

"We'll stay in touch after this?" I ask, hopeful that this friendship is another thing that I can hold onto from this place. That it is something that I am allowed to keep with me when I go.

"Oh, most definitely, yes," she beams. "Most definitely, yes."

I go back up to my room. The early afternoon sun continues to move across the sky, and the warmth of it streaming through my windows makes me feel a comfortable type of tired after this morning's excursion. I curl up on a plush chair and dial Emerson. I catch him between meetings and tell him about the morning, the way you'd tell someone a story from the outside looking in. He has the exterior details, but none of the profound ones, like reactions and emotions and perspectives to give it weight. To me, that is a rather dry way to tell a story. But he doesn't seem to mind at all, and it's all I can give him in this moment, anyway.

He tells me about his morning in the same way, and I wonder if this is always the way. If maybe I'm just noticing it for the first time. And I realize how many of the details I know about his exterior life. Every single one.

He tells me he misses me, and I tell him I miss him, too. He tells me he loves me, and I tell him I love him, too. He asks me what time I can call him later, and I tell him I will speak to him after my last session, a 9 pm class to close out the night with a slow and introspective practice.

When I hang up the phone, I realize the group meditation is to start in fifteen minutes, and I'd have to leave in the next few to be on time. The hot sun is making me feel so pleasantly drowsy that I want to sink into it. I hardly ever sleep during the day, but my body can't keep up with all this mental and emotional expenditure of energy, and like last night, I can hardly keep my eyes open.

I fall asleep right there on the chair, sleep straight through the meditation, through lunch, through afternoon tea. When I awaken, it is with a jolt, confused by how far the sun has moved in the sky, surprised by the grogginess that is still sitting on top of my eyelids. I peel myself from my seat, stretching my crunched muscles. My stomach is also grumbling against its hollowness, and after smoothing my hair, I head downstairs for something to eat.

The hallway is so quiet that even shutting my door against its frame feels like an intrusion. I suppose the group is still at the tea ceremony, and as I walk silently down the corridor, I feel drawn to the entrance of the Eye.

Considering the silence, I'd like to sit in my own meditation for a while. I know the risk I take in entering, but it is still early, and Kai had told me that his usual time to sit on the cushions is late in the evening, while everyone is asleep. All the same, after my epiphanies earlier today, it feels a worthy risk. An important one.

But as I get closer, stand near in contemplation, the air changes. The pull is tenacious. It is magnetizing me toward its center, tugging at my shoulders, turning me toward its quiet depth. And I know that any other reason I give myself for walking through the entrance would be an evasive ruse. Would be a clear disregard for the truth of it.

This time, I do not resist. This time I don't feel able. Perhaps it is a failure in resilience. Perhaps it is the opposite.

When I get to the doorway, it takes a few moments for my eyes to adjust, as the dark is in such stark contrast to everywhere else still swimming in sunlight. And as the room starts to come into focus, I feel what is like a thousand butterflies taking flight at once after a long slumber, a rush of cool air tingling at the small hairs on my arms, a head swimming drunk in the fizzing darkness. A form kneels at the front of the room, in what may appear to be prayer but is too curled up, too hunched over, too desperate. I try to inhale but it comes in like a small gasp. He doesn't move at first, although I am sure he has heard it. He waits moments, and then slowly raises his head, leaning back to rest on his heels.

I move silently into the room, touching the ground with the tips of my toes. Not because I am trying to hide—he knows I am here. I am just trying to respect the depth of the moment.

"I'm sorry to disturb you," I say with hushed voice.

"You could never disturb me," he says, putting something in his pocket that I cannot see through the dim light and then rising to his feet. He turns to me, and though most of him is muted, edges blurred, his eyes are still as penetrating as ever. They are telling a thousand stories of pain and loss and love and wisdom, and I want to go to him. I want to put my arms around his neck and let his head fall to my shoulder where he can rest. I want to feel my heart beating against his, our chests moving in mutual rhythm, alive and pulsing with shared breath.

"Sit with me a while?" he asks.

I nod and move toward him, so relieved to be in his presence again that it feels like bliss. For moments, the guilt is buried under it, and I let it be. He sits crossed-legged on a cushion and I mirror him from my own. His hair is falling over his face, and he pulls it back, fastening it so that it is held at the back of his head.

"Can I be very honest with you, about one thing?" he asks.

"You can be honest with me about anything."

"Not anything." The truth of it feels blunt and sorrowful. We are both silent, working our way through the maze of irony, me from a space of ignorance, him from his own perspective of knowingness that I want to wrap myself around.

"Let's start with just this one thing," I say.

He nods once and lays his hand across his heart, inhaling slowly behind closed eyes. When he opens his them, he lets his hand fall, and rests it across his lap.

"I've spent a lifetime without you," he says. "But now that you are here, this day that we have been apart feels like eternity."

His words combust and I am blown apart, stunned to silence by his admission, unable to make sense of the vicious mix of confusion and understanding, sadness and euphoria. I fumble to pick up my pieces and put myself back together again. But I am not the same as I was moments ago. Our cells are always changing, our thoughts giving us new life. We are never the same person we were moments before and it is always that way, just usually in such small ways that we don't notice. But there are certain moments that change us unrecognizably—the pinnacle moments that transform everything. And I am sure that I am in one.

"It's your turn now," he says.

"My turn?" I choke.

"Just one thing."

My heart is in my throat, pounding against my vocal cords, doing all it can to sing its own song as I grip tightly, holding back the words I want to speak. I look down into my lap, folding sentences into boxes, trying to pack them away, but they are forming more quickly than I can keep up with. And before I know it, I am swimming in a sea of words and they are words that shouldn't be spoken and still not one of them is good enough. Not one of them can express what is happening inside of me, what it feels like to be in his presence. This experience is nothing that can be imagined or rationalized. It is not something one can ever strive for, because it exists on its own plane. It is as mysterious as life after death, as heaven to earth, never to be explained because once you are there, the You that was is gone. You can't tell the You of before what is possible in infinity.

And because these feelings are mingling with guilt that has now returned in its full splendor, so thick it is like hot, smelly tar, spackling itself into the spaces between my ribs, I don't say the words. I let them whirl inside of me, scorching every edge and crevice until my eyes water. Instead, I reach into my pocket and retrieve the note I wrote for myself. An admission of my need. A decision I will not be able to take back.

I grasp it between my fingers, moving it from one hand to the next, and then pass it to him, still folded. His hand brushes my skin when it crosses from me to him, and again, I come undone. And it is not only me who does, because I can see it in him too. We both don't want to move. We want to stay there, connected through this small piece of notebook paper, with the words folded inside. But then he disconnects us, because he must, and he unfolds it, reads it to himself. And when he looks up, he speaks it aloud, not looking to the paper now, and I am sure this is a practiced song for him. Not the first time he has sung it.

> *Out beyond ideas of wrongdoing and rightdoing,*
> *there is a field. I'll meet you there.*

> *When the soul lies down in that grass,*
> *the world is too full to talk about.*

And then he closes his eyes, grasps the paper in his closed hand, and continues the poem beyond what I have written.

> *Ideas, language, even the phrase 'each other'*
> *doesn't make any sense.*

This beautiful wisdom is born from his lips, but it is painted on his soul. It's like he is made up of it, from something beyond the words, something true and infinite that is impossible to ignore but of which I have refused to see. And I realize, in this moment, I am understanding something I didn't know I understood. That our connection is not of this moment alone. Instead, it is something that spans eons. That we, for so long, have been a part of each other's eternity.

And with this revelation, my head starts to spin. The room moves in undulating patterns, as if I am a ship in a storm. It is too much, sloshing against my sails this way. I am so overwhelmed I can't breathe. I put one hand to the side of my head, one to the carpet, aiming to steady myself. But it all keeps moving and I am swept away in a current so strong that my only hope is to let it take me.

"Cora," he says. "Cora, it's ok." He lifts from his cushion and comes to me. He comes up close, kneeling before me, but he doesn't touch me. If he does, it might burn us both up.

"I'm so sorry." He shakes his head, the remorse obvious in the slump of his shoulders, the curves of his face.

I am shaking all over, and I look up to him. "Why are you sorry?"

"You have a life. A whole life you have built." His words are vehement and strong, but transform quickly to a whisper, as he casts his eyes down. "I am being selfish. I am hurting you. I am causing you pain."

"No." I shake my head. "It is not you who is causing me pain." The rest of the words still hang there, tucked away in corridors, begging to be seen. The pain is in our distance. Even this close is not close enough.

"I am ready to see," I say. "It's the only way." I bring both hands to my lap, the churning waters calming with my decisiveness. "And then, maybe I can go back. Maybe then I can hold this as something that will always give us life…" I pause, close my eyes for a moment and breathe there "…but does not become our life." My voice is small, devastated, pushing out words that aren't in boxes. That weren't formed on their own accord but built by me, piece by piece.

Kai is silent. His face is pained, contorting around my words but with such subtlety that I am sure he is using all his strength to hide it from me. And I am sure that he can't hide from me, and even though there were so many words that I have in fact left unspoken, I am not hiding from him either. And I am sure any of this feigned resoluteness is in stark contrast to my desire, one that is alive with such intensity that every one of my cells is screaming out. But I can't embrace this reality that I am swimming in. I must find a way to move forward.

"My true lesson may lie somewhere beyond it," I mutter through a cracked throat.

He is exceptionally still. He inhales shakily, as if he had the wind knocked out of him. His eyes fall, and he stays there for some time, and then he rises again to meet me.

"*Even the phrase 'each other' doesn't make any sense,*" he repeats.

We are silent. We hold each other's gaze in a deeper way than I have ever before experienced. There is no discomfort in the quiet of it. There is no desire to look away. We are locked there, in place, where our souls reside.

"Tonight," he says. "Come with me. And I will show you."

"Here?"

He shakes his head. "We cannot risk interruption."

He rises from kneeling, and to a stand, and I follow, shaky and unsteady.

"I have a home on the property, up to the north." He is somber but finding strength. Perhaps finding a purpose beyond his pain. "I will meet you at the studio after your last session, and we will walk together. It isn't far."

"Ok." I fold my arms in front of my chest, shivering and holding myself as if to stay warm, though I am already stifled by the heat under my skin.

"Ok," he nods. He opens his mouth to speak again but decides against it. He folds the small paper, neatly and delicately, and holds it up to me between his fingers. He gestures to return it to me, and when I shake my head, he slides it into his pocket, holds his hand over his clothing once it is secure.

And then he turns and walks away.

18

Present Day

It is now early evening. The late summer sun still lingers, hanging with the promise it made to pay homage to the season by painting its edges gold into the night. I am simultaneously weak and frenzied, energies clashing inside me and dancing around each other like opposite magnetic poles. Too overwrought to either sit still or exert myself, I move toward the studio earlier than I need to, at a slow and deliberate pace.

I wear soft cotton, matching off-white on the top and the bottom, moving elegantly around my slim curves, feeling as delicate as I need it to be against my skin. Everything seems harsh and intensified. Unnatural lighting hurts my eyes, sounds crash against my ears more loudly than I am used to, even the push of a blade of grass across my bare ankle is penetrating. Every nerve ending is alive. Waiting.

I am hungry but I cannot eat. I brought a bag of almonds with me, ate two before my throat felt like it may close around them. I am running on a mix of adrenaline and fear; something wholly natural but totally foreign moving through my veins.

Even though I had promised him a call after class, I instead spoke to Emerson before I left my room. Before I am so far removed from my usual existence that he would not recognize my voice. I am aware of the deception in my omissions, but between this rock and this hard place I have chosen the only path with the possibility of leading me back to shore.

I dread leading a class tonight. I cannot even feign presence, and

I think the only way that I can genuinely lead is to be honest with myself about my needs, too. To use the class as a curative and healing experience rather than a responsibility that I can't hold. To support myself along with the rest of the class. And I am sure now that this is always how it should be.

It will be dark by the time they arrive. The lights will be down, with moonlight and candlelight the only sources of external illumination. I will speak to our light inside. I will remind myself of it when I remind them. We will hold our poses in a restorative way. We will not push, and we will not prod. We will nurture ourselves and each other.

I sit in front of the altar, the room now properly prepared and ready to be the gentle container that it is built for. The Parvati statue sits atop the raised platform, seemingly comforted by the moon's gentle glow. To her right, a statue of Lord Shiva. I remember vaguely the story of Shiva and Parvati, husband and wife. I get up to retrieve my phone to learn about their history. I read that Parvati is representative of the continuity of life and an embodiment of Shakti, a cosmic energy that represents the forces that move through and continually bring the universe into existence. I am familiar with a type of yogic practice that is born from the feminine power of Shakti, a free-flowing and creative practice. I read on to learn that Parvati and Shiva went through many trials before they were united in love; until they became two forces in a perfect and inseparable union, neither one of whom could fully exist without the other.

Chills run down the length of my spine, everything around me suddenly appearing as if it whispers to me, its significance choreographed and divine. Every moment of my life that has led me to this one, everything I have experienced, guiding me toward these pivotal moments of awakening. Everything Kai has built, somehow, in some way, built around it. Somehow. In some way.

I hear the murmur of voices in the distance, and I am sure the group is arriving. I am not ready, but I must be. I must be here, right where I am, in the best way I can be, and only then can I move forward toward my pinnacle moment. Because these sessions, they are pieces of the story that brought me here. And they deserve my attention.

And with that, I take all the feelings sloshing through me and create a flowing current. A type of whirlwind that gives way to an undulating tide of ebb and flow and incredible potentiality. And the group becomes a part of that flow, and we move together in a beautiful symphony in a way that has its own vitality, blurred to my eyes in this vibrating state that I operate from. And when it is over, we all feel it. And the group rolls up their mats in total silence, moves toward the door without breaking the quiet.

Maralyn stays back, but just for moments. Just long enough to look into my eyes, and nod, and ensure that I know that she sees me. That she is supporting me, in the ways that she can. And with my returning nod, I am ensuring she knows that I am grateful.

And then, I am alone again. But now, I am not waiting. I am only here, right now, still wrapped in my state of flow, in the exquisite etherealness of the moment. I move slowly. I blow out each candle until I am cloaked in darkness, led only by the cascading light of the full moon. And though I hear no sound, I know when he is standing in the doorway. I can feel his hushed and barefoot steps. I can feel the glow that emits from him, warming the moonlight.

I turn to him, and with every fiber of myself, I know how deeply he is *here* with me. Our first moments of allowing. Of showing everything that dances behind our eyes. And though it is just moments, I know that the memory of it will live on for my eternity. That I will never, not ever, forget the way we stand here, touching each other without skin.

"Are you ready?" he asks me, his voice reverberating with deep reverence.

"I am ready," I say, gentle and certain. And together, we walk.

Outside of the studio, he unhooks a lantern from the veranda. The path is pitch black beyond it, the trees' canopies shielding us from moonlight, but we are embraced by our circle of light. It cradles us, moves with us, and we are silent within it. We do not speak as branches crunch underfoot, our arms are brushed with soft leaves, our hair moves in the gentle breeze. And after ten minutes of our silent pilgrimage, the light around us is not the only light I see.

"Up this way," he says, lifting his leg high onto a boulder on a ridge to the right, pulling the rest of himself up with the help of a tree branch overhead. He reaches out his hand to me, and I hesitate, wary of what will happen when they meet.

"It's ok," he tells me. "Just breathe."

I place my hand into his and close my eyes and the world spins around me, inside of my head, fast through the blackness behind my closed lids. I grip his hand more tightly to steady myself, breathe deeply once more and then again. And when I start to settle, I open my eyes to find that the world is still and has been all along. I am unstable, and lightheaded, and blurred, but he pulls me up and I float toward him on the ridge, my chest falling against his for a fleeting moment before we are both standing with both feet on the ground, higher than we were before.

"Just breathe," he whispers, his face so close to mine I can smell the sweet, smokiness of his breath, coaxing my eyes to close again simply to savor its warmth, to melt around it. And then we are moving again, my hand still in his, walking over a slim narrow path. I look up toward his home for the first time, and again, in what seems like a state that is my new normal, my breath is taken from me.

I am awed by what is absolutely the most stunning piece of architecture I have ever seen up close. Lit up with warm light against the black sky, the structure seems to unfold around itself, comprised of glass at every front and back facing facade, supported by matte metal beams, with windows spanning floor to ceiling set inside of cement walls leading out to dark wood patios that wrap around in an unraveling geometry. Each piece stacked like building blocks, perfectly balanced in their rebellious agreement. There is a bolder built into the structure on the right side, a large tree bark moving upward to support a room perched high above the rest, nature seeping in at every one of its edges.

"Oh, Kai," I breathe, and he squeezes my hand more tightly.

We approach the front door, both slip off our shoes and move inside, which is just as stunning as the rest. Modern, minimalist, and every bit considered, with clean lines, a subtle palette, and intentional asymmetry.

And life. Oh, there is so much life.

"I have never seen anything so beautiful."

He turns toward me, my hand still in his, and then he takes my other. "You have no idea," he says, penetrating me with a stare that is at once adoring and pained. He turns my hands over, moves his fingertips across my palms, touching me as if he is seeing human hands for the very first time, learning about their curves and their temperature and the way they move in the air. My fingers start to dance around his too, so gently, our touch like feather against feather, learning about the particles of skin that make us up. And then we are palm to palm, crossing our fingers over each other and back again, never still but desperately slow. I lose periphery, sparks flaring in front of my eyelids. My heart pounds against my chest so violently I wonder if it can break through.

And as if I had been hypnotized and startled awake, he is no longer on my skin, and I am jolted back to whatever semblance of reality still exists within me and around me.

"I have prepared a space upstairs."

I nod.

"You can trust me."

"I know."

I follow him up two stories, the climb a reminder of where we are headed. That pinnacle moments must be reached, not settled into.

We enter the room I had seen perched in the tree branches. It is a small, square room, two sides made of glass and meeting at a right angle, the floor a purposefully cracked concrete covered with a plush and deeply colored carpet. The other two walls are lined with shelves and artifacts, a delicate altar doused in the smoke of incense, and there are more than two dozen candles lit around the periphery. There are two chairs facing each other in the center of the room, two cushions moved to the side.

"My meditation space. Please, make yourself comfortable."

He invites me to take a seat, and he does the same. There is only half a foot of space between us, but it feels much further.

"I thought it important to have our feet on the ground during this experience. Does that sound all right to you? Are you comfortable?"

"Yes, that sounds all right," I say, grateful for the grounding.

"What are you feeling?"

I take a sharp inhale. "Everything," I exhale. I am anxious, excited, curious, and afraid. I am very afraid, not from a lack of trust or perceived safety, but because I don't know how what I am about to experience will change the course of my existence. I feel both tremendous purpose and crippling guilt, as if I am here for a reason so important it is beyond frivolous notions of right and wrong, but also that it is as simple as right and wrong—as simple as this unique form of infidelity that I am choosing to take part in.

I feel as if I am a part of everything, all at once. As if the surfaces of my skin don't touch the air in the same way they usually do. My cells feel as if they are merging with existence around me, and me and the rest of the Universe are all one thing, all somehow tied into eternity. I feel as if want my skin against Kai's, every inch of me merging with the heat of him, but this feeling is one that I try to stifle, shoving it below all my other layers, where it begs to be let out.

He nods his head, runs his hands down his thighs and back again. "The whole of this experience is in your control. If at any time you decide you want to go no further, tell me to stop. And we will go no further."

I nod.

"I don't know where you will enter. Or if you will enter. I do trust that your soul will guide you. There is much to be seen—both exquisitely beautiful and strikingly dreadful things. You must tell me if at any point it is too much. Promise me you will, Cora."

"I promise," I muster over a dry tongue.

"Let's take three deep breaths together." He leans forward, again taking my hands in his. We inhale and exhale, slowly and in rhythm.

"Do you feel comfortable with this?" He gently squeezes my fingers. "Can we stay connected in this way as we begin?"

"Please don't let go," I say, my voice trembling now.

"I'm here," he says. "I'm right here."

And we close our eyes.

"I am going to take you on a journey, into a kind of hypnotic state, with the hope that you open more gracefully to these visions. Access a part of yourself that remains dormant. Connect with your spirit and let her show you the way."

Even in my heightened state, I am lulled by his voice. Soothed by the warmth of his hands, the slight movement of candlelight that I can make out behind closed eyes.

"Take another deep breath and hold it. When you let it go, let any tension you feel in your body go with it. Again, deep breath, hold it, and release. Let any tension melt away."

I notice the tightness in my shoulders, along my jawline, sitting on each side of my head. With each breath, I imagine it wafting away, my muscles letting go, softening in its absence.

"Allow yourself to sink deeper into relaxation. With each breath you take, deeper and deeper. Deeper, and deeper."

I feel myself sinking, his voice healing and profound and dreamlike. My seat becomes softer and downy, billowing around me, enveloping me, deeper with every breath. He continues, soothing me into this trance, and I feel different in my body, again one with the air around me. It is peaceful, a gentle coolness permeating the space, so much of what I have been holding evaporating into it.

And then he brings me to a winding staircase. I stand at the very top, looking down over a forest, a hundred feet in the air. He counts down from ten, and slowly, I begin my descent. Nine, eight. I move down further, circling through the misting air. Seven. Six. Body more relaxed, more at ease. Five, four, three. Deeper and deeper still, my feet gliding across the winding stairs, meeting them like the breeze. Two and I am close to the bottom. One and I step off the last of the stairs and place my feet on the lush grass below.

"What do you see?" he asks, his voice so close but no longer coming from our seats in the room, in the house, in the woods. His voice is the wind in the trees. A warm rain against a windowpane. The ocean moving against the shore, soaking the glassy sand and then back again.

"I see a dense forest," I say. "Whimsical and alive. And there is a path."

"Can you follow it?"

"Yes," I say, and I walk.

"Continue down the path until you come to three gateways. Let me know when they are in view."

I continue walking, the vision so lifelike, so immersive, that I can smell the perfumed scents of the forest, feel the uneven ground beneath my feet, see the lush hues of life around me. I see the gateways up ahead and move toward them as if I would on this earth, with one foot in front of the other, but on a different timeline, time and space warping around each other in a way I can't recognize.

"I see them," I whisper.

"Take a moment and tell me what they look like. Are they doors? Archways? Do they all look the same, or are they unique?"

"They are portals. Bright lights and swirling. They are all the same aside from their color. A bright white light in the center, a cool blue to the left, a vibrant orange to the right."

"Behind each of these portals is an entry. A fragment of your soul's story. Moments your soul wants you to remember. Visions of yourself on a timeline that is not of your current incarnation."

I can see each portal vividly, crisp and clear in a way I have never seen in a meditation space before. I am there, in front of these spinning orbs. I am feeling their electric pulses, their magnetic pull.

"Does one of these portals call to you, Cora?"

"Yes," I say without hesitation, the small hairs on my arms, the water that makes up my cells, leaning toward the center like a plant to the light. "The middle one. The white light."

Kai tells me to walk through when I am ready, and as I move toward this swirling orb it kicks my hair up in its vortex and fallen leaves and particles of light spin around me until I am right there inside the blinding brightness of it. Everything is moving so fast and again my world spins intensely and I know I am grabbing onto my chair but I don't know when I left his hold and it feels like someone else's hands turning white from their tight grip, someone else's feet pushing against the ground. And then there is a flash and all I see is a pure white light, which may look like nothing but of which I know is everything. It is everything, all at once. And as it starts to fade, the spinning subsides, and a new picture comes into view.

"I am standing on a cobblestone street." My voice sounds different now. Deeper. Far away. "My clothes feel heavy. But my heart feels light."

I look down at my hands. I am seeing them with new eyes. They are not the hands that I am used to, but they are my own. I wear a long gown. It is tight around my ribcage. It is flowing, deep in color, swaying as I walk. "I see small shops. A bakery. A post office. A general store. I turn off the cobblestone and onto a dirt trail, surrounded by meadow and tall oak. I come to a cottage." It is warm but welcoming, a thatched roof, a wooden porch, a sweet picket fence holding it in place. I hear the rumble of a creek, I see golden leaves, crisped by the first hints of autumn.

"I open the fence, walk up to the front door, walk inside. The interior is humble, everything in its place. There is a pot hanging over a fire. A broom leaning against a doorway. A quilt laying across the foot of a small bed. I walk to the back door. There is a porch outside. It is scattered with fallen leaves. It is afternoon. Everything is painted gold."

In that moment, I look up, out toward the meadow. And, just like that, I am every particle in the Universe vibrating erratically for all eternity and then clicking into place. I am eyes that have only ever seen darkness, totally illuminated. I am a heart that had stopped beating for eons and feels its first pulse.

I am bliss. I am infinite.

I am love.

My voice shakes when I speak. I don't know how to hold this new vibration. It is bursting from my skin, mingling in the air around me because it can't fit inside.

"I see two people in the meadow. There are butterflies. So many butterflies. They don't chase them, but they dance with them. Spinning and laughing, the light of the late sun moving with them. They are beautiful. Oh, they are so beautiful."

Tears are streaming down my cheeks now and I let them fall, not abandoning the desire to stifle them but not even considering the need for abandon. They are tears not of pain, but of a joy and love so vast that there is no container that can hold them. There is no heart big enough.

"I know why the Universe is infinite. If it wasn't, there wouldn't be enough room. There would be no space for all the love that is here."

I stand there on the porch, reveling in this moment, and I don't know how long I do, because time doesn't seem to exist here. I don't want to leave. So, I stay, and I watch, until I realize that I don't need to do only that. That I can go to them.

"I am walking toward them now. I am walking toward them, and I can't wait to hold them. Feel them in my arms."

Kai speaks and his voice is a part of the air there. It is what it is made up of.

"Who are they? Who are these two people?"

I don't need to think about it, because I know who they are. "My husband, Asher. My daughter, Pearl. The loves of my life."

The tears are streaming with such force now they are splashing against my lap. My eyelids are fluttering so vehemently that I must squeeze them shut. I don't want them to accidentally swing open. I don't want to leave. I want to stay here. I don't want to leave.

And as I walk toward them, they turn to me. My daughter's eyes light up bright, and she runs to me with outstretched arms. My husband smiles the kindest smile, his head leaning slightly to the side, and he walks toward me, reveling in my and Pearl's embrace. And then he is there in front of me too, and my heart feels like it will explode. I have never known love like this. Love has not existed until this moment. Whatever I thought love was, it is something else entirely.

"Pearl is in my arms. I put her down, and she runs toward the house, still dancing with the butterflies. Asher comes close, moves his hand to my cheek, rests his forehead against mine. He kisses me on the lips, so softly it feels like the warmth of the sun's rays. Oh god, everything is spinning. I don't want to ever leave. Please. I don't want to leave."

And then, there is a jolt. And without warning, the sky goes dark. I look up, and storm clouds have rolled in, their purple-black moving fast across the sky. When I look down, Asher is no longer with me. I turn, and his back is to me, in the doorway, retreating into the house.

"What do you see?" asks Kai.

"It is dark now, and I am alone. I'm scared. I'm walking back to the house, but it is changing. The shutters are hanging. The wood rotting. The rain starts. The thunder. It pours. I am soaking wet. I step inside, a puddle forming below my feet."

"Keep talking," he says. "Keep talking."

"I hear something. A cough. Another. It sends shivers down my spine. My clothes are different. Stained and frayed. I don't see Asher. I don't see Pearl. I look everywhere. I am frantic. I am dizzy. I feel sick."

"Breathe," he says. "Breathe."

"Oh God," I say again. "There is another room. I didn't see it before. Asher is there. He is in bed. His eyes open weakly when I enter. I throw off my wet overcoat. Let it fall to the floor. I go to him. I nearly collapse. I kneel in front of the bed. I put the back of my hand to his forehead. I am sobbing. I hold both sides of his face in my hands. His eyes close for too long and a dread moves so viciously inside of me that for moments I black out. I cannot see anything. And then we are in each other's eyes again, and I cannot see anything else."

"I take his hand. He is too weak to lift it on his own," I sob. "*Please, I say. Please, take me with you.* He moves a finger across my hand, coughs once and then again. A small sound comes from his throat, and I move my ear to his mouth."

"What does he say?"

I can hardly make it out. I am panicking. And now there is utter silence and I wait. He tries again. His voice is only air. Broken but still so full. He finds the strength. I feel him, grasping at every bit of it that's left. And he speaks.

"*My dearest, Juliette. This is not goodbye.* He coughs. He stutters. I sob, my tears falling over his face. He continues, his voice finding courage. *I will go to Pearl, and we will wait for you. It will be no time at all. A short moment in our eternity. I won't forget, Juliette. I won't forget. I will come back for you. I promise you. I will remember. We will have sun on our faces again. And she will be waiting.*"

The pain I feel in that moment is excruciating. Piercing. I see it from her eyes but I feel it in my breath and I lean back in my chair, afraid I may fall from the weight of it.

"He's leaving," I wail. "He's going away. I feel him going. I am wrapped around him. I am screaming. Begging. Heaving. I tell him I love him. Once and then again and then a hundred more times, but he doesn't answer me. His eyes are open but vacant. It is not him anymore. He is gone. I am gone. She is gone. I am only emptiness. A shell that is filled with darkness. I am made only of despair."

There is silence then. "The vision is starting to slip from my fingers, turning to fine ash. Periphery is blurring, like I am in a tunnel."

"Then we must go," says Kai.

I nod, my heart disintegrating like the rest of it. Kai invites me to return to the porch, to the meadow, to the trail, to the cobblestone. He invites me to find the portal, and to walk through, back from where I came. He directs me back up the path, back toward the winding staircase. One, two, three, I climb, my feet heavy, my heart heavier. Four, five, six, weighed down by grief but rising, rising. Seven, eight, I move my toes against the rug below my feet and detach my fingers from the chair's edge. Nine, straighten my shoulders, move my head to one side and then the other. Ten, I am at the top again. I am taking three deep breaths.

Kai snaps his fingers, and I open my eyes.

The room I am in seems foreign, like I have not been here in a long time. But we still sit on these same seats, in the same light, under the same star-scattered sky. My face is soaked with salty tears, my head throbbing, my hair drenched and stuck to my forehead. I blink slowly, take a quaking breath.

Kai looks at me, does not break his gaze, holds me there. His face is inconsolable. We are both unraveled and raw. The pain within me is insatiable, the depths of love I have understood beyond what can ever be spoken. I see the same thing in his eyes. It is all mirrored there, I to him and him to me. He begs me. He silently pleads. He doesn't have to. I say *yes* without words, pleading with him all the same. And then we are both standing, frozen in place for moments, our breathing uneven but the same, our hearts beating erratically but in rhythm.

He steps toward me, closer, inches away. We are gasping for air, holding it in our lungs for too long. His hand rises to my face, cups the side of my cheek. I crumble into it, the consolation concentrated right there in that spot, the rest of me begging to be there with it. I place my hand over his, exhale there, my body limp around the place where his skin meets mine, the new center of my eternity. I look up toward his face, and move closer, inhaling the sweetness of his skin. I move my face over his, brush his cheek with my eyelashes, feel myself moving to another dimension around it, my body ethereal, made of mist that glistens and sways.

He takes both his hands and grasps the sides of my head, leans his mouth against my forehead. He breathes into me there, his warmth resting against me, in and out, his lips holding a gentle caress. I am swirling around it, falling apart and being put back together again with every inhale. Every exhale. And then his forehead is against mine in a familiar way, and we close our eyes and hold there.

Two pieces of one whole lost and finally found.

Until he squeezes his fist and rips away. And I am left raw and wanting.

Without his touch, I am cold. Alone.

I shiver.

"I'm sorry," he breathes. "I have never known a need so vast."

I swallow hard, unable to respond.

"Come," he says. "You are shivering."

The air is cooler now, but it is not only the temperature that makes me shake. He leads me downstairs, invites me to take a seat on the sofa. He removes firewood from the rack, and stacks it inside the palatial hearth, lighting it from the center and breathing into it to give it life. I watch him nurture it until it has an energy of its own, and then rising from his kneel, he walks over and sits down, tucking one of his feet underneath so that he is turned toward me. My legs are up by my side, bent at the knee, and he rests his hand there.

It feels as if my chest has at once been hollowed and filled, by something foreign and totally recognizable. It is empty and overflowing. Fragile and eternal. Lost and found.

I watch the subtle movement of his muscles, the way his chest rises and falls, the way a few strands of hair float in front of his perfect face. I place my hand over his, and we sit this way for some time, listening to the crackle of the growing flames.

And then he speaks again for the first time, and it is a voice I now recognize from now and then and wonder how many other times before—words that have been waiting an eternity to be spoken.

"I promised you that I would remember."

19

Present Day

I'm not sure where to begin; how to wade through the grandeur of it all. With every answer I discovered, I have countless other questions. I don't even begin to decipher how to navigate this new reality that I sit in, what tomorrow will bring, or the day after that. In this moment, I am fully here, paying reverence to the gift of enlightenment that I have been given, appreciating the monumental emotions moving through me, on each end of a very wide spectrum, and not taking any of this miraculous experience for granted.

I can only imagine what this must be like for Kai. I have no idea how long he has held this, if it feels like relief to no longer be alone in it, or if it feels more treacherous because of how unknown the future is. I also don't know what else he has seen. How intricate of a story has been shown to him. I want to know everything. Every single detail and joy and pain. I thought this would help me close a door but instead, it has presented me with hundreds more.

He has been silent, watching me work my thoughts through a brain that wasn't prepared to live within a new reality so suddenly, comfortable with the perspective it had functioned within up to this point, and exhausted by the thought of transforming around a new one. But my heart is wholly alive. It is grateful that I have woken up. It is mingling with my soul in a whole new way—a soul that I've just learned has been reincarnated throughout a vast and labyrinthine eternity, and one I'm sure has always tried to find its way to his.

"How long have you known?" I ask him.

"In a way, I think I have always known. I always felt this longing for something I did not understand. When I was a child, I grew up in a Catholic household, and the only way I knew to communicate with the great beyond was through prayer. So, I would pray and talk about the empty spaces inside of me. I knew there was something I was meant to discover—that there were things meant to be deciphered—but I couldn't understand the language of my soul. I was only consoled when connecting with something that I believed was outside of myself."

I feel mesmerized by his words; learning about these details of what makes him up. I can imagine him, young and searching. I can picture him as he learns to move about the world, aware that he is different than others around him. I wonder how many times our souls have nearly crossed paths, if we ever occupied similar spaces, breathed the same particles of air.

"And then, when I was in college, I had my first psychedelic experience with psilocybin. A few friends and I ate a heroic dose of magic mushrooms in the woods, and though they were just looking to get high, I was *searching*. And that is the first time, in this lifetime, that I saw you."

I swallow hard, eyes wide.

"What did you see?" I ask.

"I saw the same lifetime that you saw tonight in hypnosis. The beauty and the momentous grief of it, much of the same parts of the story. And once those floodgates opened, they never stopped. I dreamed about moments in that life, I saw them in meditation, I got flashes of visions when I saw a stunning sunset or when the light was just right. And as time went on, the visions became more insistent. There was an urgency to them. There was so much to see."

He brings his other leg up onto the couch, crossing them under himself and turning squarely toward me. I do the same, moving as close to him as I can, our legs pushing up against each other at bent knee.

"I was sure that you were here. I was sure that you were alive and waiting, even if you didn't know it. Even if you didn't see it, too." He is quiet for a moment as I let this new reality settle around me. "And then, with the visions, came the messages."

I am leaning in toward him, hanging on his words, urging him to continue. But he doesn't continue. He sits there with me, studying the curves of my face, still holding back, perhaps wary of what his truth might do to me.

"Please, Kai."

"I worry about so many things, Cora."

"What things?"

"About how overwhelming this night must have been for you thus far. About how exhausting I know these experiences can be. About how your entire reality just shifted under your feet. About how if I pour more of my truth out, you might not want to hold it. That it is selfish of me, to say too much."

"Your truth isn't only yours anymore. I am in this now." I bring my hand to my chest. "It might be hard to hold, but that's ok." I layer my free hand upon the other until I can feel my heart beating against the both of them, and I say with conviction, "I want to hold it."

He moves his fingers to his chin, runs them over his skin. "I'll try not to offer anything up unless you ask for it."

I nod my head in agreement.

"The messages," I say. "What were they?"

"They came in many forms. A sudden and all-encompassing intuitive knowing. A voice in my dreams while I slept. A startling and lovely synchronistic happening. Clues left like breadcrumbs, urging me ahead."

"These events had a certain inertia to them," he continues. "I was aware when something was charged with their truth. It seemed as if nothing was coincidence anymore, my soul screaming out at every turn." He squints his eyes thoughtfully.

"Did you listen?"

"I ignored it at first, being young and ignorant," he shrugs. "But it got louder and louder until I had no choice."

He stops, and I nod, insisting he continue.

He takes a slow breath. "I quit my job, built this home, created this center, spent my last penny—all the while sure that, someday, this is where I would find you. I didn't know when, and I didn't know how. But I knew that, if I followed the path, that this is where I would find you."

My eyes are filling with tears, the beauty of his impassioned and trusting determination so overwhelming it is almost too much to endure. I think about all the things that led me here. All of the synchronistic pieces that felt random and out of place. About the things that hurt. About the things that felt like hope for reasons I did not understand.

"I made a promise," he says, his truth so deep it reverberates, and we both sit with it for a while, letting it get down into our cells.

"I was led here, to this very spot. To this patch of land that had not been built on in almost a hundred years. It was perfect and natural and pristine, and I needed it to stay that way. I created here in a soul-inspired manner, with the respect the land deserved, always guided, always listening—always waiting, and, it seemed to me, the land waited, too."

My heart expands in an adoring and reverent way. I pause, watching him, captivated by not just his story, *our* story, but by the way he tells it. By how beautiful every breath and sigh is. By the way his eyes are always with me, and infinite, speaking his truth along with his lips. It is relieving to watch him express himself this way. To speak without the painful stifling of what is real. His wisdom is even more evident now, because it is flowing and open.

I pause, and breathe deep, utterly captivated but unsure how much of the grandeur my heart is capable of holding. "When did you know?" I ask, my voice somehow peaceful amongst the overwhelm, flowing past my lips without the recent strain.

"The moment I saw you." I watch the way his face softens. The way he holds the memory of it. "The night prior, I couldn't sleep. I was vitalized and restless, walking the grounds under the moonlight. In the early morning, before sunrise, I went to chop wood, needing to scatter the energy somewhere. And when I was done, I laid there on the grass, a peace coming over me in a way I had never known. I stayed that way for hours, until I saw two butterflies dancing overhead, and I knew it was time to rise. And then I saw you. And I was sure. Not a moment sooner, not a moment later."

I let my head fall gently to the side, feel a tear run down my cheek. "What did it feel like for you?" I whisper.

Kai closes his eyes and lets himself hang loosely. A soft smile appears on his lips, the first I have seen in some time amidst these fervent moments. "The earth spun around me. You shone like the brightest light, angelic and radiant and finally, finally, right there in front of me. Every empty space was immediately filled by your presence, like I was whole and breathing deeply for the very first time." He opens his eyes, animated by his words. "Everything was alive, Cora. My skin was sparking against the air, the top of my head tingling excessively, seeming to mingle with the cosmos. The trees swayed with it. The ground shook with it. The earth bowed to it. It was life itself, that moment. You and me, together again, after all these excruciating years apart."

It is so beautiful that I am stunned to silence. My heart opens in such an acute way that it knocks the breath out of me, and the air comes out quick and quivering. The tears continue to glide over my skin, charged like the rest of me. I again touch my hand to my heart. He does the same. I am there with him. We are there, together. And then, I watch his eyes change, his shoulders fall ever so slightly.

"The pain of discovering it would not be as simple as my dreams, that we could not fall into each other's arms in the way that every part of me needed to—the pain of that felt almost as great as the love. Almost." He leans in toward me, his voice a whisper. "Because there is nothing else in the world that could possibly be as great as this love."

That word hangs in the air between us, the truest and gentlest thing that has ever touched my ears, and still, it creates a rumbling. A turmoil in its purity against life's turbulent winds.

"You love me?" I ask, my chest trying to allow even more room but also collapsing into itself. "Now, in this life?"

"Oh, Cora. I love you," he exhales, tenderly grasping both my wrists in his hands. "Of course, I love you. I have always loved you, since the beginning of time. I will love you until the end of it."

I have never heard an expression of love so pure, so profoundly true. The fact that it is directed toward me is surreal, and it makes me feel as if I am floating through another dimension, perhaps one that is alive in a dream. My foundation is not built for something this dazzling. I am dizzy. I feel a tingling warmth from my head to my feet, my body exposing my feelings before my mind can make sense of them.

He takes his hands away. Shakes his head. "But being here with you, physically in this world? It is different."

"How is it different?" I ask, my voice cracking. The warmth that danced under my skin turns suddenly hot. My body tells me that I don't want his loving truth to turn in a different direction.

"I thought I knew what it would feel like." He puts his hand to the top of his head, leans into it and exhales. He squints his eyes, gazes down into his lap, preparing himself. And then he locks his gaze on me, and I watch him soften around it. "It is so much more than I could have ever dreamed up or envisioned. Nothing could have prepared me for this. This love is everything, Cora. Truly, everything. I am sure it is what the Universe is made up of. I am sure it is the meaning of life, a truth that so many of us have yet to discover, and humans will keep floundering for another million years until we wake up to the grandeur of what is truly possible. But I will know. And I will never go back. Even if this is the very last moment I ever lay eyes on you, even if I was to die, right here in this spot, I am forever transformed around the miracle that is my love for you."

I am shaking uncontrollably now, the intensity running up and down my spine like sound waves that are so loud but just outside our range of hearing. My body exhales, the fear that temporarily took hold vanishing into the air as if it was never there at all. I want to leave here with him, leave this world and this body and sink into each other, never again to be disentangled from each other's souls. Life's complications are laughable when compared to this glimmering truth—this reality that exists far outside of any notions of right and wrong, language and questions, waking and sleep. But without life, we would not have this. We would not have these words to speak and these hands to hold and this glorious awakening to what love is truly made up of.

Maybe this awakening is the answer. Maybe this awakening alone holds the miracle of being alive. The possibility, so slim and nearly impossible, that we may open our eyes to it someday. And here we are, eyes wide open, this energy of love overflowing beyond rationality, and becoming all that we are.

"I'm sorry," he says again, his body sagging. "I'm so sorry. I hadn't planned on saying all of this to you. I promised myself that there was so much that I would hold. But I cannot control this deluge." He puts both hands around the back of his neck, holding himself steady. "It is exploding around me, Cora. A truth so boundless that I would die if I did not let it go."

I am silent, not because I wish he did not tell me these things, but because I am so overwhelmed that I again can't move my lips. I admit that there is a part of my heart that also stutters under the weight of this loving outpouring. My life hasn't made room for this love. It is a love that seems to be defined differently—its own sparkling thing. I've never understood love in this way before. And considering what my life has been up to this point—what it still *is*, with Emerson, with our tangible, sensible love—I don't know what to do with it. All I can do in this moment is feel it. Feel the heart and soul-altering grandeur of it. Let the warmth of it dance under my skin, enlighten my spirit in a way that is so sensational that it feels like the answer to all eternal questions.

He is silent now too, waiting. Waiting for me to speak to him. To say anything. To tell him that it will be ok, or that it won't.

But instead of speaking, I unfurl my legs and rise to bent knee. I move toward him, stopping right before we touch, looking at the tears that are in his eyes and myself reflected in them. And then I let myself fall.

I fall into his arms, curl myself into him. He wraps himself around me so tightly I can burst, and it is still not tight enough. We are both sobbing, my head down in his chest, him heaving against my face that's soaked through. I grip him with my fingertips, grab him by the arm, by his lower back, digging into his skin. He holds me, rocking back and forth, my legs curled up against him and pressing into my chest.

And after we have stilled, exhausted and limp and leaning into each other, I look up to his face. His eyes are made of fire, but they are the color of deep earth, and in them, I see only love. He moves one of his hands to the back of my head, and the other to my lower back, shifting me to lean against the cushions, pressing himself against me. His hold is firm, my head cradled by him, my body secure in his adoring grasp. He lowers his face to me, so close that I can feel the energy of him vibrating against my lips.

His mouth is so close mine moves toward it like a drop of water begging to merge with the sea. I'm sure my eyes are desperate, and he holds there until they let him in, until they tell him *yes*. And then his lips are against mine. He takes me deep into his mouth, and I take him in as wholly as I can, merging through the warmth of him, exploding around him and falling into him at the same time, like two flames that dance around each other and then finally become one blinding light.

I am coming totally undone. Melting away. Being born again. The whole of me is on fire, throbbing under the weight of him, my need so all-encompassing, his body like a drug I have been withdrawing from for all of eternity. The entirety of my soul is begging for him, pleading for more. More of his body. More time. More of him in every and all ways. But with shattering abruptness, we break away, our mouths separating and then just holding our heavy breath, swallowing our want, drowning in it. Only because we must. Only because it seems there is no other choice.

"Cora," he breathes. We are trembling against each other, the air between us hot with it, particles vibrating so fast that it creates a friction that singes when it meets our skin. His forehead is to mine again, and we hold there, shaking and wanting, the desire so strong it hurts, a pressure that refuses to be contained but that somehow, we contain anyway.

He releases his hold on me, moves his hand through my hair. He gently kisses the top of my head, the side of my face, the corner of my eye, the side of my mouth, so many places I hadn't imagined I needed to be touched but I now need more than anything I have ever needed. I close my eyes, savoring every brush of his softness against me, the way the air changes with him.

He urges me down onto the couch, and he stretches out beside me. I wrap around him, he wraps around me, my head resting atop his beating heart. "I love you," he whispers, and I grip him tighter, and that is how we stay. For what might be hours but feels like moments, that is how we stay, savoring the miracle that is being here. Near each other. Denying our bodies all of each other, but at least breathing the same breath.

And we fall asleep that way. Wordless and gripping.

Entwined and wanting.

Blissful.

And anguished.

20

PRESENT DAY

The rose gold sun awakens before us, tickling our faces with its promising early light. I open my eyes slowly, wary to disturb the space we have created, and equally wary to remain. Our position has not changed since our eyes closed the night before. We fell deeply into an exhausted cocoon, melded together, not only the weight of it all keeping us wrapped up, but the lightness, too.

I had expected guilt to come crashing down on me so heavy I couldn't find breath, but when he opens his eyes, I can't be anywhere but here. The rest of it, of life, of normal human reaction and interaction, is cloudy, buried, stashed away. I know it will come later. I know it is bubbling beneath my skin. But right now, he is smiling, the morning light falling over him so gracefully that I can see nothing else.

"I'm just remembering that this warmth is real," he says. "That these mutual heartbeats aren't inspired by a dream, or a vision."

"A new memory," I say. "One I'm sure I will look upon ten thousand years from now."

The truth of that is so limitless. It is overwhelming in its immensity. Just yesterday, life was a concise thing. Now, it goes on forever, and I'm not sure where I begin or end.

I lift onto my elbow. "I'm meant to lead a class this morning."

"We'll cancel it. If you want to." He brushes his hand tenderly over my cheek. "How are you feeling?"

It's a question I don't have an answer to. Everything seems to be moving too quickly to grab onto.

"I don't know," I say, honestly. "I think I can do it. Will you come?"

"Of course I will come."

"I'll need to change." It feels so strange to talk about details this way. About life's intricacies that seem so insignificant, like which yoga pants I'll wear and what time it is on a clock. And then I feel a dusty thud in the pit of my stomach, because of clocks and time and what today is. The day that I leave this place.

"It will be ok," he says, as if he can read my thoughts, feel the same dusty thud in the same place as mine.

"I have so many more questions for you, Kai. They feel endless. The details keep unraveling, coming into my consciousness, one by one. I'm thinking about Pearl. I need to know what happened to her. That dreaded disease. The way things ended. What happened next."

I am speaking from a place of truth rather than forcefulness, and though overwhelmed by the weight and infinity of my questions, and the grief that lies in their realities that are still unknown to me, I feel grounded in the knowing that I don't have to hold them close to my chest. That I can hand my questions over to him, and he can rearrange them into answers.

But when I do speak these particular words to him, his face turns somber. It's the first time he seems avoidant since he began his truth-telling last night.

"We have a whole day ahead of us. I'll help you to understand. I promise you. We'll go out to the field after your session. We'll lay in the grass. We'll talk for hours, if you want to. We'll lay silent when you don't."

"Out beyond the ideas of wrongdoing?" I ask, eyes wide, searching for permission.

"And rightdoing," he adds with a wise shrug of his shoulders.

We both rise. He moves toward the kitchen, and I follow him. It is an obviously spectacular space, with modern black appliances, a butcher block island, a skylight with warm light filtering through overhead.

"You really built all of this?"

"My father was a carpenter." He opens a cabinet, removes two canisters. "I worked with my hands through high school and college. It made for a more well-rounded education once I decided to study architecture." He places both canisters down on the counter. "Tea or coffee?"

"I'd love some tea," I say, suddenly needing to sit down. "Thank you." I move toward a high stool behind the kitchen bar. I am lightheaded, realizing that I haven't eaten in nearly twenty-four hours. My body had been on such high alert, that it has ignored its own base needs.

He places the kettle of hot water on the stove and moves toward me. He puts his hand to my cheek. "Are you all right?"

"I should know better than to travel back through eternity on an empty stomach," I smile.

"First rule of time travel," he says, opening the refrigerator, eyebrows raised. "Everyone knows that."

His playfulness feels so natural. It makes me laugh. All we have known until this moment is intensity. I am reminded of how many dimensions exist here. How many endless dimensions that I have yet to see. I am equally awed and saddened by it, unsure how much I will never, ever know.

"Avocado and whole grain toast?"

"My favorite," I say, looking at the clock. "Though I'm not sure I'll have time."

"We'll take it for the road." He is already washing his hands, pulling slices of sprouted bread from their sleeve, working a large knife around the circumference of a large, perfectly ripened avocado, slicing into a deep red tomato. It seems that everything he does in life is filled with grace, aligned and purposeful. I love watching him move, the focus in his eyes, the life at the tips of his fingers.

He finishes layering the tomato atop the spread and pours the steaming tea into two travel mugs. "I'll be right back. Two minutes." And he glides up the stairs. I lift from my seat, move toward the sweeping glass windows, look out on his property. It was too dark to see last night, but the surrounding woods are enchanted, lined by white birch and teeming oak. There is a swimming pool out front, one so immersed in nature it almost appears natural itself, closer to a pond than a chlorinated swimming hole. A small wooden sauna sits to the left, an outdoor shower at its side, separated from the main house, connected by a raised wooden path.

"I have been creating my own little oasis," he says, walking back down the stairs. He has changed his clothes and wears a loose-fitting dark grey pair of pants, a white V-neck t-shirt that accentuates his tanned skin. "I spend most of my time at home. Home is a very important place to me."

"It's magical," I say. "I'd never want to leave."

We quiet around it. The unspoken reality. What comes next.

"Come," he says, gathering up our breakfast. "We can walk and talk."

I swing my backpack over my shoulder, and we slip on our shoes and move out into the bright early morning. There is still a gentle chill in the air, sizzling inside the warm sun rays.

I turn to him. "Can I ask you something else?"

"If you are prepared for an honest answer." He hands me my slice of toast. He bites into his, and I appreciate how much he seems to savor it. How he takes absolutely nothing for granted. I bite into mine too, my mouth watering around it, grateful for the sustenance, but even more so that it was provided by his hand.

"Have you always lived here alone?"

"I have. There aren't many who have even seen my home, to be honest. The team, of course. Some of my family. But they don't live nearby."

We walk. I blow into my cup of tea; watch the steam swirl upward into the trees.

"I haven't had a serious relationship in some time." He doesn't elaborate. He waits for me to ask him the next question, or not. We get to the ridge. He places our tea down on the rock and he hops down first, and then takes my hand and guides me down.

"Would it be too intrusive to ask why not?"

"You've seen inside my soul, Cora. There is nothing that we can't talk about." He picks up our drinks, hands me mine. We continue down the narrow path, now doused in sunlight, looking so different than it did the night before.

"I was waiting for you." His mouth rises from the corner. "There is no other way to say it."

I am flooded with tenderness. Awed, once and again, and my eyes say so.

"It's not that I've never experienced a union outside of ours. Some very beautiful, kind, loving women graced my life. But the more intense the longing became, the less I desired anything outside of what my soul was calling for. I preferred being alone, to the alternative—once I knew what was possible."

It burns, this loving sacrifice. His purity of heart, mind and soul is beyond what I can imagine, having never lived it the way he has. It hurts because I cannot fully embrace this stunning sacrifice and all its awesome grace and give it what it deserves. Because I did not have the same path, did not give us what we needed. I married another man. It seems that I cannot give anyone what they truly need. For the first time this morning, the pain starts to show itself. I can feel it cracking through the aura I have been moving within, which holds my awe but is also a means of protection.

"Why didn't I know any of this? Why didn't I experience this like you did?"

"I believe it is a part of our soul's agreements," he says. "I made us the promise. I took it as my responsibility. We each came into this life with our own lessons to learn. Our own paths toward growth. Now, we need to decipher what that growth looks like, for each of us."

We keep walking, and he continues.

"And you knew in your own way. There is a reason you are so open. So connected and filled with wisdom. And there is a reason you are here."

We see Citrine up ahead, shining in the morning light, and us, still cloaked in the trees' canopy.

"Wherever it is that this leads, wherever our lives take us, we have these moments. They will always be ours. And I am immeasurably grateful for that." He stops and turns toward me, and I mirror him. With his free hand, he places his palm under my chin, raises my gaze to his, stares deeply into my eyes. "You don't owe me anything, Cora. Anything. Ok?"

I give him an apprehensive nod. What it feels like is that I owe us everything I have, but what I have is not all mine to give. And we continue.

"Now, it might feel a little strange to be around other people. We have settled into a uniquely high vibration, and the contrast can be jarring. It helps to be aware. And to remember to breathe."

"Ok," I say again, reality starting to move in around me, creeping toward our center, and it feels claustrophobic.

We walk toward the lobby. Go inside. The light is bright, and my eyes burn. Maralyn is behind the counter, shining too, a little bit more than usual.

"My two favorite people," she says, taking note, I'm sure, of our arrival together, of my clothes that are the same as they were the night before. "Ready for your final class, my friend?"

"Bittersweet," I smile. I look at the time on the wall. "I'm just going to run upstairs. I won't be long."

Kai nods. Maralyn moves back behind her computer screen. I look back at him as I walk up the stairs. He is looking at me, too. I don't want to move away from where he is. I imagine how natural it would feel for him to walk with me, sit on the bed while I change my clothes, steal an embrace before going back out into the world. It sounds so simple, and like the most complicated thing in the world. My insides twist around it.

There will be time later to think, to process. To shower. For now, I just need to swap out my clothes, brush my teeth, and get to class on time. I place my bag down on the desk chair and open the front zipper. There is one message from Emerson, saying goodnight, but none yet from this morning. It's still early, and I'm sure he's just completing his workout, getting ready to head to the office. Sometimes, he'll go in a little late on Fridays. We'll make waffles at 8 am and eat them in bed and laugh until it hurts.

And now, it really does hurt, just in a totally different way. I text him *good morning*. I change into a sports bra, draping tank top, navy blue spandex.

Today, he responds, *is the day*.

Can't wait to see you, he continues.

Today is the day, I write back, my response too layered to begin to unpack.

Heading to class. I'll let you know when I'll be home.

Love you, C.

Love you, I type.

In this moment, I think about Emerson as if he is far away. A character in the script of my life, who I am looking upon from the outside in. There is too much here to face, and this is not the time to face it. But I can feel it threatening, storm clouds inching in from every side.

I think about how I first reacted to my miscarriage. The emotional stifling that I used as a defense mechanism in those first couple of weeks after the loss. These circumstances are starkly different, but this stifling of my reactivity to the things I am not ready to face is giving me ominous flashbacks. I have created some sort of barricade, protecting myself from the deluge. I can see the shame, the disgust, the devastation that can come with this reality, but I can only feel the rumblings of it. I've numbed myself to the cataclysm, and I'm scared to see what lies underneath.

I only have one more day here. I will have every day for the rest of my life to process things, to work through the mess I've created. But right now, I can't fall apart. I need presence. I need to sort this through. There will be regret on each side. There will be regret, no matter what.

I need Maralyn to remind me that I am not a terrible person.

I brush through my hair and leave my room, a few minutes later than I had hoped. The lobby is quiet, Maralyn no longer at her desk, and I suppose that the group has already begun their walk to the studio. I don't see Kai, either, and I am suddenly all too aware that when it comes to his presence, there is no amount of stifling I can do. My reactions to him are resounding. They have a life of their own.

This does cause a slick guilt to show itself along the back of my neck. I am grateful for it. There is relief in the discomfort, when it feels deserved.

I walk outside, and there is Kai, standing near the entrance, his face toward the sun. His arms are at his side, his palms outstretched, as if these sun rays are the source of his power. I walk to his side and look at him, the sun caressing my one cheek. He smiles with his eyes still closed, sensing my presence, and moves himself out of his standing meditation.

"Don't worry," I say. "We'll do sun salutations in today's class."

"I was just warming up," he says, his eyes laughing at the double entendre and making mine laugh, too.

He starts walking and I am by his side, our pace quick but graceful until my foot finds a small boulder. I stumble, and Kai takes my arm before I have the chance to fall. I right myself, but a fear gets loosened up. It is a constricting thought, colliding with our expansiveness. It is too tangible for our etherealness.

"What is it?" he asks, obviously sensing the disparity.

I shake my head. I can't pinpoint the fears and I'd rather not look for them. My arm is still in his grasp, as if he is still holding me up, just not in the physical sense. He releases his hold, slips down to the palm of my hand.

"You can tell me anything," he says. "Please know that."

"I do. I do know that. I just don't want to fill our time with it." I pause and bite at my bottom lip, voice sinking. "What little we have left."

"Our time." He squeezes my palm more tightly. "I am grateful that we have some to fill."

I look up at him, show him that I am grateful, too.

"Our conversation about our physical world versus the pull of our souls. I haven't stopped thinking about it. And I am afraid that..." I trail off.

He nods. Waits for me to continue.

"My fear is that I am using this experience of transcendence as a way to justify..." I lose words again. I sigh. "Justify my infidelity. And that I'm not yet acknowledging to myself the enormity of that."

Kai is quiet for moments, letting the words come, it seems. The right ones, that are aligned and not skewed by his desires. I can see it in the way his expression transforms, and then transforms again. I can feel it in the way the air moves around him. I am astonished, by how much I can see and know, in a way I didn't think I was capable of. It is so beautiful the way things move within him. The way he doesn't force them but allows them to fall into place. Allows them to make their way to the core, without the clouded voice of ego directing their path.

"We can feel the pain in each other, even through this bliss. I know that soon enough, it will make itself undeniably known, for the both of us. I wish that wasn't so. But I also know that we are worthy of it. A visceral response to the pure gravity of what we are."

He bends to pick up a fallen tree branch. He places it to the side of the path.

"I understand why you feel this way. I am sorting through my own guilt and my own fears. We don't have to sort through this alone. We will do it together."

"I feel time slipping away," I say, fumbling with a loose thread on the hem of my shirt. "At first, it seemed a years' worth of time in a single day. Now, it seems the minutes are falling through our fingers."

"I'm going to ask Soloman to cover my final groups today."

I look at him hesitantly, knowing how important these assimilation groups are to him.

"I missed you when you went up to your room, Cora. I can't imagine how it will feel when you leave tonight. I won't waste another moment."

And I wish I could freeze time, stand with him right here in this spot. Let the rest of the world pause for a while so that I can be near him, just a little longer.

The studio is now coming into view, the group congregating outside in the sun, coffee cups in hand. Kai drops my hand before we come around the bend in the path.

"Besides," he says. "We don't have anyone to fill in for you, but we have someone to fill in for me. Soloman has a gift for it, and he's been wanting to step up." He smiles.

"Ok," I concede, and then I admit, "I can't wait until this class is over. But I'm glad you'll be there with me."

"I'll always be with you. No matter what." His smile fades. "Even when it seems I am not."

I have a feeling that, at those times, this will be the hardest to remember.

21

FEBRUARY 1892

Bellevue School of Nursing is the first training school in America to follow the principles of Florence Nightingale, a British nurse who called for a supervised and trained staff of nurses at the hospital, along with strict rules of cleanliness. At eighteen years old, I joined one of the first of these training classes, built of grueling hours and even more grueling responsibilities, determined to be amongst the inspiring brigade of women who can improve care in the hospitals, in a way that is desperately needed.

I am housed in a small dusty concrete residence on 26th Street in New York City. I have two roommates, Sarah and Josephine, and though the room is really only big enough for one of us, we get along best we can. None of us are home much. We work on the ward half the time and attend lectures the other half of the time, and with whatever time left, our exhaustion sends us directly to bed and still, sleep is never something we get enough of.

This morning, I tie up my blue and white striped uniform and secure my Bellevue cap, and leave for the ward a bit earlier than usual, having been woken by the iceman pounding incessantly on the wrong door. The streets are covered with ice, too, crusted in each crevice of cobblestone, and I hold on to fence posts to keep myself upright. It snowed the night before, and then the temperature plummeted, and it seems the whole world is frozen inside a mold, not to age again until it is thawed and free.

When I arrive, the night shift briefs me on what happened while I was gone, the patients who persevere, the others who have sadly departed, and those who have only just arrived. Every bed is full, and any new admissions will have to be cared for in the corridors.

As a nurse in training, I tend to most of the duties the others prefer not to, and I spend the first hours of the morning washing urine-soaked sheets and cleaning malodorous wounds. I feel needed here, and that need bolsters me, most of the time. In this moment, however, with suffering all around me, I am gloved and wincing, dreaming of open air. A breath of something that isn't drenched in anguish.

In the next moment, he stumbles through the double doors.

Jezebel, the Head Nurse, rushes to the man's side, lends him her shoulder, and I can see by my station three beds down that his leg is broken, perhaps in as many as three places. I don't believe I've ever seen this man before, but he is strangely familiar, and I can't help but to still in place, study the curves of his face. He is quiet in his misery, breathing shaking breaths, his forehead covered in sweat even in this bitter cold.

"Juliette!" yells Jezebel. "Quickly. A chair."

I remove my soiled gloves and rush to the back of the room, wheeling the chair to the right of him as two ward assistants lead him into the seat. They prop his leg up and directly after his anguishing gasp, he loses consciousness. I am glad for it, because he won't feel the pain of it when we transfer him into the cot. If he stays unconscious long enough, he won't feel the pain of it when the doctor snaps him into place.

Unfortunately, he is awake and gasping again moments later, and I wonder how someone, in this kind of excruciating state, can possibly be so beautiful.

"Sir," says Jezebel in her firm way. "Sir, what is your name?"

He clenches his teeth and releases himself just long enough to speak it. "Asher." He closes his eyes. Breathes slowly. Stretches his fingers that were bunched in a fist.

"We are getting you something for the pain," she says. "In the meantime, can you tell us what happened to your leg, Asher?"

He keeps his eyes closed, and it seems he is able to navigate the pain better there, behind closed lid.

"I was working down by the dock." His voice is breathy, heart-shattering in its baritone. "I'm a stonemason. My leg was where it shouldn't have been, when things came crashing down."

My heart breaks for him. I imagine the rest of the details of his story, one he tells so simply through his pain, and though I am compassionate toward every ailing being that turns to us for healing, this feels different than it ever has before. And tears are rolling down my cheeks and I am sure that I would do anything to take his hurt away. Anything, as if that is the only thing in this entire Universe that matters.

"Juliette," barks Jezebel. "Would you pull yourself together?"

Asher opens his eyes when she says it and looks at me. And something happens. The room blurs around me, and it is only him, his eyes, the striking depth of them that I see. And not only do I see them, but to me, they are the only things that exist. It seems time has no meaning and all life before was an illusion. There is only now, and my body doesn't feel that it is mine and I am floating somewhere into the air, up and up into empty spaces but I am not afraid because he is there with me.

"Juliette," he breathes. "A beautiful name."

And his body seems to exhale, like he has already been given a strong pill but I am sure that he hasn't. And I am sure I never want to look away.

I never want to look away.

22

PRESENT DAY

It helped that Kai prepared me for what it would be like, to be around people in this heightened state, though I was still overcome by it. My head was swimming for the entirety of the class, my vision out of focus. Every sound was too loud, even gentle voices were brash, and music meant to be soothing pierced my ears. The smell of the incense was overwhelming, the sun reflecting off the windows blinding. I avoided balancing poses, moving around the room while the group found their center, and found solace in anything steady, grounding.

Kai's eyes did not leave me, it seemed, even for a moment. He held me, protecting me with his presence. To me, it wasn't passive, as it seemed he was actively supporting me by cushioning the impact. I wonder how far-reaching his gifts are. I wonder if his connectedness blossoms when we are in each other's presence. I wonder if this is simply my reaction to his presence, connecting to a vibration that would normally be outside my realm of awareness, like a sound too high-pitched for the human senses to grasp.

And now that class is done, the relief is palpable, and I find myself bracing against the magnetic pull that is Kai, aware that I cannot run to him, of the caution that needs to be taken around Emerson's team, and of the shameful reality of this deception. I am also aware of how breathtaking the desire is. It hurts to be even this far away from him, and though this part of my reality is terrifying, neither the terror nor the disgrace takes precedence. It is the relief that I feel most of all; the bliss of knowing I will soon be alone with him, lying amongst the wildflowers.

The group lingers for some time. Kai speaks to them about continuing a yoga practice. They ask him if he can do a headstand. He tells them he can. They ask him to show them. He does. They want to be able to do a headstand, too. He tells them that they should take the mats with them, practice on the grass. All the while, I am cleaning up the space, wrapping up the loose ends of my last class and feeling the significance of it.

Maralyn comes over to me, hugs me wordlessly. "You are beautiful," she says. "Please make sure you don't leave without saying goodbye."

I promise her I won't. I thank her, and she asks me why. I think I may cry if I respond. She understands. She hugs me again and turns to leave. And then the last of the group walks away, mats in hand. And we are alone.

We look toward each other, from our opposite sides of the room. I feel vulnerable, with him looking at me this way, with such urgency. Like I am naked, but he's not against my skin. He walks to me, determinedly, not breaking his gaze. And as if in one swift motion, his hands are again grasping the sides of my head, mine on his shoulders, his forehead leaning against me. We are inhaling sharply, gasping for air, but our lips do not touch. We use everything we have to resist it, not pretending this act of fortitude changes anything, but still, hoping that it does.

"Should we go?" I sigh.

"We should go," he breathes.

He releases his hold and instead takes my hand, leading me outside. We leave our things behind, focusing only on each other, what is ahead of us. We walk in silence, listening to the birdsong, cherishing the marvel of our hands holding on. We come upon the field, and I don't think the weather could be more stunningly perfect. The sun is soft, the breeze is gentle, the air is pure and kind.

"You pick." He gestures for me to find our place.

I wander to the center of a dense scattering of wildflowers, kick off my shoes, and lay down on my back. I extend my arm up over my head, close my eyes, and breathe in deep. And then he is next to me, two souls looking up at the few feathery clouds that are moving slowly across the sky.

"How many times do you think we have been here?" I ask.

"In this very spot?"

"No. Just, *here*. Together."

"Many," he says. "But I don't think we've ever gotten it right."

"What do you mean?" I ask, still looking up at the sky.

"I mean, I don't think we've ever gotten it right in the way that we wanted it to be right. Something always got in the way. Sometimes the big things. Sometimes the small things. The lifetime we saw, I believe that was the most pivotal. It was when we came the closest."

"I can't understand that tragedy," I say, shaking my head somberly. "How such devastation can follow such perfection."

"I've thought about this a lot," he says. He turns to me, and I move onto my side to face him, anxious to understand how he makes sense of it. "It seems that we have been searching for each other for all eternity. We have touched an eternal spectrum of experiences. Our consciousness, all along, has been expanding. We evolve through each bliss. But also, through each pain."

"But that particular pain...it was just so horrific," I grimace.

"A tragic, dreadful thing," he says, his eyes solemn.

"I wonder how we grew there," I say, pursing my lips, head shaking from side to side. "The impact it had on our souls."

"I think we are discovering that right now. I think we are discovering that, always." He rolls onto his back, bends one of his knees, watches the clouds roll slowly by.

"Do you believe a soul necessitates pain in order to grow?" I ask.

"No," he says, thoughtfully. "But I do believe pain is a route that is most often accessed for the deep and impactful growth that we witness in a single lifetime. And now, I'm sure that it is often something we access throughout lifetimes."

I nod slowly. "I've always believed that we can choose to grow in other ways, without so much pain. But there are a lot of things in the way of that kind of graceful experience. Maybe it takes an expansion of our consciousness to get there, in ways that we might not have been ready for then." I stop, feel a prickling fear. *Might not be ready for now*, I think, but I don't want to say it, make it true.

"I've always believed the same," he says. "That our souls can choose a more graceful route toward growth. But, still..." he pauses, "there is a certain amount of pain that comes with being alive. We can experience difficult things and not feel pain because of them, but to me, that's not fully embracing what it is to be human." He turns toward me again and strokes my face with the back of his hand. "And there is something about paying homage to the source of our pain, which wouldn't be possible without love."

He continues, eyes sad but clear. "I will feel deep pain when you leave. It will be a necessary part of my growth, to feel that pain, and let you go anyway."

It hurts all over when I hear these words; a blunt and expanding ache.

"It's what I couldn't do before," he chokes. "It's what I could never do."

I move closer to him. Run my hand over his hair. Feel his pain along with him.

"I know your path is so much more intricate than I can understand right now," I say. "But to me, holding on that way...it doesn't sound like a bad thing."

"It's not," he says, taking a light hold of my wrist, moving his fingers over my skin. "It's a beautiful thing. But this is pure consciousness. The core of what we have, the love that makes this up, is pure and sublime. It is part of my lesson to loosen my grip and let go of control. To embrace the interplay between fate and choice." His eyes are filled with sadness and determination. They move down to the grass below, and he holds there.

I am awed by his strength, and terrified of his resolve. I don't want him to let go. I am aware of how selfish it is for me to feel that way. I know I must determine my own lessons. That I must shift my resolve and respect wherever it is that our lessons lie. But it is hard to fathom the strength it would take to walk away from him. And the grief that would come from another lifetime spent in longing.

I can feel how much he is not telling me. He is waiting for me to ask, but there is fear, and I brace myself.

"It's ok, Kai. You can tell me. I want to know."

He looks up at me again, tears pooling. I move my hand to his face, catch a teardrop on my fingertip. I wish I could bottle it up, hold this tangible part of his humanness for all of eternity. Instead, I move my hand to my mouth, put my finger to my tongue. He is piercing the air with his gaze again, staring at my lips as I run my tongue over them, swallow around this small bit of him that is now one with my own cells.

"I've thought about it countless times, Cora," he says, voice deep and desperate. "What it would be like to become one." He moves his fingers across my now wet lips, and I feel limp, liquefying into the ground below.

He takes a deep breath, removes his fingers from my mouth and centers himself. "Something about all that pain that I am grateful for is that it brought us right here, to this place; one that has us aware of how far we have come and allows us to finally breathe the same air. It is a gift, truly. In order to embrace it, our consciousness needed to be ready. But, in this moment, it may be all we are ready for."

He swallows hard, his eyes deepening. My heart squeezes so I take his hand and squeeze it too, show him my emotions there. I am grateful and grieving, longing and overcome with desire. There is fear and dread at these moments ending, joy in the existence of them. In his eyes, I see so much—so much of the same. He exhales slowly, continues with increased vitality.

"With our continued expansion will come a forever increasing intensity. Someday, we will shake off the remaining shackles, and I am sure of it—we will merge with Universal consciousness itself. I will wait forever, if I must. Even if it is ten thousand years from now, I will wait. We had deep love then, in that lifetime, but it wasn't like it will be the next time." He moves a strand of hair out of my face, and then rests his hand on my cheek, his voice changing to a whisper. "Next time, when I am inside of you, it will be like meeting God."

My entire self is burning up, a longing so deep, a passion so indomitable, that I don't know if I will ever recover from the deluge. It surely isn't sustainable, but I can see no other way—that I will feel this impossible longing throughout my existence, until the fateful day we finally fall into each other, mind, body, and soul.

How much more time in this eternity will we spend leaning like a plant toward the sun, but never being touched by it?

He removes his hand from my face, his eyes dark. My fear mingles with the longing in a vicious and undulating mix.

"I know that I need to speak more of our story," he says. "But it will be hard to hear."

"Any truth spoken from your lips is something I want to hear," I say. "Even if it hurts."

He nods and sits up, his legs bent in front of him, his arms draped around his knees. I move to sit next to him, rest my head on his shoulder.

"You were a nurse back then," he says, fingers running over a blade of grass. "A very talented nurse, even in those times, when medical practice was so young. It was your empathy that healed people. Your presence alone was curative."

I lift my head up so that I can see him, watch our story fall from his lips.

"It's how we met, in that lifetime," he says, turning toward me and moving the back of his finger gently across my cheek. "At the hospital. I sustained an injury to my leg, and you were there to care for me. I had never seen anything so beautiful."

I pull my eyebrows together. "Were you hurt badly?"

"One look from you and I forgot my pain," he smiles softly.

I close my eyes, envision him as he was then, and a soft smile falls over my face, too. And then I hear him sigh audibly, feel the shift in his energy. I open my eyes, focus in.

"We lived in a small town at the edge of the 19th century. They were dark times. Tuberculosis was spreading like wildfire, and as the years progressed, it became clear that nowhere was safe. Disease swept into small villages and big cities alike, leaving devastation in its wake. Fourteen percent of the population perished in those years. They were truly dark times."

My eyes are wide, and I move closer to him, using his warmth for comfort.

"There were sanitariums that were hobbled together for the sick. We lived two hours from the city, if traveling by horse-drawn carriage, where the nearest sanitarium was erected. It was requested you join the coalition, to live on the grounds of the sanitarium for as long as was need-ed, to care for the sick and dying."

A chill runs down my spine. Kai shakes his head. "Oh, Cora, I wouldn't have it. I know they needed you, but I was sure we needed you more, and I wouldn't have it. You were willing, the devastation of the times pushing you beyond what may have been otherwise too much to bear. But I pleaded with you, envisaged a compromise: that you would stay back and lead a coalition of your own. Without proper medical care or sanitation, our town and those surrounding were in grave danger. You were able to convince the medical team. They agreed that your skills could be made use of at home, and you stayed behind."

I am sitting up straight, muscles rigid. The spark in Kai's eyes is so dim that I can barely make it out. It flickers somewhere behind a layer of despair so thick it is hard to see through.

"Every day you were gone from sunrise to sunset, tending to the sick, holding the hands of our friends as they left this world." I tear runs down his cheek, and then another, accumulating on his fabric. "And then one day, you got sick, too."

The sheer pain in his words is enough to break my heart in two, and my face is quickly wet with salty tears, mirroring his.

"You survived, Cora. You were so strong. So filled with love and selflessness. But because I was so afraid, everything went wrong. If you had been at the sanitarium, you wouldn't have come home to Pearl every night. And she…" He trails off.

I hear a ringing sound in my ears, and I am reverberating like a tuning fork just smacked on its side. Kai is frozen in place, the next part of our story stuck in his throat.

"I did it," I say with vacant eyes. "It was my fault."

He is shaken from his mold and turns to me. He takes my hands.

"Oh, Cora. No." He shakes his head, quickly from side to side. "It was a horrific time in human history, and our experience of it was treacherous. But you were a source of light. You saved so many. You saved so many."

My throat, my heart, my brain—everything is suddenly on fire, scorching me under my skin. My deepest wounds are ripped open, and all I can hear is a single vicious and looping declaration: *you did it again, you did it again.*

"It was me, Cora. I was the one. I tried so hard to control the situation, to keep you safe, that I put our daughter in danger; our perfect, shining, daughter with an old soul and eyes that would have stayed youthful forever. I don't want to forgive myself for that. I want to feel the pain of it, every day, as if somehow, in this atonement, I can change things. But I can't go back. It is forever etched into our story, one so tragic and so stunning. And I wonder if it would be different, somehow, if we didn't carry this weight. If right now, we could embrace each other the way that I need to embrace you."

The pain is so great that I cannot breathe through it. I feel the panic rising in my chest, my extremities numb. I wring my hands together, open my mouth to suck in air. I need to get up. I need to move and release some of this energy that is choking me.

"It was not your fault, Kai. It was not your fault." I say it with a mouth so dry the words stick together. "I didn't learn. I did it again. I didn't learn. I can't keep anyone safe."

I stand up and shake out my hands, wishing I could transfer this feeling from under my skin to the air around me. Kai rises too, aware of my panic, seemingly gauging the best way he can be present for me. When I am in the grips of panic, I avoid human touch. It feels too still and hot and confining. I need to move, pace, shake, do whatever I can to distract myself from the treachery in my mind. But this time, here with Kai, all I want is to be in his arms. I want to let the pain and panic burn through me and scorch my edges. I want him to be there with me, holding me through the fiery reaches of it until there are no more flames, but only smoke and scorched organs.

He looks into my eyes for confirmation, and then without hesitation, he wraps his arms around me. He holds my head tightly to his chest, wraps around my shoulders, and even in this erratic state, I know how perfectly I fit there. I shake and I sob and so does he, until we are once again one moving mass of emotional release, wet with sweat and tears.

And when the shaking stops, when my organs are ashy and smoking, I lift my tired eyes to his. He moves the hair stuck across my forehead away from my face. He kisses me where the tears hang, moves both thumbs across my cheeks. And the pain starts to feel different. It mingles with everything else, creating a cacophony of feeling so intense that I can no longer see periphery. It is only his eyes, and the rest is blurred, black and empty. I am wrapped up in a desire so vast that my entire being throbs around it, mind, body, and soul in rhythm, moving with his pulse. I feel him hard against me, and I need him as much as I need breath. There is no difference. I feel I would die without either one.

"I'm sorry, Cora," he whispers. "I'm sorry." He grips my skin with his hands and then exhales against me, muscles exhausted by swimming against our rushing tides.

I shake my head. "I'm the one who is sorry," I breathe. "For this. For everything."

He breaks away. It is a kindness, his martyrdom astonishing, able to do something I could not. And as my body hollows from the ripping distance, we hear a voice.

"Kai. Cora," she says. "I am so sorry. I called. I looked everywhere."

We turn and see Maralyn standing at the edge of the field, on the dirt trail.

"I am so sorry." Her eyes are pained, and I can't imagine her apologies are for any reason that can hurt more than we are already hurting.

"He's here," she says.

And then, more quietly.

"Emerson is here."

23

PRESENT DAY

I am stunned to silence. I feel Kai take my arm in his, steadying me. He speaks for us, calmly and evenly.

"I'm sorry, Maralyn. I left my phone back at the studio. Thank you for finding us."

He turns to me. "Come, Cora." We walk to the edge of the field, so we don't have to raise our voices over the distance. I am in shock. Too paralyzed for panic, too overwhelmed for clear thoughts. It is a numbing state, and I'm sure it won't last.

"He's at reception," Maralyn says.

"Did he say why he is here?" Kai asks.

"He said he wanted to surprise Cora." She exhales. "And see the team."

"Thank you, Maralyn," he says. "Anything else?"

"He'd love for you to show him around, Kai." She bites her lip, her face crunching, looking to us apologetically.

Kai nods. "May I ask a favor of you, Maralyn?"

"Anything."

"Cora and I are going to retrieve our things from the studio. Will you wait here for us to get back, and walk with Cora to reception? We won't be long."

"Yes," she says. "Yes, of course."

Kai turns to me. "Come." I look from Kai to Maralyn and back again, and then turn to walk away, eyes unblinking. Kai holds my hand, guiding me down the path, and back toward the studio.

We are silent until we are alone again, and he turns to me. "It's going to be ok, Cora. It's going to be ok."

"I'm not ready," I say, shaking my head, the anxiety starting to show itself again in my throat.

"Take a deep breath," he says, guiding me with his own. "Take another."

"This can't happen," I say. "Not now. Not yet."

There is so much to know. I need him to tell me. I need to be near him, just a little longer. *Please, please,* I think, *just a little longer,* and I don't know if I am pleading with the Universe or with Kai or with Emerson or with myself, but maybe it is with all of us, at once.

"Pearl," I say, my voice panicked. "I didn't get to ask you everything about Pearl. There is so much."

Kai stops, takes me by the shoulders. "I know how it feels. The emotions, the energies, they are demanding and all-consuming until we process them. And you are processing things from lifetimes ago. Heavy things, Cora." He is severe. Urgent. And then he softens to a whisper. "It will take time."

"But how can I do it alone, Kai?" I plead. "How have you done it all this time?"

"You are doing it. You have always done it. And I am not going anywhere. I am not leaving this world, like I did before. This is not then. This is now." He moves his hand to the back of my neck, holds me closer to him. His voice transforms into something that sounds like a song, wisdom and truth lulling me, holding me safe. "We are connected through the air we breathe, the water in our cells, the energy that moves through our seemingly empty spaces. If you ever feel separate, look up at the stars. And you will be reminded of the vast and interconnected existence that we are a part of."

I nod and I keep nodding. I breathe shakily again, rest my head against his chest. He rubs my back, calming me this way, making me feel loved and safe. But it doesn't last long because it can't. And all too quickly, we are moving again, away from the field, in step but with the ominous knowing that we will not be for much longer.

"It is not your fault, Cora," he says.

I look up at him desperately.

"It is not your fault," he says, more determinedly.

I want to believe him but I don't know how, and there is no time to try.

"I can't," I stammer. "I'm not ready to see him. I can't do this now."

He takes my hand. "I am here to support you in whatever decision is right for you in this moment. But a decision this vast cannot be taken lightly."

I nod, fear flooding me.

"If you don't know which way to turn in this moment," he says, turning toward me and making sure I am looking at him, "then that means you must go to him. Anything else, you will not be able to take back."

I am silent, eyes wide, moving my hands around each other.

"He is your husband," he says, the words exhaled and pained, a breathy reminder for the both of us. "Please. Remember who he is to you. You love him, Cora." A tear runs down his cheek, evidence of his martyrdom. "You love him."

My eyes are wide and bloodshot. I do not disagree with him. I can't. We both know it, but I am lost in my fear, and he is trying to remind me.

"There will be pain," he says. "But you will have Emerson. And a beautiful life to live."

"The pain will be so great," I choke.

"I will never lie to you. I can't tell you that isn't true."

I swallow hard, bring my hand to my head and grip at my hair.

"I'm sorry I can't make this simple," I say. "I'm sorry I can't just…"

Kai shakes his head, desperation weighing his shoulders down, silencing my words before the thought is finished. "No. I beg you." I can see how his hands shake. How he layers one on top of the other to keep them contained. "Please don't apologize for your truth." He is whispering now. He squeezes at his knuckles and his voice trembles. "I know this awakening feels like everything. And it is. But there are other truths in this life. Another soul who you have built a beautiful existence with. If you did not love him, then I would in this moment wrap my arms around you and never let go. But we know that is not the truth. We both know that this is the way it must be."

"I can only see one truth when I look into your eyes," I weep. "How can I live another?"

"Just as we have been doing, all this time," he says. The depth of his expression reverberates through the trees. I think they shudder, but in their unceasing eloquence and intrinsic wisdom, it is almost hard to tell. "Nothing has been taken. All has been gained."

"Why doesn't it feel that way?"

"Because this love is insatiable," he says. "It will always want more."

His words take my breath from me as if they are trying to make room for themselves. The studio comes into view. We are silent as we enter, gather our things. My chest is like drying cement, parched and cracking, the anxiety rushing through my veins. Kai comes up from behind me, wraps his arms around me, holds his face to mine. He turns me around, and our foreheads meet, one last time.

"I love you, Cora," he says, his sweet smoky breath mingling with mine.

"I love you, Kai," I say, for the first time, though it doesn't feel that way at all.

We hold there for moments, and then it is over. And my heart shatters.

"It's time," he says.

We walk back toward where Maralyn stands waiting, preparing ourselves for a new way of being, one with hands at our sides and so much air between us. Every step brings us further away from each other, time slipping away so quickly it seems the sparse clouds are moving across the sky in fast forward. She sees us approaching and smiles her sad smile, the only other person in this world who may have any idea of the grandeur.

"I'm going to hang back," says Kai. "Just for a few minutes. I think it will be better that way." He turns to me. "Is that ok, Cora? Just a few minutes." His voice is softer now, comforting me, preparing me.

I nod my head. I turn toward Maralyn, and she urges me to follow. I turn back to look at Kai, and he is frozen in place, a flawless sculpture of the perfect human form, with a pained and loving soul wafting around him like early morning mist, quiet and contemplative and colored by deep sunrise. He nods his head slowly, and I bring both hands to my face. I feel the tickling of tears and exhale through my fingertips, and then watch him turn away. And then we walk.

I am silent for some time, letting the dusty overwhelm settle into my cells until it is like a weighted blanket, numbing my sharp edges. Maralyn is present in my silence. She seems to hold it in her open palm. When I finally speak, she holds the space for that too, and I am grateful that I am not alone.

"This is incomprehensible," I say.

"Oh, Cora," she says, her voice laced with compassion.

I am looking straight ahead, eyes unblinking. It seems I am walking through a tunnel, periphery blurred and dark. "I didn't know that one human being could feel so many things at one time."

"There can be as much pain in discovery as there is joy," she says.

"So much," I say, "of everything."

The woods seem quieter. The earth seems to stand still, waiting. The breeze is caught like a breath held in the lungs. The trees are watching, understanding.

"I can imagine there is one thing you hold more than all others," she says.

I look toward her in question. "What's that?" I ask.

Her features are serious, but her heart seems to smile. "Love, of course," she shrugs. "If love is our guide, we will always find our way."

I know Maralyn is speaking from experience—something so tragic that in her resiliency, there is a unique magnificence. It is one that is born from wisdom. From love. And she is handing me a supportive reminder to focus on this love, from whatever direction it is coming from, to wherever I can direct it.

Though it might seem inaccessible in my current emotional state, I know this to be true—if she can access resiliency from her place, I can find a way to access it from mine.

"Living from a space of love, rather than a space of fear, is my forever aspiration," she says. "It's difficult, but only because we forget to see."

She slides her hands into the pockets of her cotton pants, swaying gracefully in the breeze. "And there are different types of love, you know? They are different, but they are all born from the same foundation."

I think about my love for Emerson. I think about how different it feels now, but that the core of it hasn't changed. It's just everything else that has changed around it, and within me. I try to envisage how I would normally act in this situation. Would I run to him? Would I be giddy with it, the surprise of his arrival, the graciousness of his company for the drive home? When I left, I'd have given so much for him to desire to join me here, and to share this experience. I am astonished by how much has changed within me, in such an excruciatingly short time—too quickly to make sense of.

But again, when you are faced with eternity, when you are shaken from the box you have created to fit your life inside of, time becomes nothing but a construct. It isn't a boundary in the way I thought it was. It is simply another plane to rest our experiences upon.

I've lived in this world for so long but craved the whole Universe. Now that I have seen the whole Universe, I am not sure how to exist in the world.

Maralyn continues. "Maybe that's the beauty of it, after all. Discovering love's layers, from its many different perspectives."

She smiles gently, the sun that drapes across her skin mirroring her inner light.

"You are beautiful, Maralyn," I say, as Citrine comes into view, and I hope she knows how deeply I mean it. "Thank you."

We wrap our arms around each other, and it gives me strength where I didn't think it could be found.

It is midafternoon, the light high in the sky, and the shadows don't stretch long and sharp. Instead, they pool around the pillars of Citrine, create a soft resting place beneath its grand structure. Maralyn nods toward me, and I take a very deep breath. I am shaking all over. I am scrambling for something to anchor me—a way that I can bring myself back to center. A new center, perhaps, but a center, nonetheless. I picture myself again as that oak tree. This time, imagine my roots stretching deep into the earth. And we walk through the door.

Emerson is off to the right, sitting at a table with Muhammad, drinking a cup of what I'm sure is black coffee. He is not in his usual workday attire and has opted instead for a pair of cuffed black pants and a casual t-shirt. In my chest, waves crashing against each other, no longer a part of one flowing sea, but two different bodies of water, moving from their alternate parts of my consciousness. He looks so handsome, so kind. I am diving deeply into my body, looking for myself, the self I knew before these few days—who I used to know before everything changed. I find pieces of her, but only pieces. If I'm being wholly honest with myself, now that he stands before me, those pieces of me feel glad to see him. I do feel that unique type of love for him, one that is simple and gracious and whimsical and kind. One that I feel for only him, and my heart doesn't know what to do with it.

He turns, smiling his genuine smile, and rises to greet me. I feel the treachery of my betrayal in the pit of my stomach. My world has shifted on its axis, but his still rests in the way it always has, in the way he believes it always will. Now that he is here in front of me, I can feel my defenses shattering. I can't separate it out anymore, this life and that life. It is becoming one thing, and in its merging becoming something dreadful. He is so strong. So resilient and steady. But in his ignorance, in this moment, he is fragile—he just doesn't know it.

A wave of panic rushes through me, and in the mere moments of quiet I have before he comes to me, I am fumbling to make sense of what I can and pack the rest away. Of course, this is impossible, but my racing thoughts are trying to defy time, trying to deliver me some semblance of clarity. I'll need to seal it all up tight, try to stay steady until I have the room to think straight.

"Surprise," he says, too suave to exclaim it, one eyebrow rising, and walking toward me with his effortless stride. And right now, in this moment, a clarity hits me, but it is one that feels dizzying.

The only thing that I am sure of, is that I am not sure. I look at him, and I can't imagine walking away.

From him. From either of them.

"Surprise," I say, smiling through it while my voice quakes.

He embraces me, but in an affable way, with a hug and a simple kiss on the cheek. I'm sure he's still aiming for some professionalism, for both of our sakes. And that would make sense to me, if the whole Universe wasn't crumbling around us.

"I've missed you so much," he says, "I couldn't stay away. And I thought you might want a ride home, after all that yoga." He grins his sideways grin, pinches my cheek with the backs of his fingers, in the gentle way that he does.

"That is pretty amazing of you," I nod, finding the things I can be honest about until I decide what to do with the rest of it.

Maralyn is back behind the desk, showing support by the look in her eyes which hover slightly above the computer screen.

"I'm not going to invite myself to any of the sessions, but I thought it would be nice to see everyone. Have a bite, talk with the team for a while, and then head out late afternoon. How does that sound?"

I smile, swallowing around the lump in my throat.

"I've heard it's been quite an experience, these last few days," he says.

I exhale audibly, and that shakes too, and I wonder if he notices. "An incredibly unique experience," I say, as steadily as I can.

"You look beautiful. And seem tired." He tucks some stray hair behind my ear. "You're ok?"

"I'm ok," I quickly nod. "Packed schedule and all that." I move my weight from one foot to the other. "I can sleep on the way home now, thanks to you. How did you get here, anyway?"

"Viktor. He left the car with us and took an Uber home. I think he was happy to get out of the city for a while. Hit the open road," he winks. "He was singing, if you can believe it."

"Viktor was singing?" I find a small laugh, and let it surface. It is genuine, and it takes me off guard. "What was he singing?"

"I told him to take control of the radio. He likes 90s pop, apparently."

"No way," I say, and for a moment, I forget. It doesn't last long. Just a moment.

"Do you have the energy for a short walk?" he asks. "I'd like to take a look around."

I consider telling him I should stay back. But aside from the fact that this would seem unusual, after he'd traveled all this way, I am sure that I shouldn't get to avoid this. Kai doesn't. And even though Emerson is unaware, he doesn't either.

"I'm hoping Kai can give me a little tour. Maralyn says he likely won't mind."

Hearing his name from Emerson's mouth is like daggers, and I wring my hands together. Maralyn looks up from her desk, saving me from response. "He's on his way, Emerson. Should be here momentarily."

And at that moment, I feel the air change direction, and Kai is walking through the front door. His hair is pulled up on the top of his head, his t-shirt is changed and fresh. I wonder if there are grass stains on the back of my clothes. I wonder if the pool of tears in our laps have dried up. I'm afraid to look, but I think they have.

He looks me in the eyes, but just for a moment. It is so fleeting that it is almost imperceptible.

He walks up to us, confidently, or at least it would seem.

"Emerson," he says, shaking his hand. "Welcome."

"Kai. It's great to finally meet you in person." He is more enthusiastic than I expected, his mood buoyant and welcoming. "Seems we've been orbiting around each other's worlds for quite some time."

"It seems so," Kai nods, and I feel the heat on my cheeks.

"I'm already astonished by what you've created here," Emerson says. "And I am told there is so much more to see."

"Thank you," Kai says, bowing his head. He is not enthusiastic like Emerson, but rather, considered. "That means a lot to me. Though I can only take so much credit. It was truly a team endeavor."

"You are lucky to have such a great team," says Emerson.

"As are you. An incredible group. It has been a pleasure to have them here these last few days."

"And how about my beautiful, talented wife?" He smiles at me, drapes his arm over my shoulder so effortlessly. Something he's done countless times before.

"Your wife is one of the most incredible people I've ever met," says Kai, matter-of-factly. I don't blush again, because my face drains instead. And I understand that Kai, too pure to tell a lie, is navigating this the same way I am. With only truths, but much omission. "She is extraordinarily talented."

Emerson turns to me. "You never cease to amaze me, Cora," he says, in such a sweet way my cheeks whiten even more.

I shake my head. "It's the space that is so special," I say. "One can't help but to become a better version of themself here." As soon as I say it, I wish I could take it back. I don't know what I am admitting. I don't know what I am avoiding. Kai looks me in the eyes again, telling me, I'm sure, that it is ok. So imperceptible, it is like we have our own language.

"So, Emerson," Kai says, moving us to more even ground. "I'd love to learn more about your most recent endeavors. I hear your firm has been wildly successful these past few years."

"It has been a crazy ride," he says, eyes widening. "A lot of hours, but also a lot of heart. I'm proud of it."

"As you should be. Congratulations," Kai says with sincerity. "And how is Natasha?"

"Oh, she's great. It's been a positive experience, to be in it together. Hard to go at this kind of thing alone, you know?"

"I do," he nods. "So, I hear you want to take a look at the space? We can have a walk around the property, if you're up for it."

"I'd like that, yes," says Emerson, nodding. "Thank you."

"We can have a late lunch on the way back." He turns to me. "Cora, you haven't eaten much today, have you?" I look toward Emerson, but he doesn't seem to react. It only seemed an intimate thing to say, because I know the truth of it.

I shake my head in response.

"Great," says Emerson. "Let's go." He removes his arm from my shoulder and claps his hands together in waiting.

"Just one moment," Kai nods, walking to the front desk. He hands Maralyn something, whispers a few words I cannot hear. And then we are walking out of the entranceway, just the three of us.

Kai asks Emerson question after question about the firm as we walk past the pond and up the path, and it provides me justification to hang back a while, stay quiet. Every word I speak, every interaction, takes energy. The exertion is not invisible to Kai, I'm sure, as he shoulders most of the conversation. I am grateful for his grace. I am stunned by his stability.

"What made you want to leave?" asks Emerson.

"The firm?"

"Yes," says Emerson. "I hear you were quite a big deal."

"It wasn't aligned with my soul's calling," says Kai. "I was pulled in another direction and had unconventional dreams to fulfill." He squeezes at the back of his neck and continues. "I believe every soul has a purpose, and this one could not be ignored." I know this language is outside of Emerson's usual vocabulary, but he is gracious. I am appreciative of him for that, and of Kai, for continuing to express his truths, so carefully, each word placed just right.

"You took a chance," says Emerson. "And it obviously paid off." He sweeps his arms in front of him, gesturing to Kai that he is impressed. And I am appreciative of that, too.

"I'm very lucky," says Kai, with a small smile. "Almost everything I could ever desire is right here."

"Almost everything?" asks Emerson, perceptively. "Is something missing?"

"Always," replies Kai. "There must be. What is life without something to dream about?"

The three of us fall silent, but all for our own reasons, letting the breeze through the trees fill in the spaces.

Lapis Lazuli is up ahead, and I am glad for the forced shift in conversation. Kai speaks to the structure in a new way, aware he is conversing with someone with architectural prowess. It is beautiful to hear him speak this way, yet another dimension I have not seen. Emerson is enamored by the structure, and I am glad he can appreciate its brilliance, in his own ways.

"Why the name?" he asks.

"Each space is named after a naturally occurring supportive substance," says Kai. "Lapis supports creativity, collaboration, and connection."

"Inspiration for this unique color blue? These splashes of color are genius. Cora is adept in the world of gemstones." He turns to me. "I can see why you love it here so much," he smiles, in a gentle way, and I am sure he is aware how much that might mean to me.

I exhale, and smile in a gentle way, too. "It's a marvel," I say.

We slip by Raw Green Opal, with the promise we'll circle back for lunch, though again, I can't imagine taking a single bite, and head next to Tiger's Eye. This space, to me, seemed almost an afterthought for Kai when he first presented it to me. But to Emerson, it is a main attraction.

"And this," says Kai, as we arrive at the yoga studio, "is Cora's office." His features are peaceful, embracing this beautiful truth even amongst the tumult. Emerson studies the angles, the woodwork, the location of the supporting beams, and I notice his ability to appreciate the space in this way, in a way I could not.

"Beautiful," says Emerson. "Just beautiful. I'm really impressed."

Kai bows his head in gratitude. "This space is very special to me."

"What do you call it?" Emerson asks. "What's it named after?"

Kai is quiet, unsure for the first time. And after all the ways he has already saved me this afternoon, I lift my eyes, ready to save him, in this small but consequential way. I speak from a place that surprises me, expressing something that I've only just come to understand, but say it as if it is something I've always known.

"The Pearl," I say, my eyes misting over. "This is the Pearl."

Kai holds my gaze again, and we are unable to break away as we did before. And then he nods his head, turns to Emerson, his voice breathier.

"Yes," he says, his eyes filling with tears of which are impossible to hold back. Mine do the same, and I bring my gaze down to hide them. "This is the Pearl. A symbol of wisdom, innocence, beauty, and sincerity."

We are all quiet, the vibrating air obvious, even for Emerson. The silence is deafening, but I want to stay there in it. I only want to be held by it. I don't want it to break. But what Emerson says next sends a chill down my spine, and the silence shatters like a sheet of ice.

His voice is low. Serious and kind.

"You've lost someone, too?" he asks. Pain recognizes pain, no matter what direction it is coming from, and he can see it in Kai, the way it drapes over his skin.

Kai's head falls to the side, his hand again holding the back of his neck. "I've lost someone, too," he whispers.

And it is then, in that very moment, that it happens for the first time.

I have my first spontaneous vision.

24

PRESENT DAY

There is a world in which this timing could not be worse. It is the world we live in, this physical world, the world of the mind and the self-imposed rules and the fact that Emerson and Kai both stand here, looking on together, so much unspoken that the air is thick with it. But in this other world, the world of the soul, this is just how it is supposed to be. And though I have been teetering between both these worlds, after being cracked so wide open these last few days, there is no way I can stifle this eruption of truth, with my soul leading the way and demanding, with all its grace, that I listen.

The room spins around me, similar to what happened before, but different in that this time, my eyes are wide open. I take a step back, stumble, dizzy and afraid, my eyes unable to hold on to one steady thing while the room undulates around me. I know I must close my eyes. I know I must let it come. But I am scared and vulnerable and trying to hold on to some semblance of normalcy, not wanting Emerson to see me this way, to have all the questions I'm sure he already has and that I won't be able to answer.

They both run to me. They both support me under my arms, bring my back to the wall, let me glide down the smooth paint and onto the wooden floor below. Emerson says my name once and again, begging for a response. Kai is silent, studying me, allowing. I close my eyes, and right there in that place, with Emerson and Kai both hovering, with the fear and the confusion and the presence all mixed up into one thing, I let it come.

I don't see anything at first. It is only blackness, the edges like smoke, slowly giving way to a pure white light. While the smoke clears, I hear her laughter. It is angelic and light and kind, and suddenly, I am not afraid anymore. The peace falls over me like a warm blanket, the laughter tickling at the corners of my mouth.

Soon, it is only bright light, and she comes into view—her curly blonde hair, her crystal blue eyes, the aura surrounding her pure and gentle. Her smile is filled with eternal wisdom, and though it would appear well beyond her years in the youthful form she presents to me, it fits perfectly on her angelic face.

Her presence alone imparts love and sagacity. It wakes up the soulful parts of me. It is breathy and light, floating in a way that is not human, for she is something else. I've lost the room I am in. I am only here, in this place, with her. It must only be seconds, but it feels as if I have been here forever. Watching her, from this place of wonder.

She speaks to me, delivers a message with her voice that is made of ethereal song. I can't hear the words, but I know them. I don't understand them, but I know them, like she is speaking from her soul and through mine, the truth shining from both of us but only one of us wise enough to see.

I chose to go. For all of us.

Her eyes comfort me. I try to ask her questions, but no sounds will come out. I try to reach for her, to decipher this wisdom. I try to tell her I love her, but I am frozen in space and the anxiety is back and she starts to fade, the blackness creeping in from the corners, enveloping what seems to be the entire Universe. I try to tell her I'm sorry. That I am devastatingly sorry. But I feel a jolt and just like that, it is over, and I am simply sitting there with closed eyes, feeling the ground beneath me, hearing the sounds of the woods and Emerson's frantic words and Kai's even breath. And I open my eyes.

The room is too bright, and I squint, shading my face with my hand. Emerson moves toward me, puts his hands to my forehead, to each side of my face. He asks me if I can rise and I shake my head and he is helping me off the ground, supporting my weight even though I don't need him to. I am back now, and I am tired but sturdy. The room is still, and so am I.

He repeats my name, once and again. "What is happening?"

"I'm ok," I breathe. "I'm ok. I'm sorry I scared you."

"We need to get you to a hospital."

I shake my head violently. "No, no, no. I'm not sick, Emerson. I'm ok. I feel fine."

"You are not fine, Cora," he exclaims. "You looked possessed."

"I'm not possessed." I'm still shaking my head, wanting to break free from his grasp which feels stifling.

"I'm worried about seizures." He turns to Kai, and back to me. "And I have this asshole over here telling me to let you be. That you are having some sort of psychic fucking experience."

Emerson does not get angry often, and when he does get angry, he is particularly good about not losing his composure. This time, his face is red and he's drowning in emotion and I wonder how much happened in those moments I was gone.

Kai does not speak and I wish he could so that I don't have to but I can see him falling apart around himself. And maybe for once he can't choose the right words, because there are endless things to say but, with Emerson looking on, no space to say them. I know he is doing me a kindness in this silence. I know he feels this is not his place, but mine. I want to soften the hurt he feels, but I can't. I can only witness his martyred silence as I turn toward my husband, and stumble to speak to him pieces of truth.

"Emerson, please listen to me, ok?" I step back from his hold, place my hand on his shoulder. "I know that was likely a frightening thing to witness. But I am not sick. I am ok. If you'd just take a deep breath, I can tell you what happened. I can tell you what I saw."

I take my hand back, look from Emerson to Kai and back again, and now both are silent and watching me, both from perspectives on each end of a seemingly never-ending gamut.

"Yeah," he says, shaking his head and exhaling. "Yeah, ok. Tell me what you think you experienced, Cora." His tone is placating, and I watch him hold his frustration tight to his chest.

The word *think* digs into my ribs and though I could not imagine him reacting any other way in this moment, though this is the only reaction that makes sense from him and something I should never hold against him, I still grieve over it. My foundation cracks just a little bit more.

"I have had deep meditative experiences here, Emerson. I have been irrevocably changed in these last few days. In a good way. A beautiful way." I look down toward the ground and then force my eyes back up to his. "And when you asked Kai if he had lost someone, too..." I trail off. He is silent. Waiting. "I thought about all we have lost, and something opened in me. And I had a beautiful vision." I smile tenderly, unable to contain the wonderment at the thought of Pearl's angelic image.

"A vision," he says, rubbing his nose and bringing his hand to his chin. I can sense his incredulity and his attempt to protect me from it. He is silent then. We all are. The tension in the air is thick. He doesn't ask me what I saw, and I am glad for it. Because not only do I not want to even try, in this moment, to explain the story of Pearl to him—but the message in this vision is unclear even to me, and I need to unravel it myself.

She told me she chose to go. Go where? And why? And still, I have endless questions and fewer answers, and my chest hollows with it, but I am cushioned by her. By the purity of love that she, in those moments, allowed me to feel.

"Cora," he says, shaking his head again. "It's ok. It's ok." He turns to look at Kai again, and then back to me. He runs his hand through his hair. "Sometimes, when we experience something traumatic, our brains try to make sense of it. You're just trying to process things."

His voice is gentle, almost too gentle, and again, I feel a stabbing sensation following his words. I am trying to grasp onto a common thread, but I know where he is going with this and hope that I am wrong.

"What do you mean?" I ask him, cautiously.

"These..." He pauses, finding a word to convey what he is thinking, it would seem, with as much tact as possible. "These symptoms can be a sign of Post-Traumatic Stress Disorder. It's not unexpected, Cora." He takes both my hands in his tight grasp. "You have been through a lot. But we'll get through it together."

His tone is excruciatingly kind. This is everything he is—caring, supportive, pragmatic—and I can see him for those things. To him, I am gentle, compassionate, and afraid. To him, I am a dreamer, and it is easy for him to see these things in me. And though all of these things are true, they are merely fragments of us. I am sure now that there are endless layers that exist that we cannot see, as if our relationship is built upon the tip of an iceberg, the rest of us waiting in shadow.

I am blind to his eternal self, and he is blind to mine.

I am silent. I look down into my lap, tears forming at the edges of my eyes. The painful edges are blunted in my overwhelm, but there is plenty of room for sadness, and it needs a way out. These moments, they are a metaphor for the things I am afraid of, and the things I grieve—still, somehow wrapped up in all the incredible love I have for him. For everything we have been for each other. And I have no idea what to do but feel it.

I look up to him, and his face is concerned, confused, stuck. I look up at Kai, and he is pained with compassion, the empathy running so deep I am sure he feels every sensation I do, every blunted edge and shattering sadness.

"Why don't we go, Cora?" says Emerson. "You can rest on the way home."

I look up at Emerson, my eyes sad, and I wonder what he sees then. If that deep connectedness and insight that I miraculously held looks like madness to him. If he is looking at his own pain, and reflecting it back at me, not realizing that we are not mirrors.

"And maybe, when you feel up to it, we can get you to a doctor in the city. Just to see what they have to say."

I feel myself choking on the words I want to say. They are too brash, too sudden. I want to tell him that I can't go home with him. That home has transformed for me, and that I am lost now, moving between two worlds in a treacherous way.

Any words I decide to say will cause pain. Deep and eternity-altering. But I can't say those words now. Because who would I be if I chose those words at this moment—demolishing this life with Emerson from under his feet in this wicked way, with another man who holds my eternity looking on? That is not what I am learning from Kai. He is pure presence, he is kindness, he is strength. If his lesson is in letting go, in this moment, he is fulfilling that with tenacity. And whatever my lessons are, they are so wrapped up in this moment they are choking me. They are clouded, and I can't see their stories, but I know that I am wrapped in them and I must stay entwined. I feel Pearl here, cushioning me. Promising me I will see. Promising me, if I just keep going.

Kai speaks then, his voice weaker than I have ever heard it, crackling under this phenomenal weight. "I can lead you back." And though I am sure Emerson understands this in his own way, I am sure Kai is not just speaking about a walk in the woods. I just don't know where *back* is; which direction I am to walk in. If I will be lost and searching, forever.

"Yes," says Emerson, curtly. "We are leaving as soon as we pack her things."

Kai nods. He turns toward the door, somberly and spent, and we follow, Emerson with his hand wrapped around mine, believing that the tighter the grip, the better he can protect me, and the surer he can hold on. He doesn't understand the lessons, and I don't blame him for that. Sometimes, it takes an eternity to see.

The way he is loving me, however well-intentioned, doesn't change the stifling feeling in my chest, but only adds to it. It doesn't evaporate the sweatiness of my palm, which is now shielded from the gentle summer air. It feels more like an intrusion into the energy that has been flowing around me, which is admittedly still merging with Kai up ahead and stuttering under all this added pressure.

The usually whimsical woods look different to me. They are darker, less intricate. The sounds are more discordant. The air sharper. I wish Kai would walk by my side and I know how terrible a thing it is to wish, as my hand is in my husband's grasp. But in most ways, it is a pure desire. It is good and kind and true. In ways, it seems it is everything; the meaning of all of it.

But still, I walk, my hand clamped and sweaty. Who is that that I am really trying to protect? I need to see where my deepest questions lie, and in what direction I can find truth deep enough to lead me. My choices are not a matter of deserving. But maybe I have made myself believe this, and have boiled things down to something that simple? I know Emerson does not deserve the pain of such sudden dissolution. But Kai does not deserve this pain, either. And what is it that I deserve? In this moment, it seems the only answer is pain.

Perhaps all of these questions truly revolve around the paradox Kai spoke of—a matter of the physical world versus the ethereal. A matter of the deepest type of recognition for the meaning of life versus my small-minded human brain. Or perhaps, it is understanding that the Universe is vast enough to hold all of it, and that, in learning to be human, there will be sacrifice. There will be choices that are outside of eternity. Eternity is meant to be spent somewhere else, out there, when these bodies are no longer filled with human life and there is only open air.

I wonder in how many lifetimes there was an Emerson. I wonder what those choices looked like, time and again. I wonder what truth I found around the ideas of rightdoing and wrongdoing, if there is really a field where those do not exist, or if all life is outside of that field, and only goodness, only kindness is the answer. But how do we define such goodness? Where is it that such kindness can be found, when whatever reality we find ourselves in will concurrently lead to hurt?

Kai turns to me, supporting me with his gaze, and I want to see the thoughts he holds. I want to shake mine out in front of him, beg him to make sense of them. I want to tell him about Pearl's message, understand its meaning. I want to learn how I can speak to her, and if I will ever see her again. I wonder, too, how many times there was a Pearl. If we only had those short years. If she was too pure for this world. If she waits for us, somewhere beyond.

Emerson catches a glimpse of our locked eyes, and he increases his grip. My eyes wander down toward the dirt, Kai turns back ahead, and even in our subtlety, there is absolutely no way that we can hide the energy that reverberates through the air. There is no way that Emerson hasn't noticed the change in pressure since he arrived here. There is no way that his heart doesn't beat against that which he feels but does not understand.

"How are you doing? Do you need to take a break?" asks Emerson.

"I'm ok." And I know that soon, I will not be able to keep up my truth-telling in the way I have. That when I can't find half-truths I will be left only with full lies. Unless, of course, I pour myself out in front of him. And he will hear only what he is able.

We are walking up the path toward Citrine now, and Kai stops at the entrance, waiting for us to reach him. "Are you sure you don't want to stay a while and rest?"

"We are sure," Emerson says sharply.

Kai nods. "Can I get you anything for your journey?"

"Nothing," says Emerson. "We will fend for ourselves."

Kai nods again, his lower jaw tense and holding his face in its vice.

"I will leave you to it, then." He turns to me. "Cora, you have brought a light to this space in a way we have not seen."

"Thank you, Kai," I croak, my voice shattering around itself. "I am eternally grateful for this experience."

"There is always a place for you here," he says, his eyes a deep, black ocean. "*Once a soul lies down in this grass...*" he trails off.

"*The world is too full to talk about,*" I whisper.

Emerson looks from me to Kai, his foot beating rhythmically against the ground, our words a mystery he has no patience to unravel. His face is a hard line in a way I have never seen from him, but he is silent, holding the words he needs to say that I'm sure will crumble over me like an avalanche once we are alone.

Alone.

The moments are slipping away so quickly now, and the reality is settling into my cells, and soon, he will be gone. *Gone.* It echoes inside of me, moving blindly through the darkness, its sharp edges ripping at my insides.

"Best to you, Emerson." He extends his hand. Emerson takes it in an obligatory way, the set of his mouth in contrast to the embrace.

When Kai takes his hand back, he merges it with his other, and brings them to the center of his chest. He bows his head for the last time and does not raise it again as he turns to walk back out into the forest. I do not see his eyes before he leaves. I only see the back of him, walking out into the woods, his gait unsteady, his golden skin sizzling against the afternoon light, his shoulders hunched and angled, the pain emanating from him in a way that shakes the tree's branches, quakes against the earth. The pain I feel, too, separating my soul from my body. Ripping me in two.

"Let's go," I hear, Emerson urging me back into the lobby. I am unsure if my feet can move from this place, if I can turn my eyes away from the direction Kai is walking in. "Cora," he says, his voice crass and unyielding, "let's go to your room," and I am pulled from it, shaken from this hold in a way that feels against my will, taking breath from me.

I nod my head and we walk up the stairs. Maralyn looks at me but I don't have the strength to look back. I can't face the truth in her eyes. I don't want to see it.

"Which number?"

"Eleven," I say, and in moments, we are behind my closed door, just the two of us.

"It's nice," he says, as if admitting something unfortunate.

"It is." I gather stray articles of clothing I have draped over the plush chair and push them into my bag.

He walks to the open windows and looks out over the property.

He is quiet while I pack my things, collect toiletries, and roll my yoga mat in a mechanical way, tighter than it was before.

"I don't like him." He does not look at me when he speaks, continuing to look toward the trees, and I can imagine they blur under his gaze, his thoughts taking all his focus. "Whatever witchcraft he's practicing here is dangerous." He is monotone, his shoulders square and still. "And don't bother to argue with me about it, because you aren't seeing clearly. He's got you under his spell."

"Emerson, that's ridiculous," I sigh.

"It's not ridiculous. You're having a fucking psychotic break and he's telling me to stop interrupting you?" He turns to me, his eyes on fire. "What in the actual fuck, Cora?"

"I wasn't having a psychotic break, Emerson," I say, dropping my bag to the floor and trying hard to appear composed. "And I'm sure he didn't say it like that."

"You wouldn't know how he said it, now, would you? Because you couldn't hear a word we were saying."

"No, I couldn't," I concede.

"And you know what else? I don't like the way he looks at you."

"How does he look at me?"

"Like he's undressing you with his eyes right in front of me." He comes in close, the muscles of his face tensed in a way I have not seen them before. "I'm glad he's stuck in this mirage of a place. I'm glad he's not out in our world anymore, fucking things up."

I cannot help but to look at him the way I do, my eyes squinted and revolting. "That is a horrific thing to say," I shudder. "I was welcomed here with incredible warmth. Supported in ways I have never been supported."

"Sure," he says, throwing his arms in the air. "That's what every cult member says while in the grasp of their brainwashed stupor."

I take a deep breath, notice the ground beneath my feet, doing all I can to stay steady, to hold myself together while I'm falling apart. The fury that runs through my veins is a welcomed distraction from the deafening pain, and it keeps the flood of guilt from choking me. I remind myself with every exhale that he is right to be upset. That I stand here, lying to his face, holding back the truth of everything that has happened these past few days that has irrevocably changed the course of not just my existence, but his too, without his knowing or approval. And he is understanding it in the only way he knows how. Trying to make sense of the pieces of us scattered along the ground and doing whatever he can to put them back together in the same way they used to be arranged.

He takes a deep breath and exhales fiercely. He paces once and again in front of the window and then walks toward me.

"Damnit, I'm sorry." His eyes soften. He puts his arms around me. Rests my head on his shoulder. "You have been through so much today. I shouldn't be upsetting you like this." He holds me tighter. "Jesus, I'm so sorry."

"It's ok," I say, my voice muffled against his shoulder. "I know you're scared. So am I."

And I'm even more afraid now, that his anger is abating. It is his kindness, in this moment, that I am afraid of.

He rubs his hand over my back, searching for ways to comfort me and himself.

"Let's go home," he whispers.

I nod into his arm.

He releases his hold, picks up each of my bags, leaving me only my backpack to sling over my shoulder. We take one more look around the room, ensuring there is nothing we have forgotten, and lock the door behind us.

Maralyn is behind the desk, pretending not to watch us as we descend the stairs. I go to her, tears prickling at the corners of my eyes.

"Maralyn," I shiver. "I am going now."

She is quiet for moments, and then comes around the desk, embracing me in a warm hug. "Oh, Cora. I can't tell you how much I will miss you." I put my arms around her too, and we stay that way for a while. When we release each other, she holds me at arm's length, ensuring our eyes are meeting so she can say there what she can't say out loud.

"Will you call?" she asks.

"Of course, I will," I say, and though my smile is feeble and shaking, I offer it up.

I swing my backpack to the front, grasp my phone, ask her to store her number. With a thud to my insides, I realize that I do not have Kai's. Perhaps typing it into this small, illuminated screen would have seemed a waste of our moments, boxing our future interactions into something far too contained. Perhaps we both knew it would be better this way. Either way, the thought of not having that connection to him makes me hollow, and I have a feeling this is something I will feel again and again, forever discovering every small detail of life that we cannot share.

"I'll make sure," she says. "That you stay in touch." And I know what she means. She then takes one of my hands in both of hers, in the same way she did when we first met, and slips something into my palm. I grasp it, press my lips together, and slowly take my hand back.

"It was nice to meet you, Emerson," she says, turning to him. "You both get home safe now."

"Please give the team my best," he says, accessing his best professional voice. "Tell them I will see them on Monday?"

"Sure, I will." And then we are walking away from Maralyn, from the beautiful Citrine Welcome and Living Center, from my home for the last three days that felt simultaneously like a blip in time and all time that ever was. Emerson puts my bags in the trunk, grasps my car keys, and then we are settled in the leather front seats of my SUV, the gravel crackling against our tires, the branches screeching against the windows.

"Rest," he says, his voice so much softer. So much more compassionate and less frenzied.

I sigh, the trees blurring in my fixed gaze, the sun flashing through its canopy and then hiding again, over and over in a rhythmic and hypnotizing way. I squeeze my palm, feel the small piece of paper against my fingers, folded delicately, and waiting. It burns my skin and I cannot help myself, yearning for the comfort of the words I know are written there. I open it and see that familiar poetry etched there, reminders of our infinity. But below that recognizable message, there is another poem, not written by my hand, but by Kai's.

> *The minute I heard my first love story,*
> *I started looking for you, not knowing*
> *how blind that was.*
> *Lovers don't finally meet somewhere.*
> *They're in each other all along.*
> —Rumi

"What's that?" asks Emerson, looking at me out of the corner of his eye.

"A farewell from Maralyn," I say, creating a fist around the paper and casting down my eyes that have misted over, watching the road move beneath us.

And then I let my eyes fall shut, allowing the hurt to sit in my cells and feeling grateful for it.

Just like he knew I would.

25

PRESENT DAY

I sit awake with closed eyes for most of the ride home, and stare out the window for whatever is left. Emerson is silent, his hands gripped on the steering wheel more tightly than usual. He puts on the radio and shuts it off. He seems to be mesmerized by the road moving beneath us.

When we get home, Viktor comes to retrieve our bags and parks our car in the underground garage. I have the inescapable feeling of being on a movie set. Like I am pretending to live this life, but that it is not really mine. That right behind our four walls the real world unfolds, and we are just tucked inside of it.

"Finally," Emerson exhales. "We are home."

He seems so relieved. Like the rest of it can be left in its place, behind us now that we are here. I move through the familiar but parched air, the emotions almost too big to feel, refusing to let myself unravel around them now. Not now.

Emerson takes my hand and leads me to our bench by the front door. He removes my shoes for me, tucking them into their place on the wooden rack. Then, with my hand again in his, we rise, and walk to the bathroom. The tile feels cool against my feet, the air-conditioned room prickling at my skin. He takes the edges of my tank top, lifts it over my head, followed by my bra, revealing my bare breasts, pale against my slightly tanned skin. He moves my pants down over my waist, carefully inching them over my ankles; so gently, as if I am made of thin glass. He lets my underwear fall to the ground, bunch around my feet.

He leaves me for moments to start the water in the shower, the steam quickly wafting upward into the chilly air. He lifts his t-shirt over his head, unbuttons the pants that hang low on his waist. His flawless form moves toward me, holds me close. I am aware there are different types of flawless, and he is one of them.

He motions for me to follow, and we step into the steam, letting it swirl around us. He washes me, moving his hands across my shoulders, the small of my back. He massages the shampoo into my hair, loving me this way, telling me he is here to keep me safe. And I do feel loved. I do. But I also can't see straight, his kindness slipping off me with the soapy water, clashing against my shame and swirling down the drain.

When we are clean, or at least when we appear to be, he turns off the water and wraps me in a long robe. He dries my hair in his towel, and then wraps it around himself. We walk to the bedroom, sit upon the bed that is ours, and it is all comfortable and foreign, practiced and novel. I cross my legs atop the blankets, and he lays on his back, his head resting on his crossed arms.

"Thank you," I whisper.

He pats the bed near him, invites me to lay by his side, props a pillow under our heads.

"I really am sorry, Cora. I was scared back there. And pretty furious, if I'm being honest with you."

"I know," I say. "I know you were."

"For starters, I won't rest until we rule out every possible cause of whatever it is that happened to you back there. You know that, right?"

I sigh. "I would tell you if I felt I was in danger, Emerson. You know *that*."

"I'm not saying you feel that you are in danger." He tucks my wet hair behind my ear. "I'm saying that you might be, anyway."

We are both quiet again. I feel the dampness of the pillow, cool beneath my cheek.

"We see the world in different ways," I say.

"I think that is one of our strengths," he says, eyes soft and thoughtful. "We offer each other a unique perspective."

"I agree with that." I prop my head up with my arm, leaning my elbow on the bed. "But sometimes I feel you don't value mine."

"I might say the same about you," he says, lifting his head and mirroring my pose. "I'm normally ok to agree to disagree. But not when it comes to your health." He shakes his head adamantly. "Humor me," he says. "Just a checkup. You're overdue for one, anyway."

I swallow around a lump in my throat and force myself to soften. I'm eager to put this behind us.

"Ok."

"Ok?"

"Yes," I concede. "I'll make an appointment for next week." .

"Good," he says, wrapping himself around me, curling his legs between mine, breathing into my hair. And then he pulls back, his face changed. "If I ask you something, will you tell me the truth?"

My stomach flips. My throat contracts.

"Yes," I say, voice cracking in my flaring intuition, so I try again. "Yes, I will."

"You know you can tell me anything, right? And it will be ok."

"I know," I say, the heat beneath my robe suddenly overwhelming.

He rolls onto his back, his hands clasped on his abdomen, deep in thought. I wait, curled up in myself.

"Are you attracted to him?" He asks me calmly, any emotion associated to his question kept tight to his chest.

My stomach stops flipping and seems to drop out from under me, leaving a hollow space.

"To who?" I ask, giving myself time to find my breath.

"To Kai. I know he is attracted to you, and I don't blame him for that. It's something that can't be helped, believe me." He turns to me again and I wish he didn't. "But I just wonder, if the feeling is mutual."

He notices my quiet, aware of the hesitation that I cannot possibly hide, and he continues.

"It's ok if you are. He's a very attractive man," he says matter-of-factly. "You are human, after all. It's not like I've never been attracted to another woman. It's totally normal. If that's as far as it goes."

My head is swimming around his questions and admissions, expressed in a way I have never heard him speak before—with his usual confidence and assertion, but with an openness that is unfamiliar.

"Just tell me the truth, Cora," he says, simple and concise. "That's all I ask. And we can put it behind us."

The truth. I am irrationally tempted to laugh out loud, so overwhelmed by the breadth of that request. And since the full truth seems like it would make the entire Universe quake, this simple admission suddenly seems small in comparison. And it feels important to speak it. To let at least this much of it spill out so that he can hold it.

"I'll make it very simple for you, ok? I'll ask you straight out." He straightens, braces. "Are you attracted to Kai?"

He is looking into my eyes now, searching. I look down at the sheets, bite the inside of my lip.

"Please," he says.

"Yes," I say. "I am." The word *attraction* has never been the right one, but it's a truth in the way he can understand it, and that is enough right now.

I look up again, and he is nodding his head, seeming somewhat grounded by the admission.

"Ok," he says, still nodding. "Ok. Thank you, Cora." He rests his hand on my hip. "See now?" He lightens, it seems, in a forced way. "Doesn't that take some of the charge off it? Doesn't that help?"

I nod, knowing the buzzing fear of this admission may have subsided, but the charge is otherwise still blaring in my ears. "This conversation means a lot to me," I say. "I appreciate your openness, after this difficult day."

"Me too." He runs his hand down the length of my arm, plays at my skin with his fingers. "It's kind of a turn-on, you know. Want to know the part I like best?"

I nod my head.

His voice deepens. "That he doesn't know what you taste like." He moves closer to me, puts his mouth up to my ear. "That he wishes he did." He brings his mouth down and brushes them against my lips, breathing heavily. "That you are here, in bed with me. That you are mine, and no one else's."

He kisses me hard, moving his body against mine. He rolls on top of me, dropping his towel onto the bed, ready and wanting to give himself to me, to hold me in the best way he knows how. He opens the front of my robe, moves his mouth against my breasts.

"All mine," he breathes.

My body responds, alive with a life of its own. My soul cries out, confused and gaping, trying to fill empty spaces with something that seems to fit. I am at once wanting and laden with guilt, loving in an over-whelming way but not knowing where to place it. And then he slides into me, moving in this practiced dance, and tears are falling from my face. He lifts them from my cheeks with his thumb, and I am sure he thinks he knows where they are coming from. But he doesn't, because not even I am sure of their source.

"This is how much I love you, Cora," he breathes, pushing hard. Loving me with every thrust. And whatever is there between us, we both unravel around the pleasure of it, and in that moment, I understand that infidelity no longer has a contained definition. It is something I will feel, every day, for the rest of my life. Betrayal is not something I will solely hold as the ultimate disrespect for my vows; for this man, who loves me the way he does, and who I love the way I do.

It is something I will hold in these moments, too, in the other direction. For my stark disregard for the very meaning of life. For entwin-ing my soul with someone who is not him.

Who is not my eternity.

That night, when Emerson has fallen asleep, I retrieve the small, folded paper from the pocket of my clothes that are lying on the bath-room floor. I place it in a small, black pouch, and scrunch the drawstring.

I tiptoe into our bedroom and lay it in the back of my dresser drawer, underneath a pile of folded t-shirts.

26

December 1900

The whole world is blanketed in snow. I know it's not true, but it seems that way.

That's how vast it feels. That's how quiet.

We pull on our wool socks and our boots and fasten them tight, and crunch three sets of footprints into the downy white. Someday it will melt, and they will be gone. So I make sure to add our trail to my memories.

It is early winter, the creek still moving under the ominous promise of icy stillness. Pearl runs up ahead. Her favorite place in the world is by the water. Her favorite trinkling sounds. Her favorite jutting rock, hanging over, high enough to get a good view of things. Treasures arriving and receding with the moving water, transporting sparkling things from high up in the mountains.

She hops up onto the rock, puts her hands to her hips, studies the day's conditions. Every day, something new. Every day, a fresh work of art that she is a part of.

"Be careful, my girl," says Asher. "It's mighty slippery today."

Pearl nods once, lays down upon her stomach on the jutting rock's face, peers over its edge. Her feet dance in the air behind her, swinging in the cold breeze.

"I'll just lay here like this," she says. "It's a safe rock. I'm always safe when I'm on it."

"Laying there like that is just right," says Asher. "Let me know if you find anything."

Asher and I sit down on a log along the bank, huddle up into each other. I can feel the warmth of him through all these layers. He is always warm. I can always feel him.

He puts his arm around me. Pearl hugs the rock, her small arms hardly reaching around its most narrow curve. We rest there, watching.

"She has a gift," he says.

"I know," I say. "I'm trying to understand it."

"She's very connected. Very pure."

I lay my head on his shoulder. Watch our breath swirl in front of us as one moving thing.

"She reminds me of you," I say.

He leans his head against mine. "She reminds me of the both of us, together."

We are quiet. Almost as quiet as the snow, but we can't help the beating of our hearts.

"Juliette," he says, his voice so feathery it doesn't break the quiet, but drifts within it. "I've been seeing things."

He lifts his head, opens his palm out in front of him, catching stray snowflakes as they fall.

"What kinds of things?" I turn toward him, in waiting.

"Things about us. Things I can't quite explain. Things from another time."

I squint my eyes, shake my head. "I would have remembered if we'd met before. Seeing you for the first time—it was my greatest miracle."

"Oh, that was the first time," he says, looking out toward the creek and then to me. "In this life."

I try to remedy his words, but I don't know how. Still, my heart feels peaceful, and I let curiosity linger on the tip of my tongue. I watch him, turning things around in his head, and I wait. Because I can see he is painting a beautiful picture in his mind, and I don't want to disturb his creation. I want to see it when it's ready.

"We both know how it felt," he says. "Like nothing else. Like its own thing. Like a miracle."

"A miracle," I agree, taking his hand.

"I've been having these dreams. We were living different lives. But living them together."

I lean my head to the side, letting his enigmatic wisdom settle around me. I let it find its place, accumulating on my eyelashes like the snow until it makes its way in.

"And I think I didn't just meet you, on that fateful day." He moves his cold hand to my rosy cheek, kisses me softly. "I think I remembered you."

My heart burns in a way that is at once foreign and familiar.

"It has something to do with our souls, Juliette. I believe they have been one for a very long time."

I am quiet, and so is he, and it seems the earth is recalibrating around us. Like we are falling into place. Like we too are drifting down from the sky, watching time move with us.

"What do you think?" he asks.

"I don't understand it," I say. "But I can't imagine it any other way."

He nods thoughtfully, the flakes accumulating in small bunches in his hair.

"I don't know if it's meant to be understood. I think it's meant to be felt." He takes my hand and places it on his heart. Holds us there. I can feel the heat of him. I can feel it, the way our hearts beat as one.

"Where have we been?" I whisper.

"Everywhere."

"Will you tell me what you've seen?"

"I will tell you," he says, with a sincerity that feels weighted. Important. "I will tell you everything."

I bite at my lip. "Have we always been this happy?" I ask him, only wanting one answer but knowing it's not one he will be able to hand over. And he exhales, his eyes falling.

"Not always," he says. "But happiness has a funny way about it, when you think about eternity."

We sit together, looking out upon the glistening earth, my eyes blurring with the fleecy sky. Pearl waves at us, smiles and turns back toward the water.

"Think about the snow," he says. "It falls to the earth this way, so temporary, so pure. Think of everything it took to get here. It was water once. Maybe it was one with the creek. Maybe it was a teardrop. A bit of morning dew. And now, in this moment, it is a beautiful crystal, formed only from the perfect conditions. Every bit of its unfolding leading to its present state, in this very moment."

I look at Pearl, her tongue reaching out into the chilled air, the crystals becoming one with the soul of her.

And I think that maybe this moment is all we need. Until the next one. And the next.

"Are we the snow now?" I ask.

"We are the snow now. And we will be again. And we will be the sun, too. And the trees. And every other beautiful thing this world has to offer."

I lay my head back on his shoulder, breathe there, close my eyes there.

"Every beautiful thing," I say.

27

PRESENT DAY

It is Monday morning, and I am exhausted in a new way—in a way I never have been, a way and didn't know I could be. I have held myself together all weekend, ensuring my disparate pieces created the illusion of cohesiveness. I have feigned stability, and sometimes even vitality, whenever I could muster it, concealing the monotonous pounding in my chest and the pain that is tangible, taking up space in my lungs.

If observing from any other perspective than from within the tumult of my heart, it was a perfect weekend. There was succulent red wine and pristine weather and open windows and long walks with burnt honey ice cream dripping over the sides of our cones. And there is a part of me that applauds my strength. My presence, although counterfeit, was in part a kindness toward Emerson that I was determined to deliver, and I did so in a way I didn't know I was capable of. But that is only a small part of me, because most of what I am experiencing is disgust. My ability to deceive to this degree frightens me. To feel this grief and find a way to smile through it—love through it, even—is difficult to remedy, and there is something in the deceit that is in stark contrast to the soul of things. To the truth of things.

I was taut, pulled from one direction to the next, and just when I was about to rip open, I changed course, finding the space where my skin stayed whole so that the rawness of it went unnoticed. Whenever I did slip, he was not blind to it. "Cora?" he'd say. "Are you ok?" And I'd tell him, yes, I was ok. And I was, in the sense that my heart was still beating.

It was the only way I knew how to breathe. If I let my grief show itself to him, it would lead to our dissolution. And then, there would be more grief layered on top of it, for the both of us, and it would be too much to hold. I didn't have the strength, or the clarity, to face this yet. If we had to face this in the state I am in, I would dissolve. And until the clarity comes, I don't even know what it is we would be facing.

Moreover, my awakening—what I believe I experienced because of Kai's presence—while it has opened me to love in an all-encompassing way, has also shined light on my old wounds. They have surfaced in a vicious way. The loss of my little girl, a grief I have been moving through life with, but which I have shoved as far down as I could since the initial deluge, has now become crippling. It is augmented by what I have learned about Pearl, and what I have done to her, and it has become one sloshing, dark, tar-like entity. The shame is thick. The grief makes it feel too large for consolation. The only way I can see through it is to accept it. Accept that my life is now made up of it.

I am sitting in the living room, watching the clouds move slowly across the sky. Emerson just left for work, earlier today than usual, having missed the day on Friday and needing to catch up. I'm not scheduled to go back to the studio until tomorrow and have the day to myself. It worries me, all the space I'll have to sit with my thoughts. But I am too tired to do anything about it.

I hardly slept last night. It is incessant, this wretched mix of longing and despair, of gratitude and love, of peace and war. I rise, unblinking. Steep lemongrass tea. Sit at the counter in the kitchen, sipping the too-hot liquid, staring into the space between molecules of air. My mind is overwhelmed to obscurity. Everything is muddied and unclear.

When it comes to Kai, it wouldn't be enough to be aware that I miss him. It would be the most magnificent understatement ever thought up. My entire soul longs for him. Even from this distance, I am magnetized to the space he takes up, my soul reassembling itself around the possibility of being even infinitesimally closer to him.

If there could be any possibility of consolation to ease this treacherous state, I know it would come from him. But to speak to him would mean his voice would etch into my soul in new ways, and I don't know if I could survive it, that small taste of his nirvana while I am here in my alternate life. To see him again would mean such active deception that I don't know if I could live with myself. To be consistently in his orbit again would mean divorce, a reality I had never thought I would even fathom less than one week prior.

The pain is far-reaching, as complex as an ever-expanding shape, infinitely building, unfolding, being discovered. It is built around him, but it is also made of him. It is what he has done to my soul. This grief is a reminder of what I must now navigate alone: a spiritual awakening that has cracked me open in every place at once. I must figure out how to live alongside it, how to see with new eyes, feel with a new heart, move through this world with a soul that I now hear screaming out, pulling me in directions my feet are not moving and have never before tread.

I am grieving many different things and I know Kai is, too. I wonder if we'll just keep stuttering around our pain for all of this life, ultimately understanding there will never be a reprieve from it. That we'll only learn to live with it. Learn to breathe around the shape of it.

I am hyperaware now of how few close relationships I have in my life. Even those whom I could possibly talk to about the inner workings of my heart, I could not talk to about this. Until last week, none of my relationships were on the soul-infused plane that I craved. And now, there is Maralyn, in our ways. And Kai, in every way. But both of these relationships feel out of reach and the silent contrast of these losses makes the isolation of my soul feel even more palpable.

I get up to retrieve my phone. No messages or missed calls. I think of Maralyn. She is likely behind her desk already, shining all her light. Maybe she is in a group, with a new team of eager soul-searchers who have filtered in. I send her a message, knowing what I risk in connecting there; in breaking a silence that feels necessary but of which I don't have the resilience to maintain.

Hi Maralyn, I text. *It's Cora.*

I continue to sip my tea, now cooled. I look at my phone, once and again. I pace the floor near the window, forward and back again. The anxiety is kicking up, showing itself in my throat, in the wringing of my hands. I am horrifically uncomfortable and starting to feel ill in the way anxiety weaves its way through the body, bit by bit and then all at once. I need some air. I dress quickly, and head for the door.

After a week of sunshine, there is finally a grey sky. It appears gentle, but it is deceiving. It is totally unyielding, protecting the ground from the sun so vigorously that one cannot even guess where it hangs in the sky. July in Manhattan is normally very warm, sometimes almost suffocating, but today, there is an unusual chill in the air. I suppose we are waiting for rain, and I think I will feel at home when the sky opens.

I walk a distance down to the water, a favorite stretch of park running along its edge, quiet today on a Monday morning, most of the city already where they are meant to be for the week ahead. As wary as I am for this time to ruminate, I am most often grateful for my flexible schedule—for the space to stretch my legs at odd hours while living outside of societally-imposed workplace norms.

The anxiety is still pulsing within me, shivering inside my bones. The mind-body connection is most evident at moments like these, thoughts showing themselves in visceral ways. The soul-body connection, however, is more difficult to understand. In the past week, I have felt my own spirit in extraordinary ways. The spinning visions, the tingling head, the energy in my chest rising like champagne bubbles. If I didn't know any better, I'd imagine I needed a doctor, too.

I told Emerson I'd call my generalist today and make an appointment. I will do so to placate him, but I am avoiding it, and plan to put it off until this afternoon. This doctor's visit, Emerson's need to have me examined—it is representative of our discord, and I don't want to face it.

The path turns up ahead, still following the water, and opening to a wider stretch of open space. Normally, this area is especially populated, even on the weekdays, tourists congregating to see the famous views of the bridges and skyline, enjoy the shops and the notable carousel with its hand-crafted horses and spinning colors. This morning, even here, it is quieter than usual, and I stop to watch a few children climb atop their chosen steeds, readying for their whirling transport.

The carnival music starts, and the children laugh, and it is so simple, their joy. It is calming, and I am lulled by it, hypnotized by the movement and the sounds. I stand there until the ride is done, and until the children hop down from their horses, run back to whoever awaits them on the sidelines. As I turn to go, a small boy nearly collides with me. Startled, he drops the change that he has grasped in his hands, and his mother apologizes, bending to retrieve it. I help them gather the coins that have rolled in each direction, and while scanning the ground, I see the glimmer.

I squint my eyes and get closer. I see it catching the city's movement in its graceful way, reflecting on the spirit of things, and leaving the rest to its sheen and to the imagination. My heart flutters, and I reach down to pick it up, a single pearl gently clasped between my two fingers.

I roll it around in my hand so that I can study its intricacies. I am immersed in the wonder of it, so when my phone rings against my hip, I too am startled.

I ensure the pearl is safely tucked away in my breast pocket, and only then do I retrieve the phone. It continues its ringing vibrations, my hand shaking as I move to answer.

"Cora," she says warmly. "Hi."

"Maralyn," I exhale. "It's so good to hear your voice."

"Is this ok? Is this an ok time?"

"Yes." I touch my hand to my pocket and continue along the water. "I was just taking a walk. Clearing my head. Trying to."

"I was in a group earlier," she says. "I thought it would be better to call."

I nod my head even though it is something she can't see. I am wary of what she might want to tell me, and simultaneously wanting to ask her a thousand and one things.

"How are you?" she asks. "How are you, *really?*"

"I'm not doing very well," I sigh. "But I'm trying my hardest to maintain some semblance of normalcy."

I am already unsure how long I can sustain it. I am grateful for this space to be honest, rather than hiding in the dark corridors of my heart.

"That sounds exhausting," Maralyn says.

I exhale, moved to tears by this simple act of empathy. I'm so easy to unravel. My emotions sit at the tips of me, waiting for every opportunity to seep out. I try to speak but my voice breaks around it.

"Oh," she exhales. "I am here. Let it come."

The permission is all I needed, and I walk toward the railing, overlooking the river, and cry out loud. The tears fall from my face, making their way into the churning water below, which is moving faster under the threat of storm. Maralyn holds space for me. I can picture her, sitting behind her desk, her hand to her chest, her compassionate face breaking in a kind way, from all the love she has.

"I'm so sorry. I've just had to hold it together these last few days, in a way I didn't know I could. It's frightening, really. I've discovered I'm rather good at keeping up appearances, when I feel I have no other choice."

"Do you dare apologize," she says, with strength and tenderness. "You are very brave."

"I don't know," I breathe. "I don't know."

I grip the railing.

"How has it been with Emerson?"

"Oh, he's been wonderful," I say, shaking my head and then moving to a whisper. "His kindness is deafening."

"I understand," she says, and I know that she does.

We are silent for moments, me afraid to ask, her afraid to share. I continue to look out toward the horizon, bits of it poking through the skyline. The wind is picking up, lashing across my cheeks. My pearl sits securely on my chest.

I take a shaky breath, as deep as I can muster. "Is he ok?"

Maralyn is still silent, her hesitation creating a sharp fear in my gut.

"He is struggling, Cora." She is so soft, the truth hard to hear but laced with compassion. "It's as we can imagine it would be."

I swallow hard, let the wind smack against me.

"He asked Solomon to cover his groups for the rest of the week."

"Has he ever done that before?"

"No," she says, honestly.

I stand unblinking, looking out into the sloshing water.

"I haven't spoken to him since Friday," she continues. "Not long after you left. But I will be here for him when he is ready. I promise you."

"I know you will," I say. Regret hits me like a tidal wave, and I feel it rushing under my skin, showing up in dampness across my chest, along my forehead. I wipe my face with the back of my hand, try to clear it away, but it is no use.

"Do you think I should have stayed?" I ask her, though I'm really asking myself, and with this question there is no answer to, the regret changes form and feels like panic. "I abandoned him." My voice is shaking with the weight of it.

"Cora," she says, calmly and with deep kindness. "I miss Bryan every day, but never once have I felt he abandoned me. Because someone doesn't have to be here physically to love and support us. As long as there is love, he is always right here." She pauses. "Kai knows this. He knows it better than anyone."

I close my eyes, feel the beauty and strength of her expression swelling in my heart space. I feel deep empathy for her, for what she has been through. I am awed by how pristine the light of her soul is, amongst it all. How it not only continues to shine but seems to always shine brighter.

"You are a beautiful, courageous, and generous soul, Maralyn," I say, "and I love you."

"I love you too, my friend," she says. "I love you too."

I am quiet again, my heart mesmerized by her wise and expansive perspective, this reminder of infinity. I am connected to Kai more deeply through not just the love, but our pain too, and there is comfort there. The pain does not need to be treacherous from this place, but a bridge to his soul that I can embrace with devotion.

I continue to look out toward the horizon, the sky muted but alive, the light seeping through its grey sheen.

"I found a pearl," I say. "Right before you called."

"A pearl?"

"Yes," I say. "It means a lot, to have found it. Kai was telling me about these messages. About how they show up."

"Ah," she says. "I see. A beautiful thing, those synchronicities. I believe they come when we need them most."

I know she does not know the story of Pearl, but she understands there is a story there. And we both know she doesn't need those details, to hold space for my soul in this way.

"Yes, I think so," I say. "And maybe, when we are ready to notice them."

My hair is moving erratically in front of my face, whipping around me. I pull it back, try to contain it.

"It sounds to me like you are being guided, Cora. If you just keep listening, you'll find the answers you need. I'm sure of it."

Her words are warm. I close my eyes, savoring them, and then turn around, leaning my back against the rail. The dampness in the air is telling me it is time to go home.

"We miss you," she says.

"I miss you, too." I take a sharp inhale, walking back from where I came.

"I'm here, anytime," she says. "Truly."

I tell her how much it means to me, and how grateful I am for her presence. And then we hang up and there is silence, and my connection is severed. The pain continues to hold me to him in its piercing way. It shows me that in order to feel him, all I must do, is *feel*.

When I get home, I stash the pearl in that black pouch in the far corner of my dresser drawer, with the small, folded paper is kept safe.

That night, it hurts too badly to pretend it doesn't. And even though I've awakened to the importance of the hurt, Emerson hasn't, and he is so worried about my mental state, that he persuades me to not only call my general practitioner, but a psychiatrist, too.

I have both appointments on Thursday afternoon.

28

APRIL 1901

The bell chimes in its brass and cheery way, and with it, her face is alight. "Mr. Hutchinson!" she squeals, her tiny hands in excited fists, her eyes glowing in the early evening light.

"Well, well, well. If it isn't that time again." Mr. Hutchinson reaches over the counter, rustling her bouncing curls.

"It's treasure hunting time, and I've got my treasure hunting boots on." She points down at her feet, bounces on her heels. "Mama says it's always good to be prepared."

I laugh. "I did. I did say that."

"Well, let's get to it, then." He walks around the counter. Pearl grasps his fingers, and he looks toward me. "Will it be the usual?" he asks, just as he always does.

"Oh, yes," I smile. "Pearl was wondering if there was anything new to lay her eyes across. And I'll need some grits, as well."

"You are in luck, little one," he says. He directs her to the glass-encased countertop. "Would you take a look at that?"

Pearl is standing on the tips of her toes, her small hands clutched over the edges of the wooden counter. She turns to me, mouth agape, blue eyes sparking with wonder. I walk toward them, lean over, place my hand on her shoulder.

"My goodness," I say. "That really is something."

"Got it on trade from an older couple passing through. They were moving on into the countryside. Planned on getting some goats. Some sheep, too." He unlocks the glass enclosure, lifts up a golden chain. "They needed all kinds of supplies. Wanted some extra penny for it, too, and I obliged." He removes it from its small stand, brings it into the light. "Do you want to hold it, my dear girl?"

Pearl squeezes her lips together, her eyes bulging with excitement. She looks up at me, hoping, and I nod. She turns back to him, shakes her head quickly. "Oh, yes," she says. "Oh, yes, please."

He drapes it over her delicate fingers, and she treats it as if it is the most fragile thing in the world, spinning it slowly in circles, watching the light change within its golden weave.

"Try it on," he says. "I bet it will look mighty fine on you with those golden locks of yours."

"You really don't mind?" she whispers. "I'll be so careful."

"Oh, I know you will. Now spin around. Let your mama clasp it there for you."

I clasp the necklace behind her, let the golden chain cascade over the lace of her dress. Mr. Hutchinson hands her a mirror, and she looks at her reflection there.

"It might be the prettiest thing I've ever seen," she says.

"Almost as pretty as you," I say.

When we get home, she asks Asher a hundred questions about gold and where to find it and how it's woven into something so tender and fine. And he tells her stories and she glows and I hope that someday, we can drape that necklace around her neck for good.

Make sure it's always shining with her.

29

PRESENT DAY

It is Tuesday, my first evening back at the studio, four days since I returned home, less than a week since my life was transformed irrevocably. The evening is stiller than it was yesterday, but there is a dampness that lingers, and I am craving the warmth and slowness of a gentle practice. The familiarity of the space is more comforting than I expected, and I am glad to have this respite. Though I have been wary to move back out into the world—a world I have trouble recognizing but that I must remind myself that I am, in fact, a part of—this is a place that I belong.

The class starts to file in, changing from sandals to bare feet, unfurling mats, stretching tired muscles. We start right on time, as we are almost at capacity, this hour a popular time for movement, the workday having just ended for many. A few minutes after we begin, I see Natasha walk in, tiptoeing to a space in the back. I give her a small wave, and she returns my welcome with a nod, one that is cold and concise.

I am jarred by her presence. She is another connecting piece of this destined puzzle, and since I've been home, I am quick to separate it out. There are pieces that are connected to Kai, or pieces that are not, and I know which I am drawn to, even if it feels threatening. I am shaken by her lackluster response, my intuition flaring in a poignant way.

Now practiced in the art of emotional deception, I lead class with a straight face, though grace is hard to find. With the monotonous heaviness already sitting in every bone, and now, with the additional severity of Natasha's glare, it is particularly difficult to compartmentalize. I am grateful when it is over—when arms and legs are sprawled out in Savasana, and the lights are low, and I can let my eyes be honest.

The group files out, and in usual fashion, Natasha hangs back. It doesn't seem usual, however, as the intensity that is her natural state is not buffered by any of her gentler sides—her benevolence, her whimsy, her glow, and as she walks toward me, I notice what it does to my chest. It is suffocating and confining and contracting, and it makes my breath shallow.

"Natasha," I say, steadying myself. "How are you?"

"I have been better." Her voice is flat, her eyes dark. Her hair is pulled back, tight and slick.

My fear is rising, holding me where it hovers.

"I told Emerson we'd be going for a drink," she says bluntly. "So that's what we're going to do. Yes?"

I nod my head, unable to form a sentence in reply. We take a moment to put on our shoes and gather our things in uncomfortable silence. I hold my bag from its handle and follow her out the door. Her stride is confident but weighted. There is more silence as we walk, and I know better than to break it. We come to a bar that is half a block away, and she turns in without warning, sure that I'll follow.

It's a dark and moody place, and we find a seat in the corner. I place my bag in my lap, hug it and lean forward in my seat, bounce my legs up and down in a rapid rhythm. I feel small, a child afraid of getting found out, scolded, destroyed. I tell myself I am fearing the worst, but it is not just fear that is telling me this story, but intuition, and that cannot be denied.

She knows something. I just don't know what.

"I'll have an Old Fashioned," she says. She raises her eyebrows toward me.

"A glass of Cabernet, please." The server nods, leaves to collect our drinks. Natasha leans back in her chair, crosses her legs, moves her hand to her chin.

I clear my throat. "What's going on? What's the matter?"

"You tell me," she says, bringing her shoulders up toward her ears in a way that doesn't seem curious, but taunting.

My fear is in my throat. A sweat is forming along the back of my neck, the creases of my forehead, in the spaces where my skin rests against my skin. I hope it is too dark for her to notice.

"I'm not sure I know what you're talking about," I say tentatively.

She shakes her head, slowly from one side to the other.

"Sure you do," she says.

I watch her, unblinking, and she continues.

"Sure you do. You're terrified." Her voice is unnervingly matter-of-fact. "You're wondering if I know. You're wondering how much I know. And you're afraid to admit anything until you're certain."

I feel dizzy, my world that was holding on by threads starting to make fracturing sounds at its edges.

"Oh God," I say, eyes barren. I'm not sure which direction to turn in. What to hold and what to release. I move my hand to my face and collapse against it, mirroring the rest.

Natasha is quiet, watching me unravel.

"So?" she finally asks. Her mouth is a firm line, chin slightly raised.

The bartender returns with our drinks. Natasha spins hers around, ice clinking against the thick glass. I raise mine with a shaking hand, bring it to my lips, wishing I got something stronger.

"I'm not here to torture you." She sighs, her words slightly softer but her voice just as rigid. She raises her glass to her mouth and takes a long sip. "I just want to talk."

"Ok." I take a deep breath, straighten in my seat, my pulse pounding in my temples. "Let's talk."

"I know about Kai. I know you two have something going on."

I am silent. Surrendering. There is no use in hiding anymore. I can sense her resolve. She waits for a response, the quiet agonizing. The fear of this eventuality was one thing. The reality of it is another—paralyzing, breathless, as if I have been punched in the gut.

Finally, I nod blankly.

"I'm rather close with Emily. We went out for drinks last night. She wasn't trying to cause trouble. She's my friend."

She swallows hard, pauses, eyes cast down at the table, and with a breath, brings them back to me and continues.

"She said she went back to the studio for something after class. Saw you two in an embrace. One that most definitely was not platonic. She said it was, and I quote, *incredibly sensual.*"

I take another sip of wine, choke it down. Natasha slumps into herself, shakes her head pleadingly. "How *could* you, Cora?"

"Oh, God," I say again, my breathing labored. The panic is rising again. I wring my hands together, trying to swallow over a parched tongue but the muscles in my throat stop working.

"I could hardly believe it when I heard it," she says. "I wanted it not to be real. It didn't make any sense to me. But it seems it may be even worse than I'd feared."

I breathe through an open mouth. I am trying to contain myself, the panic oozing from my organs.

"Hey," she says. She reaches out her hand, grabs mine. I want to run outside and gasp the clean air, the dark room wringing me dry. I need to move. I feel trapped by her hand, held there in this place.

"Listen. I just want to talk, ok? Take a breath."

I nod, sure with all of myself that I deserve the hurt of this. And again, with all of its irony, I am comforted by this realization. I may as well hand myself over to the destruction. It is too much. I am ready to just break under it and be done with it.

"Talk to me," she says.

I breathe, the energy moving through, and out. I find the slightest dampness on my tongue, allowing me to find words.

"I can't explain it, Natasha. No one would understand it."

She takes her hand back. "Try me."

"How could I express this to you, of all people? Emerson's partner? His closest friend?"

"That's why you need to," she shrugs.

I nod, biting my lip, swirling through the burning anxiety. I look down, searching for my resolve.

"It wasn't a lustful experience," I say. "Not like you might imagine it was."

"Then what was it?" Her eyes narrow, searching me.

"It was…" I close my eyes for a moment, look for my truth, remind myself that at its core, it is graceful. "It was deeply spiritual. It was soulful. I left there changed."

Natasha sits back in her seat again, seeming to throw my words back and forth in her mind, making sense of them.

"It has eternity wrapped up in it. It's bigger than I am. Than who I thought I was. Our story is not a concise thing. It's not of this world. And I don't know what to do about it."

I don't say any more. I can't bottle it up that way, and I don't have to. Somehow, this seems to be enough for her.

She bites the side of her mouth, nods, her thoughts quiet and unfolding.

"I love Emerson," I continue. "You know how much I love him. I never imagined being in this place. I never imagined it."

"He doesn't know?"

I shake my head. "No, he doesn't know."

"Are you going to tell him?"

"I don't know," I say, exhaling, and then shifting to a more grounded reality. "Yes. Yes, I'm going to tell him. I just needed time. To work it through."

She runs her finger along the rim of her glass, around and then around again.

"Did you sleep with him?"

"No," I say.

"But you kissed him, at the least?"

I hesitate. Force myself not to look down. Force myself to face her.

"Yes."

She takes her hand to her neck, rubs it across her chest. She pulls a thin silver chain from under her shirt, moves it around between her fingers. I squint my eyes. A single pearl hangs from its weave. My heart flutters, somehow breaking through the weight of the anxiety in the way only a heart can.

"Did it feel like something totally new, Cora?" She drops the necklace, lets it dangle in the air as she leans toward me. "Like the fucking meaning of everything?"

I am so thrown by her words that I physically shift back in my seat. I am feeling ironically seen, by someone I didn't imagine would ever see me this way, and I am thinking that I should perhaps be more careful what I wish for.

I look toward her, my mouth slightly open, my eyes searching, desiring to discover what perspectives and experiences have led her here. What has allowed her to speak to me about this in the way that she does. I see a truth there that I can't quite make out. Something that feels familiar, in the way it quakes the ground below our feet. And then, I nod, confirming with this simple motion that it did, in fact, feel like the fucking meaning of everything.

Her face is somber, her eyes deep and reflective. She exhales hard, moves both hands to the table and lays her palms flat.

"It hurts," she says. "Because it will hurt Emerson."

"I know how much you care about him," I say, grateful for her allegiance, a consistent presence in his life. "And I appreciate you caring enough to have this conversation."

She takes a sip of her drink, leaving only ice behind. She leans both of her elbows on the table, her head resting on her hands.

"What are you going to do?"

"I don't know," I say with a despairing exhale.

"Emily won't say anything to him. They don't have that type of relationship." She leans back again, hardening and defrosting, over and over. "I tried to downplay the whole thing as much as I could. It puts me in a terrible position, but that's beside the point. I don't know who else she's told, and I don't know what anyone else saw. It's something to be aware of. That this can come back to him. And aside from all else, it'll mortify him, you know. His team, talking about his personal life in this way."

"I know." I look down, unable to hold myself up. "It was horrific enough, without all of this."

"Whatever you decide to do, he deserves a say in it." She turns around, looking for the server, trying to get his attention.

She's right, and I know she's right. The words I speak to him, and when I speak them, don't change the reality of the recent past. No matter what, he deserves the truth. Because it is a truth he is a part of.

"You know what he deserves," she says. "Someone who loves him madly. We all do."

The word *madly* feels less like a loving reminder and more like a punch in the gut. Do I love Emerson that way? Have I ever? And is his love for me that deep and far-reaching? It seems easy for me to say that I love Kai this way. It seems diminutive to even consider it a question, and simultaneously absurd in its reality, being that I am a mortal in this world, having only ever understood love in my mortal ways.

I lean my head to the side, see an opening, and ask her. "Have you ever loved anyone that way, Natasha?"

Her face softens, and she closes her eyes. When she opens them, she holds my gaze, the sadness and pain and depth and beauty of it inescapably recognizable.

"I have." She flicks her hand in the air. "How can I judge you? If I was given the opportunity. I don't know..."

"What happened?"

The server walks over to us. Natasha orders another Old Fashioned. I ask for the same. She shifts in her seat, uncrossing her legs and moving the opposite one on top.

"Nothing," she says.

"Why?"

"It's complicated." She shrugs. "Life can get in the way."

I take a deep breath. Watch her. It's easy for me to recognize her sadness.

"Should we let it?" I ask.

"Let what?"

"Should we ever let life get in the way of its own meaning?"

We are both silent as we weigh it, our perspectives painted by our experiences, pains formed through regrets or missed chances, untapped possibilities or roads not traveled. It is through our faulty actions and flawed understandings that we learn what it means to be alive. It is only through our living that we can learn that we haven't really lived. Not in all the ways we can. Not in all the ways we are meant to.

"Probably not," she says. "But we're human. So, we'll keep doing it anyway."

The server returns with two drinks and places them down in front of us. My bag is still on my lap, and I'm still clutching it. I move it to the seat next to me. My phone buzzes. I don't check to see who it is. Natasha's phone buzzes. She doesn't check, either.

She continues. "Sometimes I can't decide if we are more afraid of feeling pain, or of the possibility of causing hurt in someone else."

"It is probably always varying degrees of both. But we often hurt either way. And, maybe, that's ok. Maybe it's the way it should be."

"Maybe," she says. "I don't know. I'm tired of it."

"Of what?"

"Hurting."

It is one simple word, but it's the way she says it that shakes me. It holds so much. She holds so much. And she is trying to tell me.

"Maybe truth is always the way," I say. looking down at my lap, and then back up to her again. "Even when it might appear otherwise."

Natasha moves her pearl around in her fingers. It catches the low lights and reminds me of the moon. My phone buzzes again.

"We need to learn to take our own advice," she says.

Buzzing, again.

"I'm sorry," I say. "I just need to check on this."

I rummage through my bag, pull out my phone. There are five missed calls from Emerson.

And one message. One simple yet earth-shattering message.

My heart is in my throat before I can comprehend it. But the world has again shifted below our feet. The air changes around it. Our cells are reconfiguring.

And we are all falling, falling.

Cora, it reads.

It's time you told me the truth.

There is suddenly not enough air. My lungs are searching for oxygen and coming up short.

Natasha is eyeing me inquisitively. She picks up her phone, too. Looks down at the screen and then back up to me.

Truth, unspoken, rumbles below our feet, percolating with volcanic liquid. It has a way of pushing its way up through the earth, breaking granite and shifting tides. To face this ashy earth is the only way. To remember what it is to be painfully human.

"Emerson," I choke. "He's called you, too?"

She nods.

"I need to…"

I can't finish the sentence, but I don't have to. Natasha seems to be putting the pieces together on her own. I am shaking from the tips of my fingers to the depths of my soul, my mind clouded but my body warning me of what is to come. I know tectonic plates are shifting.

"Hey," she says. "It will be ok. Just talk to him."

I squeeze my lips together, my eyes showing gratitude in a way my voice cannot. I grasp my phone, take my bag under my arm. I remember the bill, but she stops me when I reach for my wallet.

"Go," she nods. Her eyes are compassionate, and terrifically sad. I stay with her for moments more, the noise and the lights and the smoky smells around us falling somewhere outside of perception, and then I walk into the night air.

I take a breath, look up into the blackened sky. The moon is waning, creating an irregular shape, its iridescent glow familiar and kind. With shaking hands, I lift the phone to my ear. It rings once. Again.

"Hello?"

There is silence on the other side, but I feel him, breathing with me.

I take another deep breath. Another. Panic rises again, feeling all too familiar now. The world spins, but in a different way. In a way that makes me feel seasick. Tears are forming at the edges of my eyes, but they are stuck there, every part of me too tense for movement, too contracted for flow.

"Emerson," I shiver.

"Come home," he croaks, his voice shattering as if it is made of thin glass.

"I'm coming. I'm coming home."

He hangs up the phone. He does it without warning. And then it is just me and the sky. A dark cloud floats in front of the moon, the glow illuminating its edges, refusing to be snuffed out. In this moment, I can't understand why it cares to stay alight.

30

PRESENT DAY

I pull up to our apartment less than ten minutes later, my heart pounding fast and hard, my hands still shaking around my keys. I close my eyes in the elevator, feel the momentum of the climb, the sinking feeling of arrival. The door opens, and he is standing with his back to me, painfully still and looking out over the city.

The door shuts behind me as I remove my shoes, move slowly into the room and toward him. I place my hand on his shoulder, and he shudders. Something we have never been before. A new thing, that we have never felt. A damp hurt hangs over the room—a heart-wrenching abhorrence from him, clashing against my contempt like storm clouds.

When he turns to me, he appears barren, his mouth a straight line, his eyes looking somewhere beyond me. But I know how much is there.

"Come," I say, leading him to the couch. He shakes his head and does not follow. Instead, he begins to pace the floor, the same floor I paced just yesterday. I move back toward him, following him with my eyes.

"What's happening?" I ask, my voice and the hunch of my shoulders hushed and overwrought.

He continues to pace the floor, silently for some time. When he finally speaks, his voice is more even than I imagined it would be, but his eyes are piercing.

"How many times have you spoken to him since you left?" he asks.

"Who?" I ask, foolishly and out of overwhelming fear, and I immediately regret it.

"God damnit, Cora," he says. "How many times have you spoken to Kai since you left?"

"I haven't spoken to him," I say weakly. "Since I left."

He stops in front of me, and he looks tired. His usually bottled-up emotions cannot contain themselves, and they are showing up in any way they can—through his unblinking eyes, the twitch in his left cheek, the way he grabs at his neck.

"I found your fucking love letter," he says. "I saw you hide it, when you thought I was asleep." He takes an exaggerated breath, and I stand before him, trying to control the shaking of my limbs. "I wouldn't have gone looking through your private things," he says, "but Muhammad said something to me that didn't sit right."

He shakes his head, clenches his jaw. He continues, imitating Muhammad in an eerily cheerful way. "*Your wife and Kai must be quite close, yes? I thought they must be very old, very good friends.*"

I hang my head down. I can't breathe. I try to gasp for air but it hurts too much when it enters my lungs, and stutters on the way out.

"But that's not what he really wanted to say, Cora. That's not what he *really* wanted to say." He leans his head back, looks up to the ceiling and back again. "He just didn't want to be the one to tell the boss that his wife is fucking someone else."

I shake my head frantically. "It's not like that, Emerson," I choke.

He guffaws, starts pacing again. He pulls a small, crumpled piece of paper from his pocket, throws it to the ground at my feet. I leave the paper there, burning a hole through the floor. When he finally stops walking, he takes an exaggerated breath, looks into my eyes, and forcibly evens out his voice.

"Can you do something for me?" he asks.

I nod. I say *yes* without sound.

"When I ask you a question, don't try to save my feelings. Just tell me the truth." He moves his hand through his hair, exhales. "I won't be able to handle it, I know that. But this is worse." He makes a tight fist and releases it. "This is lethal."

I nod again.

I am disgusted with myself—for the things I have done and for holding them from him. That he had to find out in this treacherous way, deceived by the one person who should be doing all I can to protect him.

I want to give him what he needs, but I am terrified of what it will do to him. What it will do to us.

I will give him what he needs, but I am so afraid that my teeth chatter.

He moves over to the couch now, sits down on the edge, puts his head in his hands and then looks up again. I sit down next to him, carefully, wary to disrupt the particles of air that move around us.

He turns toward me, hardening, preparing himself.

"Were you unfaithful to me, Cora?"

I close my eyes for moments, the pain of speaking this truth to him so vast that I need to connect to something beyond myself to speak it. I need to hold truth in my hand as gently as I would the most fragile thing in the world, as if it is a soap bubble that contains all meaning, and it is up to me to keep it safe.

"Yes, Emerson," I whisper. "I was unfaithful to you."

He squeezes his lips together, shakes his head, letting it sink into his cells. I force myself to keep my gaze on him, while my shame begs me to look away.

"In what ways were you unfaithful to me?"

"In most ways."

"Be specific," he demands, his voice becoming stern and unyielding. "Did you fuck him, Cora?"

"No," I say, definitively enough for him not to question it. I see a subtle relief in his shoulders. At least I can give him this small thing, whatever it is worth.

"But you were intimate," he says. "Close to him."

"Yes."

"Did you kiss him?"

"Yes," I say, weakening, looking down at the floor.

"How many times?" he asks.

"Once."

He nods.

"But it seems that is the least of my worries." When I don't respond, he changes it to a question, his forced composure unnatural and frightening. "Is that the least of my worries?"

"I'm not sure what you're asking me," I say.

"I want to know what happened. I want to know *how* this happened, in three fucking days," he says between gritted teeth. "And I want to know if you care about him, the way I fear that you do."

I take such a deep breath it burns the corners of my lungs. I hold it, exhaling slowly to calm my pulse. "I will tell you whatever you want to know."

"I need to know everything."

"You won't like what you hear," I say, my voice as heavy as lead and my heart heavier. "And I am quite sure that much of it will sound absurd to you."

"Try me," he says, and I am positioned to do just that for the second time tonight.

He rests his elbows on his knees, his face looking down toward the floor below. He is exquisite in his pain. Chiseled from marble as an expressive and contained work of art.

"I don't want to make excuses for my behavior. We both don't deserve that. I'm just going to tell you what happened." I swallow hard. "What it was to me."

He waits, silently, still not looking at me. I am silent too, feeling unable to cross the threshold between unspoken and spoken. Between unknown and tangible. Between his imagined reality, and what is true, which I am sure is going to burn even worse than he fears it will.

"It is going to hurt," I choke.

"I know," he says. "But how much?"

I am silent again.

"How much, Cora?"

He looks at me now, his bloodshot eyes weary and angry and distraught. He shakes his head from side to side as he inhales, steadies himself with an exhale.

"This isn't…" he trails off. "You're not…"

His throat seems to close around the words, and I don't ask him to continue, but his eyes tell me what he fears most deeply.

This isn't the end, is it Cora?

You're not leaving me here, are you?

"Just tell me what happened," he says.

I purse my lips, steady myself.

"Kai and I…" I stutter, breathe, then continue. "We have a unique connection. It is a spiritual and soulful thing that neither of us could deny. And I've been trying to make sense of it."

He looks up, his face showing disgust, and it digs into me. "Spiritual and soulful? Sounds like excuses already."

I bite my lip, lower my shoulders.

"Just keep going," he says, shaking his head and reassuming his position.

"It is hard for me to put it into words. I believe our souls have traversed many experiences together. In this lifetime…" I trail off, wring my hands. "In this lifetime, and in others."

He is smiling now. I can see the corner of his mouth, the way he sways as he leans on his legs. It is a vicious smile. It makes my insides flip.

He raises his head, moves his tongue across his teeth. "Oh," he says, in a mocking and too-light tone. "Now it all makes sense. You know his ghost! It was just like seeing an old friend." And then his eyes glaze over, his lips turn thin. "Give me. A fucking break."

I collect myself, holding my desperation tight to my chest.

"Please, continue," he says, bringing his hands together and smirking in a way that mocks me. "This is just getting good."

I sigh. "I'm just expressing what this was for me. You don't have to see it like I do. You asked for my truth."

"No," he said. "I didn't. I asked you to tell me what happened. We all know your *truths* are not always the same as reality."

"Fuck that," I say.

"Excuse me?"

"Fuck that," I repeat. "I know I deserve no sympathy. And I'm not asking for it. But you need to stop calling me crazy."

"You don't think this is crazy?" He is yelling now. He stands up, hovers over me. I am not afraid, but I am breaking—the hurt I am causing, the dissolution I am watching right before my eyes, is not something the human body knows what to do with. Tears are streaming down my face, and there is no stopping them, though after so many days of them, I'm unsure how I have any left.

"Maybe it is crazy," I cry. "But that doesn't make it less real."

"Real for *you*. You're forcing a reality on me that I haven't chosen. You're hypnotized by him. You'll believe anything he tells you."

He is blurring in my tears. I wipe my face on my shoulder.

"And you're terrified of just calling it what it is," he says, astutely. "You're terrified that you can't excuse your behavior because of some enlightened fantasy bullshit."

I'm silent, fumbling around in my heart for my truth, my sacred resolve dissolving as my soul is silenced. He's probed a core fear of mine—that I've used the premise of this soul connection as an excuse for my infidelity.

"And you know what?" he asks, without looking for a response. "The reasons don't matter. What matters are the choices you made. What matters is you risking everything—the life we have built, the love that we have—and not giving a damn about the man you are supposed to love."

The man I am supposed to love. I am drowning in paradox. Layers of it are stacking on top of me, keeping me under. The earth and sky. The shoulds and the should nots. The ethereal and the physical world. They are separate things that shouldn't be. We have parsed them out and forced ourselves to choose. And all our souls want is to be in both places at once.

"You are my wife, Cora! My wife. I adore you. And whatever happens, that's not going to change." He clenches his fists, presses his lips against each other. "I don't understand this. I can't."

"I love you, Emerson. You know how much I love you." I shiver, lips trembling. "It kills me. To be hurting you this way. That I have done this to us."

"Just didn't kill you enough to stop it," he huffs, pacing again but in a quick and dizzying way. "Didn't you think of us when you looked at him?" He stops then, looks me right in the eye. "Didn't you see the possibility of destruction right in front of you?"

I am sobbing now, my breath coming and going in gasps, my face warping around the tears.

"Of course, I did. I was weak. I was terrible. And then I held it from you. I was terrified of the wreck it would cause." I collapse into my hands, tears and words finding paths around my fingers. "I'm sorry, Emerson," I sob. "I'm so sorry. I was flooded by these visions of the past. Of beauty and of pain. Of all these pieces of my shattered soul."

He is quiet as I cry. I feel the couch slump and I know he has sat down next to me again. I look up through my rain-soaked eyes and he is slumped into himself, his stature loosened in places I didn't know it could be. My tears give way to quivering breath, and I wait.

"I won't pretend to understand that," he says. "How that felt for you." He winces, and then turns toward me. His eyes look barren in a way I have never seen them look, and it is so devastating to see him this way that it quiets me, my cries strangled by it. He takes a breath, allows himself a pause as if he is on the same kind of precipice I was on—trying to find the strength to utter whatever it is that he has been holding.

"What I can understand is that this isn't enough for you," he says. "We aren't enough." He squeezes his eyes shut, keeps them closed while he continues. "Why can't I be what makes you whole? I never have been. We both know it."

When he opens his eyes again, he finds me there. He has softened, and it hurts more that way, because the pain is kind and hard to delineate.

"We have always known it," he says. The words feel as if they could move mountains. They seem to quake the earth that way.

"You have always known this?" I whisper.

"Of course I have. Your head is in the clouds, Cora. And I'm not saying that is a bad thing. It makes you beautiful. It's one of the reasons I fell in love with you. But it's a language I don't speak. It's not who I am."

He looks at me pleadingly, begging for something that we both can't grasp. An answer. A solution. Something to make it hurt less. Reality seems to have shifted again, and it happens so rapidly now that it is only the soul of myself that can keep up. To the rest of me, it is blurred, but I can feel it. And as our unspoken becomes spoken, as our internal worlds become each other's, I feel less alone, and even more afraid.

It is only fair that I ask him. It is only fair that he has the chance.

"Do I make *you* feel whole, Emerson?"

"What?" he says, seemingly shaken.

"Do I make you feel whole?" I say it slowly. I say it with the weight it deserves.

He moves closer to me. I see the lines of his face, the same lines I have seen countless times, but which have become so commonplace I have forgotten to notice them. He is not a sketch, but an impeccable line drawing. He is detailed and strong. He has always stayed inside the lines. And now things are messy, and his features have new life to them, and I wish I could tell him that it makes him even more beautiful. But now is not the time.

"I love you," he says. He cautiously takes my hands.

"I know you do. And I love you, too. That is something we have always been sure of." I squeeze his hands, run my thumbs over his fingers. "But that wasn't my question."

He is quiet, tears prickling at the corners of his eyes, his shoulders hunched.

"We were getting there, you know? We were learning." He takes a deep breath, continues. "It's just taking us time, to learn about each other in the deepest ways."

"Should it be that way?" I ask, my voice small, the tears halted but choking me.

"I don't know," he says, shaking his head but never leaving my eyes. "I don't know." He is deep in thought. His forehead crunching around it, his whole body gripped.

"It's not that way with him, is it?" he asks, his voice terrifically sad.

I lean my head to the side, feel the burn in my chest of the stuck tears that again break through and exhale in an audible sob. It is a question I don't need to answer any other way. He lifts his hand, runs it over my hair, his tears now streaming down his face, too.

"You love him," he chokes. "You love him, don't you?"

I squeeze my face, knowing I need to say the words. Knowing I need to, but I don't want to. I don't want to shatter him with this final blow. I don't want to shatter us, even though I can already see fragments of our former life scattered beneath our feet. I feel the acuteness of the moment. One that will change everything.

He repeats his question, his voice deliberate and grave.

"You love him, don't you?"

I am silent aside from the sounds of my sadness.

"Please," he whispers.

My voice is a whisper too, shuddering and spent.

"I love him."

We both still, fall into ourselves. The silence is deep and unyielding. It goes on, and on, and neither of us can even find the resolve to blink, until he finally lifts his head.

"How?" he says, pleadingly.

I am quiet.

"How can something happen that way, so fast?"

I shake my head. "I don't know."

"Please, Cora. Try to explain it to me. I need to understand. How you can be my loving wife one day, and less than three days later, you are in love with another man?"

"I think..." I trail off, not wanting to demand a point of view that he does not want to hear, but still, needing to be all of myself if I am to be genuinely present in this fragile moment. "There are things that exist outside of the way we understand the rules of this world."

The moonlight hits him just right, and I see a glimmer in his eye, iridescent and shimmering. To me, it is a pearl, plucked from his heart and showing itself in the way a soul does—born from pain and friction, opened and raw.

And it does something to me, my heart fluttering as if filled with champagne bubbles, making their way up through the neck of their bottle. My chest is overflowing with pain but making room for other things. It's telling my soul it's ok to speak. *He* is telling my soul it's ok to speak. And the words pour out of me, our hands holding each other, the hurt untamed and cascading, wafting around us with incredible weight.

"There are some things that aren't born from this world. They exist in an infinity. We experience them here, and they feel too vast. Too strange and overwhelming. They cause destruction because we believe we are too fragile, too small and insignificant. We flounder through this world, holding on for dear life, avoiding pain at all costs. We think we are protecting ourselves. Protecting those we love. Because we don't know another way."

I wipe a tear from my cheek, take a stuttering breath.

"And then maybe, someday, something might awaken us from this haze. We may begin to understand how much we are truly capable of. We may finally see the truth that is at the core of all life and life beyond it: that love is endless. That it is not a concise thing. That it is an energy that permeates everything. A connecting piece that brings us all together in this eternal tapestry. It isn't outside of us. It is what we are made of."

I squeeze his hands more firmly, this wave of truth giving me a strength I did not know I could find.

"Meeting Kai has awakened this in me," I say. "When it comes to the soul of things, I..." I trail off, close my eyes for a moment, let another tear roll down my puffed and reddened face. "I didn't fall in love with him quickly. Not really. I think I have always loved him. I was just remembering."

The pain in his eyes is transparent. I can't see to the bottom of it, because it seems to go on forever. I wish I could take it from him, but I have just as much of my own, and it's taking up too much space.

"This love we have for each other, you and me, it is a part of the whole of it. A dazzling part that keeps the world spinning. But sometimes," I say, my voice changing to a whisper, "love's awakenings must show themselves in twisting ways. In terrible and excruciating ways."

He sobs, hangs his head. Our hands are still entwined, our tears mingling as they evaporate up into the air. I feel love for him in such a profound way that, for the very first time, for us, it is visceral. It is vibrating in the same particles of air as our tears are. It is blossoming deeply within us, in spaces of one another's that we have not yet seen.

"But where does that leave us?" he finally says. "I'm not as strong as you. I'll stay here forever, even if it isn't whole. Even if it isn't everything. I don't know what life is without you. I don't want to know. For me, this love is more than enough."

I am awed by his admission; by his expression of these things that we were before unable to speak. He looks up, his blue eyes bloodshot and worn, sad but alive. They are so alive, in a way I have never seen them before. The love moves over me tenderly.

"Don't you feel it, Cora? The love, the way I do?"

"I do," I breathe, placing my hand to my heart. "I do feel it the way you do."

He straightens up, squeezes my hands again, speaking an imperative.

"It's beautiful," he says. "Don't you think it's beautiful?"

"I know it is," I whisper. "It is so beautiful."

"But," he says, his shoulders again receding, "it's not like that love." He stays with me for moments and then casts his eyes down again. "It's not like that."

We are quiet again, teetering between acceptance and denial. I am the one to break the silence. I wait until our breath steadies, and I ask him. My words are gentle but transcendent, holding both the fear and the grandiosity of all we are trying to embrace but of which our bodies are not sure how.

"Have you felt it before, Emerson?"

He is still. He doesn't breathe.

"Felt what?"

"That entirety. That eternity. The possibility of that kind of love."

He responds silently. He looks into my eyes. He holds me there. There is a world in him that I am now seeing, in a true and whole way, for the first time. It is a brilliant world, so vast and expansive. And I am sure he can see mine, too—the Universe within me. We tell each other that way, with our eyes, in the way our hearts are beating. We are drowning in its gorgeous paradox and loving each other there, in a new way, deeply and in all directions.

"I can see you," I whisper. "All of you."

"I can see you, too," he says, in a way that tells me he is opening to the existence of such a thing for the very first time.

And we stay there for moments more, lavishing in this enlightenment, and I know that the truth is showing itself undeniably. That this is good and pure and enough. That we always have this special place that is ours alone. In this eternal universe, we are, no matter what.

That this is us, saying hello and goodbye at the same time, for the first time.

There is something I know I must hand over to him. I know I must tell him that it is ok. Tell myself it is ok.

I move my hand to cradle his face. I make sure he is looking at me. Make sure he hears the words in the profound way they are meant to be heard.

"She loves you, you know," I say. "She loves you that way."

And I can only see it because I am, in this moment, a part of his soul. I can see something that would have been otherwise blinded by his tears, by the pained way his muscles move, by the heaviness of his exhales.

I can see it. I can see it.
His soul smiles.
I am sure of it.
"I know," he says. "I know."

31

NOVEMBER 1901

It has been a week since she left. It has been three days that he's been gone. I have died along with them. My body just keeps acting as if I haven't. I haven't fed it, or let it rest. But my heart just keeps on beating as if it is mocking me. As if it is trying to prove to me that we aren't really that fragile, after all. That even with these resilient masses of blood and bone, they are still gone.

Because of me. Because of the hurt I brought. Because I couldn't save them.

And I just keep on breathing. One breath after another after another, even though I'm begging for it to stop.

I've only left his bed to lie in hers. I've only left her bed to lie in his. They are my tombs. Back and forth, I wander. Just to be closer to them. Their smells linger, but every day, they are fainter. And I am sure, once they have faded for good, so will I.

Or maybe I won't. Maybe I won't.

It is six o'clock in the evening. The sun is setting, hard and fast. The air is colder now, late autumn quickly falling into winter's icy grasp. Without the fire, I am numbed. If only I could ice over. If only I could freeze my grief in place, store it away until the world thaws, or smash it into a million little shards and let myself shatter along with it.

He loved the light when it was this way. And because he loved it, she especially loved it too. There are many types of souls, and they surely have the same one. A type of soul that's filled with wonder and wisdom. A type of soul that loves first and lives later. A type of soul that is led by the beautiful things. A type of soul that sees only beautiful things.

The whole house seems to be on fire, the magenta-red-orange sunset painting our walls in its smooth strokes. Is it true that light, when it leaves, is the most alive? I squeeze my eyes together. I don't deserve to see it. It is so beautiful, and my soul is not. I squeeze them so tightly that my body shakes. And I think if I just stay this way a little longer, it will go away. I'll see the same thing I see behind my closed eyes. Just a little longer.

But the usual darkness I find there, behind closed lid, looks different. Like the color is trying to make its way from the outside in. And I am scared, because even here I am not safe to choose, the colors swirling in front of my eyes in an undulating oil painting of light. And I can feel the tears falling from eyes that I thought were forever dried up, a chest heaving with guttural cries from a place I thought was forever breathless.

And that is when I hear her.

I know it's her because her voice has always been one of an angel. It has always sounded that way, like she was far away even when she was right there in your arms—speaking from the heavens, singing her words like she was an instrument of the Gods.

We found you a treasure.

Chills break over my skin and again, I am reminded of how alive I really am. She is reminding me, how alive I really am. And I am too overwrought to be surprised. Too awestruck to be disbelieving. Too grateful and indebted to her miraculous kindness to be clouded by the marvel of it all.

And I inhale once more, deeply into my hollow lungs, my face in her bedding. I smell her sweet smell and I open my eyes and I still smell it, see the colors still coloring the walls. I rise. I rise, unsteady and weak, but I rise. And I walk toward the water.

The creek is slower now, following the pace of the season, which is moving toward hibernation. Its shores have grown with its contraction, the weathered stones smoothed from the dancing water now doused in cool air. Pearl loved the creek in every season, each for its own reasons. At this time of year, she loved how these spots of land, once submerged in freshwater, showed themselves. She loved having access to more ground to rest her feet upon. To scan with her eyes in her hunt for treasures.

I balance over the smooth stones, my muscles weak but flowing, and climb toward our favorite spot: the jutting rock that hangs over the creek, even when the water is rushing, giving us a better view of the whole of it. I stand there at its edge, the cool damp air prickling at my nose as I bring it in. I find a seat, dangle my legs like I have so many times before. Pearl used to lay on her stomach, hang her head over the peak, squint her eyes, searching. And if she spotted something, she'd wade out as Asher held her hand.

So there I find myself, lying against the cold rock, my chest burning with it, squinting my eyes the way she would through the dimming light of the coming evening. And there, wedged between two of those smooth stones, the water moving over it in trickling and dancing patterns, I see life.

And I know.

I climb down, wade out in the ankle-deep waters, wish Asher was holding my hand. My weak muscles shake, my head pounds, but my heart flutters, feeling them, so close. The water rushes gently over my boots, making their way inside and swirling around my toes. I reach down into the cold water, shift it one way and then the next until it loosens. Until it is in my hand, large enough to grasp my fingers around and have it fill my soft fist. I have never seen one like it, its shell dark and painted, much like the sky is. Much like the last moments before sunset.

I climb back up onto the jutting rock, my legs again dangling, dripping the creek back into itself, and I inspect the mussel, turning it over in my hands. I feel around in my hair and remove a clip that has been matted around, that hasn't been moved since a week prior. I rip it from its knot, move its sharp end slowly into the tight space between its shell, prying it open as carefully as I can with shaking fingers.

It resists at first, but then it is like the heavens opening, the light this time making its way from the inside out. The iridescence dances in front of my eyes like the pastel rainbow that slips over a soap bubble, the way the colored air reflects from a snow-capped bulb. I hold the creature in my cupped hands, revering it, thanking it for its life. And then, as gently as I can, I take two fingers, and pluck it out.

She found me a treasure.

She found me a treasure.

32

PRESENT DAY

When I was eight years old, my parents cleaned up the dinner table and then brought out a box of chocolate truffles. "For dessert," they said, which to my eight-year-old self was exciting, but more so, disconcerting. They were obsessed with the modern concept of an organic diet, had taken to blending smoothies before it was cool, and aside from special occasions, they weren't going out of their way to buy a box of chocolate truffles for a regular Wednesday night. And a school night, at that.

When they told me they were getting a divorce, I was sincerely stunned. They didn't seem to possess any of the usual symptoms of a soon-to-be-divorced couple. I rarely heard them argue, they put on a good show at birthdays and holidays, and for my practical father and prim and proper mother, the idea of admitting a failed marriage seemed incomprehensible.

I had just bitten into a truffle, the gooey goodness leaking out onto my tongue, and my father said it, straight out.

"Your mother and I are getting a divorce."

I remember holding the half-bitten truffle in my hand, the chocolate shell cracked, the rest of its sticky insides leaking down my fingers. In an instant, my whole world had changed, and my brain short-circuited around it. I tried to quickly reassemble the pieces in my head, tried to understand what it would look like, what we were about to lose. But I couldn't grasp anything, the stickiness moving slowly down my wrist, my parents speaking words that blurred into one high-pitched buzzing sound.

That's not what this was like for Emerson and me. It's only what I feared it would be like. Endings, in my experience, were only shocking and dreadful things. But endings aren't simply endings. They are also beginnings. They are transitions. They are portals to new dimensions of living.

We weren't stunned to silence. We weren't gasping for air. Once the turmoil of the initial conversation was behind us, there was deep reverence—a reverence that came with sadness and mourning and nostalgia and beauty and grief and understanding and terror and freedom and a thousand other things that we didn't need to sort through, but only needed to feel. Together.

We knew that what we were doing was right, and though devastatingly painful, the truth of it kept us buoyant, trusting that things can fall apart, but they can also come back together in totally new ways.

We talked deep into the night. We cried and we pleaded. We sat in confusion and basked in understanding. We even laughed, not only mourning the end of our marriage but reminiscing about what made us so magnificent. The piece of cake that hung from my eyelashes on our wedding day, of which we have everlasting photographic proof. The time Emerson sang karaoke at a bar in Jamaica, tripped over a loose nail, and somehow landed on his knees with the microphone, poised perfectly for the song's finale. The way we always knew how to make each other laugh, the full-body kind that tickles at your core.

We fell asleep that night wrapped around each other, two parts of our own sort of whole, wearied and surrendered. The next morning, we held each other in a long embrace. We gripped each other more tightly than we ever have. I think about sunsets, and seasons, and goodbyes. I think about the shift, inevitable, from light to dark, and back again. The pain was tremendous. It was brimming with fear which told us stories, beguiling us to give it what it wanted—for us to stay right where we were and disregard the rest. But we found strength in our burning hearts.

Because we knew we had to feel the peak of this pain, in order to heal from it.

And now, I watch Emerson walk out the door. He turns, once more, speaking an infinity of things in his silence, and then he is gone. When he comes back this evening, I won't be here. My body begs me to run for him, but my soul keeps me there in place, my feet adhered to the floor beneath me. The door closes, and our world shatters into shards of shimmering glass, everything we have been glinting under the morning light. Everything we could have been, disintegrating before us, left to other times, other dimensions.

It is excruciating, and gorgeous, in only the way the most tender and true pains can be. And I will grieve, fully and without abandon. It is a type of hurt I have never felt. A new hurt, only possible with our particular type of love, one that is unique to us, only us, maybe not made of the same type of infinity, but infinite, nonetheless.

I pack a small bag of my things. I'll come back for the rest. We have seemingly endless things to straighten out, but that will happen in time. For now, we can't stand the pain of it, being here together, while knowing we have been ripped apart at our seams. We will take things one step, moment, breath at a time. Most of our shared items will stay behind, with Emerson. This feels like more of his home than mine. It was ours, while it was ours. And now it isn't.

For two nights, I will stay in a hotel room, a short drive outside of the city, where there is more open air. It will give me the space I need to look inside myself, to grieve deeply, meditate deeply, and cry deeply. I'm not sure where I will go from there. The future is always unknown, but we build our lives around this illusion that we have some semblance of control. I am being forced from this denial. I am being forced to embrace the unknown with the simultaneous knowing that I am safe. That I am guided. That we all are.

Once this heavy dust settles and the thick pain starts to recede, I can see a hopeful horizon for Emerson and me—only with a different view than we are used to. I will be conscious of whatever it is he needs to make this more graceful. I will be here if he wants to talk. I will hold silent if he doesn't. This is a process that will need to unfold on its own terms, and one I will try my best to be gentle with, especially while we are in these trenches.

It amazes me, how much we were not facing. We were two shapes that fit together in many ways, but not some of the most important ones, and we both knew it. The love we have for each other kept us adhered, two hearts trying to keep up with each other's rhythm, afraid to think the thoughts that could send us reeling in opposite directions. Amongst all the rest of it, I was surprised by the relief I saw in him. It is probably the greatest gift. To know, in my heart, that he will be ok.

When I get to the hotel room, I feel the heaviness in the way anyone would expect I would. The way anyone would imagine these first hours would feel. The quiet and the solitude are particularly over-whelming when compared to the vivacity that was our marriage, which, even amongst our discord, was still a shining thing only one week prior. The soul follows its own timeline. To me now, this truth is absolute. This could not make sense any other way.

I cry for hours. I cry until my cells are dry, and then I take big gulps of water, and cry some more. It is pure release. Screaming release. It feels awful and incredible and important. I think of the seed that rips itself open and breaks through the earth to remember: there is always light on the other side.

I don't sleep that night, fear laying over me like a lead blanket. I don't eat the next morning, my throat too taut to swallow. But that second night, my breath gradually begins to even. I sit in meditation for long spans of time, a quiet, surrendering type of meditation that allows me to move my energy but not manipulate where it is going, just simply trust that it is going where it needs to. It allows me to sit with myself wholisti-cally, my soul and my skin meeting again, merging in a new way. It allows me to hear my Spirit speaking, comforting me with the reminder that I am on my own unique path—and that through the hurt, it is right and good and aligned.

Before my eyes open, I pluck a pearl from the sky and place it before me, see my reflection there.

When I open my eyes, the air feels different, and I know it is time.

I walk to the window, open it as wide as it will go, and lean my face toward the sky. Stars rain down on me like mist—gentle light resting weightless. The pain feels beautiful here, the burn inside lighting me up like the rest of it. A prism shines through my eyes and wanders to the edge of the sky, his light reflecting back at me. Kai was right to remind me that I can't feel separate here. Even at the sky's edge, the sprinkling of this ethereal connectedness doesn't end. It goes on forever, dancing through the air the way our souls move.

And my soul is moving toward him.

33

PRESENT DAY

The Catskills Retreat Center is blanketed in silence. Darkness had fallen shortly after my departure, and it is nearing eleven o'clock by the time I pass the entrance to Citrine, drive on the outer road around the edge of the pond, and up toward the Northeast corner of land.

I pull up a winding driveway, nearly obscured by elegantly hanging trees. His home is dark aside from a single light, perched up high in a small square room on the third floor. My body exhales, the grieving and tense pieces of me pardoned in this moment of pure alignment.

I walk up to the front door, and stand there for moments, staring at this threshold that will soon lead me to him. I notice every intricacy of the moment—the smell of sweet dampness, the darkness that hangs in every corner like velvet, the way my skin meets it, soothed in its embrace. The coolness of the late mountain air moves through my hair, cleanses my lungs.

It is ultimate presence, devoted to savoring the moments that come before the miraculous. The anticipation feels almost otherworldly, as if it might be too extraordinary for my small heart to hold. But I can hold it. I expand with it. And I notice, for the first time in a very long time, even amongst the tumult of the past few days, in this moment there is no room for pain. I stand at this threshold in wonderment, savoring the soulful space I'm residing in. And then I am knocking on the smooth wood, gently so as not to disturb the enchantment. There are footsteps, delicate and melodious. There is a surge of energy, tender and strong, resounding within me, enkindled by the knowing that in moments, he will be in front of me, breathing the same air, sharing the same patch of deep earth.

The door opens, and he stands there, cloaked in a profound mingling of darkness and moonlight. He is so still and so am I, awed by this actuality and taking it into our cells. His breath is taken like mine is, our hearts waiting for their next beat. When mine finally pulses his must too, and together, we crack wide open. I feel the rush of it deep in my bones—totally flooded with him to the point of overflowing, doing all I can to make more space for him. For his eyes, and his breath, and his soul.

And then he is moving toward me, and I am moving toward him, and with pure surrender we fall to each other, two magnets finally embracing the amaranthine pull toward our cores. The love is resounding. Its vibration is so stunning it could bring me to my knees, and until that moment, I thought I knew joy, I thought I knew peace, I thought I knew what it meant to feel the whole of myself, embodied, enlightened, and alive. His hands are on my face and mine are on his hips and we grip each other tightly, gasping for air, inhaling each other, tremoring in each other's heat.

"You're here." His breath stutters. His face is to mine, our bodies pushing against each other wherever there are parts of us that can meet. My muscles disentangle and move toward him, their rigidity drifting outward and away until they are fluid and filling in our empty spaces. I am bigger than my body, bigger than the particles that make me up. My head swims with it. It tickles at my skin, the top of my crown, the depths of my insides, my connection to the divine.

He cups my jaw and slides his fingers across my lips. I let my mouth fall open, feel my nerve endings exploding around his touch. I take his finger into my mouth, gliding my tongue over it, savoring the sweet taste of him and every soft curve. His breath shivers, and he slips his finger back through my lips, places it between his own. I moan softly. He tastes me on the tip of his finger, drinks me in, merges us there, and then moves the same glistening fingertip down my jaw, down my neck, stopping where my heart is, my skin reacting and rising to meet him.

"If I put my mouth to yours," he whispers. "I won't be able to stop."

"Don't stop," I breathe, so close we can feel each other's words. "Please, never ever stop."

And with that he pushes his lips against mine, and it is as if we are made of pure light. We hold there and we are formless. He pushes my mouth open with his, and the softness is nearly unbearable—the urgency and the heat merge in such an infusion of sensations that I can't tell if I will burst or crumble or melt away. We pulse around each other in rhythm, and the whole of me is on fire. I am gripping at him, pulling his head closer, loving him in a way I never knew possible. In a way that takes every part of me to exist. In a way that could not be possible without our mirrored souls, dancing with each other in synchrony, our throbbing in unison, our mouths fitting too perfectly for coincidence, created in each other's image.

For a moment, we break away. We don't just look at each other but into each other; see the mirrored passion in our eyes and deeper. He pulls me further inside the room and shuts the door. And then we are connected again, breathing into each other's lungs, surrounded by darkness and the light of each other. He moves his hands down my neck, down my shoulders. He grips me on each side of my rib cage, where my heart is doing all it can to break free. He moves down my torso, slips his hands under my clothes, opens his palms to my skin. It burns there, where he touches me, and everywhere.

He separates us, extends his hand, takes mine. Even that long is too long to be apart, but I savor the need, drink in the inescapable desire. He leads me toward the stairs, walking backward so that he does not have to look away. When he finally does turn as we rise, I hold tightly to him, studying the way his every muscle expands and contracts.

Alone for this small pocket of time, without the grip of his stare, I find myself fully aware, wholly present, and fiercely grateful—for the bliss that is these moments, for the miracle that we are here. Not just physically in each other's presence, but truly here, together. Without anything between us. I am sure that I love him in a way that is boundless. That to me, his entire being is something that is divine and ethereal, but still, fully here and human and tender and alive. I am sure that if the whole world were to go black, I would still find him, glowing in the dark. I would always be able to find him. I would always be able to feel him that way, his aura reflecting softly across my skin.

At the top of the stairs, he leads us through an entrance of large sliding doors, two-story ceilings, and wide-open space. Amongst all the airiness, the space holds a cradling warmth. There is a king-sized bed with its pristine white linens, two large Birds of Paradise reaching up toward the ceiling. There is a sprawling hearth, downy faux fur throws and plush pillows arranged before it.

"This way," he says, inviting me to rest on the billowing furs. "Is it too warm for a fire? I want to see the firelight across your skin."

"Please," I say.

He pulls three pieces of wood from a stack recessed in the wall, arranges them in an alternating pattern. He ignites the stack, blows gently to bring the fire to life until he is silhouetted by the orange glow, and returns to settle alongside me. He touches his face to mine and I shiver, desire unfolding around me, appreciating every wisp of his feather-like touch. My body is behaving in new ways. The way my skin sparks against his is totally electric, kindled in the places we meet and then everywhere else, reverberating out in every direction. There is so much movement, a melodic throbbing of pure energy demanding to be let out, and I can feel the same things moving under his skin, matching the beat of my heart.

He brings his mouth to my ear, breathes there, grazes me with his lips.

"This will be very intense," he whispers. "But you are safe with me. And you don't need to be afraid."

I close my eyes, his words as inflaming as his touch. He trickles his fingertips down my spine, and holds his palm against me at its base, where my root chakra is spinning in its fiery red and burning me between my legs. His palm is unmoving, though what it does to me is anything but, and he lifts it the moment it becomes nearly too much to take. Our faces are brushing against each other's, moving over our curves and dancing with our breath. And then, he is against my mouth again, leaning me back onto the softness below us, cradling my head in his hand. He pushes against me, and the weight of him sends me reeling. I feel him, hard through our clothes, and I move to him there, grazing against each other where I am wet and begging, where the burn is incomprehensible. He presses into me, and I cradle him between my legs, wishing there were no fabric between us. He retreats and returns, and I must remind myself to take in breath, all of my energy moving to the parts of me that are connected to him, that are thirsting to become one.

He lifts himself up, grasping the edges of my shirt and raising it over my head. He studies me, sensual and adoring, falling over me, burning into me. I move my hands behind my back, unclasp my bra, let the straps fall over my shoulders. He removes each one until I am bare, and then lifts his shirt off, too. He is impeccable, glimmering. I sit up, run my fingertips over his smooth muscles, put my lips to the salty sweetness that mingles there. His hands move to my breasts, playing gently and then taking them fully into his grasp. Our mouths are together again, and I lean back, begging him to follow. He is on top of me, and there is so much skin, so much warmth, so much softness, so many places where we touch. I shudder, the energy tickling at the base of my spine, rising up and retreating, over and over again.

"Do you feel it?" he whispers.

"Yes," I breathe. "I feel it."

He moves down, hooking his fingers on my pants, pulling them away from me. I lie naked beneath him as he undresses, needing him now more than I have ever needed anything in my life. Anything in all of my eternity. But when he is only bare skin, and I can see the whole of him for the first time, for moments, I can't help but to still, my breath taken, mystified by his perfection.

"Don't be afraid," he says again, leaning back down against me. He sweeps his hand down my torso, down my stomach, touches me where I am drenched for him. I moan and so does he, the pleasure too much to be restrained. I feel him between my thighs, and my back arcs into him, pleading for him. His fingers glide across me, and I nearly come undone.

"I'm not afraid," I whisper.

His eyes lock with mine, and he kisses me softly, right there in the center of the velociously spinning air. And then, for just a moment, we are lying motionless aside from our uncontrollably pounding hearts, our need and throbbing so intense we may in fact wither around it, and we know it is time. And slowly, gently, aware that anything more would be the end of us, after an eternity worth of longing, countless years without the whole of each other, we unite in our eternity. He glides inside of me, holds there, the intensity of the stillness and the most intimate inches of our skin sparking against each other alighting every single nerve in my body and fizzing against the air. It is a pleasure like I have never known, didn't know could be human. I am filled with him, in every way a person can be filled, pressed so tightly against each other that there isn't even air between us, so deeply enmeshed that I can feel his titillating heat against the inside of my belly.

Our eyes are still locked on each other, our breathing erratic but exactly the same, and when we cannot physically stand the stillness for even one moment more, he pulses, and we both shudder uncontrollably, shaking around each other, gripping at each other's skin so that we can survive it. He pushes into me again and pauses. Pulses again. I pull him to me, bringing him deeper. We are dancing together, around each other, one with each other, our soul's reunion blissful and erotic and drenched in adoration.

The energy at the base of my spine surges more quickly, coiling and uncoiling, every time he moves. I know he feels everything that I feel. I can see it in his eyes, the way he gasps when I gasp, the way he pushes when I reach for him, recedes when we are about to fall to pieces. And then, he stops again, holds his hand in my hair.

"Close your eyes," he whispers. "Breathe. And together, we will meet God."

And with that, he thrusts into me, once, twice, three times, and I am exploding and imploding, unraveling and being built again. I scream out loud, the pleasure too large for my body, climaxing around each other in clenching waves. The energy is rising up my spine, but this time, it does not stop. Up, up through to my heart and love pours from me. Through to my throat and I yell out his name. Up to my third eye and for moments I am blinded by light. And then, up to my crown, and I am no longer a soul in a body, but a soul itself, one with the Universe, the meaning of life, a pleasure so great it reverberates through each and every piece of me.

Kai falls over me, breathing hard, his sweat mingling with mine, our bodies shaking but the firelight laying peacefully on our skin, creating deep and elegant shadows.

"My love," he breathes. A tear runs down his cheek. "My love."

I wrap myself around him. I feel the rise and fall of him. With closed eyes and limp muscles, we remain in rhythm.

"You're here," he says again.

"I'm here," I whisper.

He puts his hand to my chest, feels my trembling which matches his.

"You're all right?"

I nod, overwhelmed by the sensations in my body that are still pulsing, lightheaded and blissful and here.

"Kundalini rising," he says. He is grounded in his wisdom, in his usual way, but this time, it is met with a tone of astonishment. "We were awakened."

He moves his hand from my chest and traces me with his finger, remembering.

"The pleasure wasn't contained," I say, awed and breathless. "It was everywhere. It was everything."

"Miraculous," he says, his head shaking in peaceful wonder. "The feelings of infinite love showing themselves through our physical forms.

It will be cascading. This universal connectedness is wrapped up in us. This is divine union, at its most pristine."

He reaches over and drapes a blanket over our merged and amatory forms.

"How did you know it would be this way?" I ask.

"Because I know how I love you." His voice is gentle and sure, speaking this truth as if it is the most obvious and most beautiful thing in the world. His hand is moving up and down my arm, my skin still reveling in the simultaneously titillating and tranquil sensations, as I drift into the softness that is enveloping us. "I've experienced whispers of it when immersed in an intensive vision, but never this. This was beyond all preconceptions."

He wraps around me again, cradling me as our trembling recedes.

"It can only get more powerful," he says, our mouths so close they brush against each other. "All of it."

I cannot imagine anything more powerful than this. But then again, I could not imagine this, either. "It is beyond what the human mind believes we are capable of," I say. I wrap myself more tightly around him, around the miracle of it. "Most of us are not versed in the miraculous."

He shifts slightly, presses his forehead against mine, and this time, it won't be the last time. He moves his lips to the curve of my neck and I am still so charged that I again lose my breath. He whispers there. "There are endless things still to discover."

We are silent for some time, relishing in our moments, the feel of our skin, the crackle of the fire. I can feel my consciousness expanding around it, the soul of me running as deep as expanding eternity. These miracles, this love, bringing us both deeper and higher. The earth and the sky. From our souls and into our bones. For ourselves. For the collective. Love is the answer. It has always been the answer. It is in this love that we will wake up to our fullest potential, over and over again.

Always deeper. Always higher.

And I am learning that letting go doesn't mean what it once seemed to mean—giving up, losing our grip, or failing to do what is right or necessary. Letting go means letting the soul of us in. Letting it lead the way. Being certain that it will always guide us.

I am reminded of what it feels like to dream. That reality can feel that way too. Peaceful drifting. Glimmering hope. Endless and cascading possibility.

Kai lifts my chin, kisses me delicately.

"Do you want to tell me what happened?" he asks. "Do you want to talk about it?"

I nod. "I want to talk about everything. I just needed to feel you first. I'll need to feel you that way for the rest of eternity."

There are tears in my eyes, but after endless shedding, I find these are a new kind. The fire of our lovemaking is now burning embers, serene and prodding the deepest gratitudes to show themselves across my face, love overwhelming me in a way that confuses my heart and changes its melody. When he kisses me again, his tears join mine, and I'm sure this merged substance is a panacea. An elixir that holds the Universe inside of it.

"Did it end?" he asks, his tenderness softening the truth's sharp edges.

"In a fierce and beautiful way," I say. "It was in our wreckage that we found each other. Which made me sure that it was, in its ironic way, exactly how it was supposed to be."

His eyes are locked with mine. His hand is gliding over my skin.

"Emerson was so angry and broken. I was so afraid and filled with remorse. But we transformed around the pain of it. It happened so quickly, as we got closer to the core of things. We unlocked something. We saw each other. I swear, we saw each other for the first time. And I learned that it wasn't just me that didn't fit. It was both of us. I don't know how I didn't see that before. If one piece doesn't fit, the whole can't fit together."

His hand stops where my heart is, and he holds there.

"These truths, the ones that make up our stories, are the same as the rest of it," he says. "These Universal things are true for the brightest star which cannot thrive without the right conditions, to two small but mighty hearts trying to bend around each other."

"As above, so below," I say.

I lay my head on his chest, listen to the rhythm of his vitality.

"You were very courageous. You both were." He continues to move his hand over my skin. "I am so sorry for his pain. But he can thrive in new ways now. He can find his place. And I am here, to hold you while you grieve."

I lift myself, missing the eternity swirling in his eyes. I unclasp his hair, letting it fall around his shoulders, and move my hand through it. It is smoky like the heat from the fireplace, like our embers.

"I didn't know that grief had the capacity for such beauty," I say. "That it could be filled with such wisdom. I always saw it as a barren thing. A dry and empty thing. But without love, grief cannot exist. It is born from love." My body exhales in this serene knowing, and I whisper, "And that can't possibly be empty."

He nods slowly, wipes a tear from my cheek.

"That is what kept me breathing, all this time," he says. "Knowing that the hurt was born from my love for you."

I put my palm to his face. "I couldn't even bear it for this tiny echo of time, Kai. How did you hold it for so long?"

It seems a boundless thing to imagine—how long he has shouldered this longing alone. Not just in this lifetime, but beyond it.

"Oh, you held it, too," he says. "Just in your own way. We both carried it, all along."

"You may be right. But it was different. Once I woke up to the truth of what we are, the pull toward you became the most pivotal force in my Universe."

I move my fingers over the smooth skin of his face, watch the ways his eyes swirl in the firelight.

"It had to be that way," he says. "It couldn't have been a moment sooner. I couldn't force it. I couldn't reassemble fate's plan. I could only navigate it in the best way I knew how. And the best way I knew how was pouring myself into this place. Creating something beautiful for you.

Languishing in the yearning, day after day, knowing that even the smallest possibility of reunion would make every moment of it the most important thing I have ever done. And if you decided you could not stay, then I would have had to accept that, and just keep on living and keep on hurting. Until next time..."

He trails off. He squeezes his lips, as if remembering. Shakes his head slowly from side to side. "Though, to be honest, that may have been too much to bear."

"Oh, Kai." I hold him tight, legs and arms and faces folded over each other. And then my eyes are to his again, and I ask, "What happened when I left?"

"I broke," he shrugs sadly. "Over and over again."

My heart shatters and comes back together, hurting from his experiences, blissful for our current moment, waves of emotions that seem conflicting merging into one grand thing that there are no words for.

"She was with us, Cora. Did you feel her? It comforted me to know that. That no matter what, she connected us over the ethers."

"I kept seeing pearls," I say. "I found one on the ground. Saw one hanging from Natasha's neck. Saw one in Emerson's eyes when they showed their greatest pain."

"The messages," he says. "She is always guiding us."

I am struck by the wonder of it. That somehow, there is even more love. Understanding, with absolute certainty, that it is endless. That there can always, always be more.

"What did you see, in that vision?" he asks me. "In the studio?"

"In the Pearl, you mean?" He smiles and I mirror him. "It was so beautiful." I exhale, closing my eyes for moments so that I can envisage her light. "I saw her, Kai. She is an angel, in every form. She spoke to me. She delivered a short but powerful message."

Kai is silent, his eyes penetrating, a gentle smile still resting upon his lips. "What did she say?"

"You've known this," I say, pieces of our puzzle solidifying in his presence. "For a long time. Haven't you?"

The wounds that were ripped open are being salved, treated by this wave of love's pure vibration, the truth showing itself in this healing and magnificent way.

"I didn't know it," he says. "But I believed it was so. This was not mine to hand over to you. These were her messages to you. She knew when it was time. I knew that she would."

"It was her," I say, tears of awe resting upon my lashes. "It was her soul that I held in my womb for those seventeen short weeks, wasn't it?"

He nods again, stroking my hair.

"But it wasn't time. It wasn't right." I lay my head down and he follows, our faces touching each other with feather-like grace.

"It wasn't you," I say.

"It wasn't us," he says.

The sharp ache. The devastating loss. I carried this for so long. Not just in this lifetime. But before and through the in-between. And in moments, it transforms and in its place, there is light. A wisdom beyond what I could have ever comprehended. A significance that was for so long invisible, but that I am now able to see.

"It is all part of our story, Cora. The laughter and the pain. The love and the tragedy. If we didn't have what we had before, we wouldn't have what we have now. And now that we are here, in this moment, the gratitude is immense—because even amongst the memories of those excruciating experiences, we know the whole of our story is bound to the miraculous."

"And as we grow, we'll need less of them," I say, more confidently than I had before. "The excruciating experiences. Maybe we need less of them now."

"I'm sure we need less of them now," he says. "In this love, anything is possible."

And with this gentle reminder of our infinite potential, the awareness falls over me, sweet and soft and alive.

"She can come back to us now, can't she, Kai?"

He smiles, in a more all-encompassing way than I have ever seen him smile.

There is not only one love, but I am sure, there is only one love like this one.

"She's been waiting," he says. "For all of us."

34

PRESENT DAY

I wake up with the sunrise and Kai's beautiful face inches from me, his still-naked body pressed against mine, the hearth filled with ash but the fire still alive in me. We make love again, this time with extraordinary slowness, reveling in each new way we can love each other, knowing we will forever discover more. We lose ourselves in each other, ascending and climaxing again and again, a cascading symphony of passion that, at least this time, we are determined to hold gentle. We will learn each other from the inside out, every cell and curve and pulse telling our story.

When we finally rise, my feet touch the ground with new grace. My muscles move like water, flowing and strong, trusting and vital. It is a deep peace; one deeper than I have ever known. I am reminded of the feeling of relief after a particularly panicked experience, of the peace that comes over me, more obvious in its dichotomy. This peace is so much deeper than that, and I'm sure it is because I have lived in this state of unrest without him for so much of our eternity, and now, I understand this contrasting tranquil relief in a way that is beyond description.

We walk down to the kitchen, Kai lavishing in the opportunity to make us our first proper meal. It doesn't feel usual, watching him move around the kitchen, watching him toss onions into a pan and inhale their sizzling sweetness. It is comfortable and right, but not usual. This is extraordinary.

He turns to me, spatula in hand, bare chest and sweatpants laying low on his hips. "I want to know absolutely everything about you. Every single little detail I have so far missed about you in this life."

I laugh, the reality of this hard to fathom—how few of these details we know about each other, and how I still know him better than anyone else in this Universe. And we learn about each other, one small detail at a time. We spend the day in the details, the small parts of our wholes. We speak about our families, our dreams, our favorite colors, and for whatever else we missed, we'll have all of eternity to keep learning.

That evening, when the sun is hanging colorful in the sky, he tells me it is time. And when I ask him what it is time for, he only takes my hand, and we walk.

The air is gentle and sure, a kind of supple warmth that feels like it will last forever. We come upon the field. I think about the way the grass tickled my skin, the way he held me there, the way we loved each other, in the only way we could, even when the world said we shouldn't. I am comforted knowing that the next time we lie in that grass, we don't need to hide.

When we come to the bridge, arching over the creek that trickles by, its sound seems an even more beautiful melody. I run my hand over the smooth wood, my fingers tracing the stories told across it. "These carvings. What are they? Who carved them?"

"These are our stories, Cora. We lived them together. For each vision I had, I carved a new image. To remember it. To memorialize it."

My eyes scan the railing. There are so many stories I don't remember. So many for me to discover.

"Will you tell me the stories? Every one?"

He drapes his arm over my shoulder, two souls standing together on a bridge, the creek moving beneath our feet the way time does, moving things forward but never sweeping them away. "I can show you. Every one."

I smile, curious and content. I recognize the small house. The family of three. The butterflies. I wonder about so many others. The shell, the river, the snowflake, the necklace.

He gestures for me to follow him, and together, we walk back toward the bank. The earth is vital, cushioned with moss and downy below our feet. "I could lay down right here. Fall asleep right here in this spot."

He smiles softly, lifts my face to his, kisses me.

"It would not be the first time."

I look up at him, eyes wide, searching, my heart again growing in my chest.

"Come," he says. He directs me to the small wooden altar at the foot of the jutting rock, one that I had marveled at before. That opened my heart space when my fingers grazed its smooth surface. We sit down in front of it, our knees in the cool earth. He puts his hand in his pocket, retrieves a small gold key, and slides it into the ornate wooden box that sits below the elegant statue of Aphrodite. The box is so expertly made, that I had not noticed the fissures, and that there is a keyhole waiting for its perfect match.

The box opens from the front, folding out from itself, rearranging, the two corners swinging to the sides and the center pushing outward toward us. Inside, there is a small velvet pouch, cinched at the top. Kai removes it with reverence, places it on his palms, closes his eyes, bows to it.

"I found it," he says. "Right here in this spot. Just as I said I would."

He loosens the hold on the top of the pouch. With deep care, he removes what is inside, holding it gently between his fingers. The earth spins with it. And in that moment, I am transported.

In that moment, I have my second spontaneous vision.

When I open my eyes again, both of us are streaked with tears, both of us hunched and kneeling on the cool, lush earth. The creek sings near us, the jutting rock residing in its steadfast way over the trinkling water, just as it always has. The delicate gold chain is lying across our fingertips, the single pearl that hangs from it nestled in my palm.

And we know we are home.

We are finally home.

35

NOVEMBER 1911

It has been ten years since she's been gone. Four days shy of ten years since he's been gone. From the golden chain, our treasure of pearl hangs, dangling from the most delicate clasp, perfect in its organic asymmetry, born from life and the earth and the water and her. It is always with me—grasped in my hand, hanging from my neck, stashed in its small satchel and tucked neatly into my pocket.

And so are they.

Always here. Always here.

I speak to Asher. Sometimes, I am sure he hears me. Sometimes, I am sure he speaks back. Those are the most miraculous of times. The times my soul knows joy. Other times, I only hope he can hear me. These times, I am not sure but I speak anyway. I wish he could have taught me, before he left, how to always be sure. How to open myself up enough to let my soul out. I wish I asked him, when I spoke of memories and where they go. I wish I could have learned what would seem impossible to most, but to him, came easy.

My body is tired. It has been tired all this time, but now it is different. I see my sickness as a gift. It hurts enough to bring me to them. It hurts enough to rip me away.

And I'm sure my memories will come with me. Asher said he believed it is so, so it is so. But it is not just the memories that I need.

I walk toward the creek, a satchel filled with treasures in my hand. I am much slower now, my limbs accepting their fate. I am a peony. I am ready to become the soil.

The air is crisp. Still and clean. The sky is light lavender blue, the afternoon sitting softly in waiting. The rock juts over the water, just as it always has, and it makes me know that it will for much longer.

At its base, far enough from the rumbling waters even in the Spring, but still, close enough to be fertile and lush, I descend to bended knee. I pull a small gardening trowel from my satchel, and I dig.

And I dig.

And the light is leaving and my arms are weary, but still, I dig. I curve my arm under the jutting rock, tunneling through the earth until I can reach no further. Until it is just right. Until I know it is just right, the soil prepared and ready for the miracle that it will keep safe, but not yet. Not yet. There is something I must do first.

With my arms back at my side, the hole I dug in the earth before me in waiting, I place the trowel on the soil, retrieve the small pouch from my pocket and open it slowly. I let the chain fall into my palm, turn the pearl over with my fingers, loving it. The way I always have. The way I always will.

And with my knees bent underneath me, damp with earth, and the sky turning a deep navy blue, I close my eyes.

"Asher," I whisper. "Asher."

There is only the sound of the creek. The blackness behind closed eyes. I rub the pearl between my fingers. I hold it to my heart.

"Asher," I say again.

And the way the first soft light shows itself at the edges of dawn, as soft as a daffodil field, as kind as the sheen of our precious gem, I see the first whisper of his eyes. First, only his eyes. And then he is there in front of me, his head leaning slightly to the side, his smile at once as pure and more pristine than it has ever been. And the whole of me is there with him. My soul holding my body in its ethereal embrace. Finally. Finally.

"My sweet Juliette. You're here."

"I'm here," I say through my tears, my body overwhelmed by this wholeness. By the soul of it. By this love. "I've missed you so much."

His head leans to the side, his features made of light now, but still exactly the same. "I am always with you," he says. "Always."

"I know, my love," I whisper. "Sometimes it is hard for me to find you. But I know you are there."

"It just takes time," he says, his voice the same as it always was, just the way I remember it. "It is mesmerizing, to watch your soul from here."

I am studying the curves of his face that have not changed, knowing that all of mine are different. I press the pearl with my palm, feel it against my beating heart.

"I will be with you soon," I say. "I am coming soon. Will you tell her?"

"She knows," he says. "But still, I will tell her." He lifts his hand toward me, and though he cannot touch me that way, I feel him. Across my cheek, in my hair. "She is always with you, too."

We are silent. I am breathing, tears streaming down my cheeks. I am almost ready, but not yet.

"Did the memories come with you, Asher?"

He smiles. "Every one."

"They'll come with me too?"

He nods. "Every one."

"And when we come into the next life?"

He closes his eyes slowly, opens them again. He puts his hand to his heart, and I feel him there.

"I promised you, Juliette. That I would remember. I promise you, now."

My body is quaking through my sobs, and it is beautiful. It is love and it is pain and it is truth, all wrapped up in our astonishing divinity. Here, in this body, my consciousness is alive for a little while longer, while my soul is holding me, rocking me to sleep.

"I am going to keep this pearl safe for her, Asher. I am going to keep this safe for us, right here in the earth."

I reach down, touch my hand to the soil, move it along the edge of the place where I dug deep.

"I am watching, Juliette. I am making a memory of it. I promise you."

"You'll find it again?" I ask him. "You'll find it for us, right in this spot?"

"I'll find it for us," he promises. "I'll find it. Right in this spot. Under her favorite jutting rock. By her favorite trickling steam. Deep within the lush soil that was so many times imprinted by her delicate step."

I take a shaking breath, my tears soaking into the soil. "And someday, we will remember," I whisper. "Both of us."

"We will remember," he says. "All of us."

And all too suddenly, he starts to fade away. The edges of his face are blurring, his hands becoming mist and then the rest of him, until I can hardly make him out.

"Asher," I say again, reaching for him.

"Open your eyes, my love," he says without form. "Hold the pearl and then keep it safe."

"I will keep it safe," I cry, reaching.

"I will see you soon," he says. "There is no need to be afraid."

And when the blackness again descends, I open my eyes. I move the pearl to my lips. I hold it there, the love immense, all life and memory moving in gentle succession in my heart. And then, when it feels just right, I open the steel capsule that Asher had gifted Pearl, all those years ago, where her most precious treasures are held. I scatter the glistening stones, the calcite, the Sphalerite, all her treasures born from the earth back to where I know she would tell me they belong. I drop them gingerly into the creek, watch the clear water run over their already glazed forms, let my heart feel the enormity of it. Remembering that in letting them go, I am only giving them back.

I place the gold and pearl necklace into the mussel shell, into the pouch, into the steel, and then into the earth, where I dug a place for it under the stone. It is safe there, one with the lush soil, the jutting rock holding it just like it held her. Just like it held all of us. And I know he will find it there. I know he will.

And when the earth is in place, fertile with new soul, I lay upon it. I lay my cheek to the soil, feel them there. I close my eyes, and it is only peace. One I have never known.

And I don't open my eyes again. Because when the light comes, I become it.

And there is only love.

Because there is only us.

This brilliant eternity.

For all of us.

EPILOGUE

TWO YEARS LATER

"Oh, Emerson," I say. "You didn't have to."

He is standing in the entrance of Citrine with his polished shoes and clean-lined linens and fresh-smelling skin.

"It's nothing," he says, handing over the small gift package, expertly wrapped.

I shake my head. "It's not nothing," I smile.

She comes up behind him, her black stilettos dusted with earth's powder. He turns to her, holds her gaze, and I see the spark in his eyes. I see that he can see to the bottom of hers.

"Come in, come in," says Kai, approaching behind me. "It is truly an honor," he says, "to hold witness the new Mr. and Mrs."

Emerson puts his arms over Natasha's shoulder, thanks Kai with a knowing smile that says more than his words could.

"It's good to be here," Natasha says. "It's very good to be here."

It is two years, almost to the day, that our lives transformed. All of us. It took time for our dust to settle, but with the depth of our shared and undeniable happiness came a dissolution of life's usual decorum. We may not be there yet, but I can see it, what the four of us can be—our histories so entwined that it would be a terrible shame if we were too afraid to try.

This is the second time the four of us are all in the same room, the first being Emerson and Natasha's wedding, and though it may seem ironic nearly to the point of impossible, it also seems just right.

Kai and I didn't have a big wedding—we held a small ceremony in the woods, invited a handful of our closest friends and family. Maralyn held my flowers, overjoyed to tears. Soloman presented our rings made of Pearl. Avery married us right there under the trees.

I moved into Kai's home right away. We never talked about it or made any plans—it was as natural as the way a leaf drifts down into the perfect space between blades of grass. I never did meet Jarrett in person, as he meant it when he said he wasn't coming back. And he was elated when he found out, from his Balinese Hut, that I would be here to lead our guests through the profound yogic experience.

It has been bliss since the moment Kai and I reunited, and if I thought it was enchanted at the start, I could have never imagined how it would grow with us. Every day is a new miracle, an expanding and augmenting and magical thing that I'm sure now has no absolute. I'm sure the love will just keep growing, on and on, for all of eternity, just as it always has.

"My loves," he whispers, leading me out to the garden to join our other guests. "My loves," he says again.

Pearl will be here soon. Today, we celebrate her near homecoming. My belly has been growing with her for more than nine months. I am blessed to nurture the miracle of her wisdom, and to feel all of her angelic love in this tangible and extraordinary way.

And we know she'll choose to stay. Because we know it is time.

I wonder how she will be in the world, her wisdom so vast, her love so eternal. I wonder how she will change this world. I know how she will change ours.

I touch my hand to the single pearl that hangs from a golden chain around my neck. It was ours, but not really. We were just there to keep it safe.

Kai places his hand on top of mine, the other to my belly, our eyes reflecting each other. And for moments, we are the only ones there, the very center of the spinning Universe.

Of everything.

ACKNOWLEDGEMENTS

The writing experience is often a solitary one. It can feel selfish and indulgent because when you are moving with its flow, periphery blurs. You utter, to whoever may be there in the room with you, more often than you'd like to admit, "hold on a second, I have to finish this thought," knowing damn well it is never just one second, and never just one thought.

And then, when the work is done, it suddenly becomes anything but solitary. It is released into other hands, to do with it what they will. Resonate, perhaps. Scoff, maybe. Be inspired, we can only hope.

So I'd like to thank everyone in my life for supporting me through the solitary, with every hour and unanswered utterance, and for encouraging me through its release, which I have a feeling is the most difficult part for any writer.

Thank you, too, to my early readers, proofreaders, co-brainstormers, and idea-bouncers. It may not seem a very big thing to you, but it is everything to me.

Thank you to my editor, Sara Oestreich, for taking my spiritual musings and helping me to ground them into this tangible story.

And thank you to you, my love, who inspires me to write about love. And not just any love. But this kind of love.

www.ingramcontent.com/pod-product-compliance
Lightning Source LLC
Chambersburg PA
CBHW020246180626
46810CB00006B/2390